Series by Julie Johnstone

Scottish Medieval Romance Books:

Highlander Vows: Entangled Hearts Series
When a Laird Loves a Lady, Book 1
Wicked Highland Wishes, Book 2
Christmas in the Scot's Arms, Book 3
When a Highlander Loses His Heart, Book 4
How a Scot Surrenders to a Lady, Book 5
When a Warrior Woos a Lass, Book 6
When a Scot Gives His Heart, Book 7
When a Highlander Weds a Hellion, Book 8
Highlander Vows: Entangled Hearts Boxset, Books 1-4

Renegade Scots Series
Outlaw King, Book 1
Highland Defender, Book 2
Highland Avenger, Book 3

Regency Romance Books:

A Whisper of Scandal Series
Bargaining with a Rake, Book 1
Conspiring with a Rogue, Book 2
Dancing with a Devil, Book 3
After Forever, Book 4
The Dangerous Duke of Dinnisfree, Book 5

A Once Upon A Rogue Series
My Fair Duchess, Book 1
My Seductive Innocent, Book 2
My Enchanting Hoyden, Book 3
My Daring Duchess, Book 4

Lords of Deception Series
What a Rogue Wants, Book 1

Danby Regency Christmas Novellas
The Redemption of a Dissolute Earl, Book 1
Season For Surrender, Book 2
It's in the Duke's Kiss, Book 3

Regency Anthologies
A Summons from the Duke of Danby (Regency Christmas Summons, Book 2)
Thwarting the Duke (When the Duke Comes to Town, Book 2)

Regency Romance Box Sets
A Whisper of Scandal Trilogy (Books 1-3)
Dukes, Duchesses & Dashing Noblemen (A Once Upon a Rogue Regency Novels, Books 1-3)

Paranormal Books:

The Siren Saga
Echoes in the Silence, Book 1

Highland Avenger

Renegade Scots, Book 3

by
Julie Johnstone

Highland Avenger
Copyright © 2019 by Julie Johnstone, DBA Darbyshire Publishing LLC
Cover Design by The Midnight Muse
Editing by Double Vision Editorial

All rights reserved. No part of this book may be reproduced in any form by any electronic or mechanical means—except in the case of brief quotations embodied in critical articles or reviews—without written permission.

The characters and events portrayed in this book are fictitious. Any similarity to real persons, living or dead, is purely coincidental and not intended by the author.

The best way to stay in touch is to subscribe to my newsletter. Go to www.juliejohnstoneauthor.com and subscribe in the box at the top of the page that says Newsletter. If you don't hear from me once a month, please check your spam filter and set up your email to allow my messages through to you so you don't miss the opportunity to win great prizes or hear about appearances.

Dedication

For my brother, Marc Joseph Darbyshire ~ December 20, 1968 to May 26, 2019

If you've ever read any of my other novels, you will recall that sibling relationships are a huge part of many of them. I think this tends to be so because my own brother meant so much to me. He was a warrior in his own right, and he is missed every single day. He passed away quite unexpectedly during the editing phase of this book, and I like to think he was watching over me as I finished it. So this one is for him with fond memories and much love.

I also want to say a special thank you to my editor, Danielle Poiesz. I don't think many editors would spend two hours trying to find the answer to an eye color question! Danielle smoothes the bumps out of my prose and keeps me sane.

Author's Note

If you're interested in when my books go on sale, or want to be one of the first to know about my new releases, please follow me on BookBub! You'll get quick book notifications every time there's a new pre-order, book on sale, or new release. You can follow me on BookBub here: www.bookbub.com/authors/julie-johnstone

All the best,
Julie

Prologue

1296
Valley of Blood
Borderland between England and Scotland

"Eve!" A rough hand to her shoulder shook her out of her lovely sleep. All at once, the field full of purple heather, the warmth of the sun, and the bright blue sky disappeared.

Eve Decres opened her eyes, startled by the absolute darkness and cool air that permeated the room. Gooseflesh peppered her arms, and she frowned as she stared into the dead fire. That was odd. The fire in her and her younger sister's bedchamber had never been allowed to die out. Her father always lit it himself, and Clara tended to it through the night.

"Come, Eve," a deep voice commanded as someone grabbed at her arms.

Eve instinctually reached to her bedside where she kept the prized sword her father had only just given her on her tenth birthday, but the sword was knocked out of her reach and clattered to the floor.

"Eve, I'm scared!" Mary's warm hand grasped at Eve's. But then someone lifted her younger sister from their bed, the contact of their fingers breaking.

"Let go of my sister!" Eve demanded, trying and failing

to twist out of the iron grip upon her arms. When that didn't work, she bent her head and sank her teeth into the intruder's arm as John, the stablemaster, had instructed her to do should she ever have need.

"Damned squirmy little hellion!" The man grabbed a fistful of her hair and yanked her head back, causing tears to spring to her eyes. She shot out her fists in an attempt to pummel her assailant, but her wrists were caught in a viselike grip, and she was tugged violently forward into a hard chest. Whiskers tickled her nose, and the heavy, sweet scent of strong mead filled her lungs when she inhaled.

"If ye fight me again, I'll kill yer sister," her captor said.

Immediately, Eve stilled, icy fear shooting through her veins and freezing her ability to move. With a satisfied grunt, the man pulled her off the bed, and her bare feet met with cold, rough wood. Before she could even properly stand, she was being dragged toward the door of her and Mary's bedchamber. Moonlight streamed in from the window and cast a bright glow that illuminated two large men. Eve and Mary screamed in unison.

The men looked like savages. Long, wild hair grazed their shoulders, and only a loose strip of material covered their muscled chests. Eve felt her eyes widen at the brazen state of shocking half dress. A jagged scar travelled diagonally down her captor's shoulder and disappeared under braies that hung low on his hips. Each man held a sword, longer than the ones her father and his knights used, and the stranger holding Mary had slung her over his shoulder.

That man turned toward Eve and her captor while jerking a wailing Mary off his shoulder and slapping a hand over her mouth. Eve opened her mouth to shout a protest only to have a hand, calloused and smelling of smoke and horses, placed over her own mouth. She fought the urge to gag as she struggled in vain against her enemy.

"What do ye want me to do with this one?" the man holding Mary asked, his heavy brogue revealing that he was a Scot.

"We'll take her with us," Eve's captor answered, his brogue not nearly as thick as the other man's. "It'll be amusing to have the great Decres's offspring as my servant. Mayhap she'll grow to be a beauty."

Something in his voice made Eve's skin crawl. She kicked back, but when her foot smacked into his thigh instead of his groin, fear lanced through her. She had miscalculated his great height.

He spun her to face him and reared up a hand to smack her, but suddenly he stilled and nodded at his comrade, who inclined his head in a silent understanding that set terror in Eve's heart. He moved his palm from Mary's mouth and whirled her around. He backhanded her so hard Mary slumped in the man's arms, her head lolling forward.

"No!" Eve shrieked, only to have her chin grabbed and squeezed.

"Listen to me, wench. Ye're the one he wants. Ye're the one who was named the heir to yer father's castle, nae yer sister. Ye are the one who will bring me a boon. Yer sister will live or die by my word and my word alone. Do ye ken me?"

Eve sucked in a sharp breath, tears flooding her eyes and making her throat ache. Where was her father? Her mother? They would never allow harm to come to her and Mary. The man's words echoed in her ears.

Ye're the one who was named heir.

Papa had only made her the heir to Linlithian Castle two nights ago. How could this man know that?

A man appeared in the doorway, taking up the whole space. "We need to flee. Decres's soldiers are returning, and if we're to get ahead of them to meet—"

"Enough," Eve's captor snapped. "What of Decres and his wife?"

"Decres awaits ye in the great hall, on his knees as ye requested, and the wife is dead."

Shock slammed into Eve, and her lungs seemed to close. She tried to suck in a breath, but no air would come.

Mama, she mouthed silently as sobs ripped through her body and merciless, talonlike fingers sunk deep into her chest to tear her heart in two. Her mother. Her good, kind, sweet mother could not be gone.

As she was dragged through the bedchamber door and into the corridor, her foot brushed against something warm, almost fleshy, but that made no sense. Suddenly, a torch appeared at the end of the corridor by the stairs and cast light down the long corridor. Eve could do no more than stare in horror at what she saw.

The bodies of her father's knights littered the corridor all the way from her bedchamber to the stairs. A wave of sickness cramped her stomach, and she swallowed repeatedly until it passed, but as she was tugged down the stairs past another body, she feared she would pass out. She fought the darkness threatening to consume her, desperate to see her father.

Within moments, she was being shoved into the great hall, and there, before the dais, kneeled her father with a circle of savage warriors around him, swords drawn and pointed to kill. The circle parted to make an opening, and Eve screamed at the sight of her mother lying motionless before her father in a puddle of her own blood. A terrifying certainty that her father was about to die filled Eve, and when the Scot who held her released his hold on her and stepped toward her father, she cried out, grasped the dagger sheathed at the man's hip, withdrew it, and plunged it into his lower back. He spun toward her and knocked her so hard across the cheek that the dagger flew from her hands as she stumbled backward. A bellow of rage came from her father, and he surged to his feet, but the men surrounding him forced him back down. Eve's head hit a bench, and the room swayed before her, bright specks of light dancing across her vision and darkness consuming the edges of the room. The Scot drew his sword back and her father yelled, "Avenge me, Eve!" And then the sword hissed through the air and plunged downward.

Eve's heart stopped as her breath froze. Silence fell in the great hall, then a horrid gurgling from her father, followed by silence once more. Her ears began to ring and heat enveloped her just as she fell sideways into oblivion.

They were dead.

Eve squeezed her eyes shut, tears coursing down her cheeks as she was jostled by the fast pace of the destrier her captor was commanding. She would never see her parents again, never talk to them, never hear them laugh. The pain robbed her of the ability to breathe. It made her bones ache. Sudden shouting around her shot fear once more to her heart. She opened her eyes just as an arrow whistled by her, and the movement of air tickled her cheek.

Behind her, her captor's hold around her waist suddenly loosened, and he grunted, then fell sideways off the horse they rode. The beast reared up, neighing. Terrified, Eve grasped the reins, while beside her, the same thing happened to Mary's captor. When the man fell off his horse, Mary began to cry, and Eve moved her destrier as close to her sister's as she dared and reached for the reins, trying to slow both horses.

"Whoa," a familiar voice commanded, and both beasts came to a jarring stop.

"John!" Eve cried out as the robust stablemaster stepped into the path with Clara, Eve and Mary's lady's maid, by his side. Tears flooded Eve's eyes at the sight of two people she could trust.

"Mount with Eve, Clara. She rides better than you do. I'll take Mary," John instructed, the urgency in his tone making Eve's heart race. He climbed onto Mary's horse, and Clara mounted the destrier Eve sat upon. "If we become separated, ride to the cave at the pass. I'll come for you there as soon as I can."

"All right," Clara said as she settled behind Eve and gave her a quick hug. "It will be fine, Eve."

"My father's dead," Eve sobbed, her voice cracking.

Clara's chest rose and fell with a deep sigh. "I know, child. I'm sorry."

"Eve Decres!" came a rage-filled roar from behind them.

John called out for the horses to run, and Eve tightened her hold on the reins and urged the beast to flee. They took off at a gallop through the woods, jumping logs and ducking branches as they rode hard toward escape. Eve had no notion where John was leading them, but behind them, the thundering pursuit of what sounded like hundreds of horses filled the air. Her body tensed as she kicked the horse in the sides, forgetting all she knew about riding. Terror took over as she urged their horse past John and Mary.

John reached for her reins and missed. In her mind, she thought to stop, but fear would not allow her to do so. The horse surged forward out of the woods and through the valley, while behind her, John's shouts to halt resounded through the air and Clara's frightened cries surrounded her. Eve's blood roared in her ears, and her heart beat painfully within her as the valley blurred by and the horse began to gallop up the mountain.

Eve glanced behind her, horrified at how close the Scots already were. When one raised a bow, she screamed a warning, but the noise of the horses drowned the sound. The man let loose the arrow, and then another. First her sister and then John fell from their horse.

Something broke inside Eve, and her voice cracked as she cried out, "Mary!" But her sister had disappeared under the onslaught of horse hooves. This couldn't be happening…

Wake up! This is just a nightmare. Wake up! she ordered her mind. But nothing changed.

"Eve! Halt the horse! Halt it! The mountain ledge is not far!" Clara shouted. "Halt! Halt!"

Eve tried to form words, but her throat closed, and she could no longer see anything but her father being killed, her mother lying dead before him, and Mary being trampled while Eve abandoned her. The horse neighed and came to a violent stop, shooting Eve forward over the mount and into nothing but air, plunging her toward the depths of water below.

Chapter One

**Tyndrum, Scotland
September 1306**

Thousands of horses' hooves pounded against hard dirt, filling the thick misty air of Grant Fraser's escape route with the deafening sound of betrayal. His breath lodged in his chest as he pulled up sharply on the reins of his galloping destrier in the same moment that his elder brother Simon, who was riding beside him, did the same. They came to a halt, their horses neighing, dust swirling up around them.

What was left of his comrades, the newly crowned King of Scots's warriors, rode close behind them. Fear rolled off the group. He understood it. He felt it as well, but he could not, would not allow fear to consume or defeat him. He had to not only shield his king but also aid Simon in protecting their younger brother, Thomas, who rode behind them alongside his best friend, Allisdair MacLorh. Just thinking about those two young fools and how they'd ridden to the battle of Tyndrum, despite being ordered not to by everyone but the king, made Grant clench his teeth until pain danced across his jaw.

He tightened his hand around the hilt of his sword. The motion caused the dried blood to crack over his knuckles. He had felled the English knights not long ago.

"We've been deceived," Simon growled.

"Aye," Grant agreed, his chest tightening with a mixture of anger and worry. "Ye ken it's the MacDougalls." The powerful Highland clan, who shared his clan's border, had said they would support Robert the Bruce as the king, but they had lied. They'd ridden this day against Bruce and his followers, which included Simon and Grant.

"I ken it," Simon said as he withdrew his sword, a savage look twisting his features. "After we survive this, I'm going to hunt down the MacDougall and rip out his black heart with my bare hands."

Grant nodded, and they both spat toward the ground. They had no respect for liars and turncoats, and this day, Laird MacDougall had proven to be both. "I'll be by yer side to help ye, Brother. I vow it."

Simon clasped Grant's arm, and a swell of emotion tightened Grant's throat. "Bruce approaches," Simon said. "We must act quickly."

Grant looked behind him to where the king fast approached with his young wife by his side. Three bloodied, battered Scots rode in front of Bruce and Elizabeth, and three more rode behind, as well as the two foolish pups who should not have come here and put themselves in the middle of the danger. Every warrior was armed and prepared to give his life to save that of his new king's. Now, weapons even weighted Thomas and Allisdair, as Bruce had knighted them before the battle. Bruce represented the Scottish people's greatest hope to defeat the tyrannical King Edward of England, who wished to subjugate them with an unmerciful iron fist.

Urgency tensed Grant's muscles. He glanced swiftly to his left to the steep impenetrable rocks of the mountain. They'd find no escape there. To the right, then. One look down the plunging cliffside was all it took to understand they would not all make it. But most of them could escape, and he'd give his own life to ensure Simon and Thomas lived. A nearby ridge looked close enough to the ledge that would lead to slanting, scalable rock and freedom. Those who made their way down the mountainside could jump to it. Someone would have to drive the horses back toward the scene of the last battle so the approaching Englishmen would follow the decoy while the king, his wife, and the other warriors escaped, ferreting Bruce to safety. Then they could gather new allies and take down Edward.

Grant jerked his rope out of his sporran and jumped off his horse.

"Grant, what are ye…" Simon's voice trailed off as Grant held up the rope and pointed at the ledge, then looked to the king, the queen, and what was left of the king's army.

"Grant Fraser, I could kiss ye," Ross MacLorh said, dismounting his horse.

Grant winked at his friend. "I'll thank ye nae to. If I die today, I dunnae want the lips of a big, burly Scot to be the last I recall."

Tense laughter rippled around the group as the rest of the party dismounted. The king stepped toward Grant and clasped him on the shoulder. "What do ye intend to do with the rope?"

"I'll lower each of ye down to the ledge and then drop the rope to ye, Sire," Grant explained. "I'll remain to drive the horses back the way we came and ensure the English think they are following all of us."

Even as the king nodded, Simon said, "Nay," his unyielding green gaze locking on Grant. "Ye'll go with the king and the others, and I'll lead the horses."

"The devil ye will," Grant protested. "I'm staying, and ye're going. Ye're laird of our clan. Ye must leave."

Ross snatched the rope out of Grant's hand. "We will all die this day if ye two stand here bickering."

"Bruce." Ross waved at the king. "Come. Ye must go first."

"Take Elizabeth before me," the king said, his voice like steel.

The queen opened her mouth to protest, but Bruce silenced her with a kiss. He cupped her cheeks and whispered something in her ear, to which she nodded and then turned to Ross. "I put my life in yer hands, Ross."

"They're steady hands, my queen," he vowed.

As Ross slipped the rope around the queen's waist, Grant faced Simon once more. "I'm staying. The rope is mine. The idea was mine. Ye and Thomas must flee." This was his moment of restitution for failing to always be there for Simon, as they had vowed long ago as boys they always would be after their parents had died, and only the four siblings had remained.

Simon slipped his hand to the back of Grant's neck and gripped it, bringing them so close that their foreheads touched. "I'm yer laird," his brother said, the intensity of his tone humming in Grant's ear like a thousand swarming bees. "Ye will do as I say."

"Nay," Grant argued. "Ye will be outnumbered." He did not state the obvious that whoever stayed had little chance of living.

"Aye." Simon nodded and squeezed Grant's neck. "But ye ken these mountains better than any man here, myself included. The king has a better chance of escaping with ye leading the party, as does Thomas."

Damn his brother for being right. The desire to deny

the truth clawed at Grant, making him feel as if someone slashed at his innards with a jagged dagger. If he refused, Simon would simply argue, and Grant once again would have failed to trust his elder brother, his laird, as he had done in the past when he'd believed Simon a turncoat for the English. After they had been reunited and he had learned that Simon had been working as a spy in King Edward's court and had not really abandoned the Scottish cause, Grant had vowed that he would never doubt his brother again.

Grant looked over his shoulder to where the king was being lowered to his queen. "I'll lead them to the pass." Simon's exhalation of obvious relief nearly caused Grant to recant his words. His brother expected to die. That's why he wished to be the one to stay and not let Grant. Grant would die for Simon, just as Simon would him. "I'll be returning for ye," he said and glared at Simon when he opened his mouth to protest. "Ross kens the route from the pass as well as I do."

"Aye, I do," Ross confirmed.

Grant gripped Simon by the shoulder. "Dunnae get yerself killed before I come back for ye."

Simon offered a smile. "Dunnae get yerself killed trying to save me."

Grant jerked his elder brother into an embrace. "I kinnae think of a better way to die than giving my life for ye, Brother."

Simon nodded. "Same here, Brother."

They broke apart, and Grant made quick work of lowering Ross, the only one remaining, to the ledge. He then slipped the rope around his own waist and gave Simon one last look as his brother braced himself, feet apart, ready to lower Grant.

"I'll see ye soon," Grant assured him. "And then we will hunt down Laird MacDougall together and kill him for betraying us."

"I'll hold ye to that promise," Simon said.

When Grant reached the ledge, he looked up, expecting to see Simon, but the rope came flying toward him, and then shouted commands from Simon to the horses to retreat came from above Grant.

He maneuvered to the front of the party and waved them onward. "We'll move fast. Watch yer step and stay close." He had to get the king and the others to safety, and then return to aid his brother. He'd not prayed since the day he'd learned his mother had been taken by their enemies, but as he scaled the rocks, he began to plead to God to shield Simon, and all of them, this day.

Chapter Two

Hawick-upon-Tweed, Scotland

People crowded the market, but Eve weaved her way through the tables where goods were being hocked, determined to buy the best fruit and vegetables for the convent. She tugged on her itchy novice habit, which she had not, in eight years of hiding, ever become accustomed to wearing, and continued on through the throng of bartering townspeople.

She bowed her head and folded her hands in front of her, as if in prayerful consideration, while she passed a group of knights who donned capes emblazoned with the King of England's coat of arms. She stole a sideways glance at them, not surprised when none of them spared the slightest look for her. Men never took notice of nuns—or women feigning to be a novice as she was. It was why Clara always had Eve wear her habit. It was the perfect disguise. Clara vowed it made her practically invisible to any man who might be searching for the lost heiress of Linlithian Castle.

Eve didn't see how any man would even recognize her. She'd changed much in the years since she'd escaped from the Scots who had stormed her home, murdered her family, and intended to force her hand in marriage to gain her father's castle. But Clara insisted that she was recognizable, and Eve's uncle agreed. And because Uncle Frederick had been ruling both the castle and her father's men in her stead until she reached eighteen summers, she'd had no choice but to relent. She had not seen her uncle in the years since she'd fled, but they had exchanged many letters, and any time Eve disagreed with one of Clara's dictates, her uncle always sided with Clara and reminded Eve that she was obligated to heed him.

Eve had long dreamed of the day she could leave the confines of the Sisters of Saint Cecilia Convent and return to her home, and as today was finally her eighteenth birthday, she had every intention of making the journey to Linlithian within the sennight. She knew her uncle only sought to protect her by keeping her here, but she wanted to take her rightful place and rule fairly and wisely as her father had. She would take her uncle's counsel, of course, but she had her own mind and would use it the way her parents had raised her to use it. And thanks to King Edward's declaration when he had gifted her father Linlithian for saving his life, her father's heir, should it be a girl, could rule the castle in her own right upon reaching eighteen summers *and* choose her own husband. She intended to pick a husband as soon as possible, and he would be a man she could love who would love her in return.

Eve plucked a berry out of a basket and sampled it as she thought about the possibility of marrying. She had long imagined it. Of course she had. Her parents had been very much in love, and she wanted that, as well. She frowned as she bit into another sweet berry, worry niggling at her. As the heiress to a castle that stood strategically between the border of Scotland and England, many men would wish to wed her for her home and not her true self. She would have to be careful and wise if she was to find real love. God willing, she would not wed for less.

"Let go of me!" a woman screamed from behind Eve, instantly sparking her protective instincts. She slipped her hand inside the slit she had cut into her habit for easy access to the dagger sheathed on her hip. Eve turned, her temper flaring at the sight of a gypsy woman in the clutches of one of the knights and surrounded by his comrades.

The knight jerked the dark-haired woman to him. "Help me!" she cried out, trying and failing to strike him.

"Sir," Eve pleaded, turning to the fruit seller behind the nearest table. "Surely, you will aid the woman?"

The older man shook his head, remorse in his eyes. "If I aid her, I could lose my home or my life. My wife and children need me."

Eve bit her lip in frustration. She could hardly argue with his comment. It was true. The king's knights who traveled through these parts were often violent to the Scottish people of the village. Though Eve had no love for Highlanders, she had gotten to know the Lowlanders of these parts, and they were a civilized, kind people. Even the gypsies never hurt anyone and were generous with their knowledge.

She glanced at the woman again and tensed when the knight began to drag the crying gypsy off toward a side road. She swept her gaze around the crowded square, but the few men who were there were clearly averting their eyes from the knights. Eve curled her fingers around the hilt of her dagger as her heart began to pound. Clara would be furious if Eve involved herself, but what choice was there? The woman was helpless against so many men.

"In the name of King Edward, halt!" Eve shouted. She ran toward the knights, who had all stopped and were turning her way.

"Sister!" the fruit seller behind her cried out, but she did not look back as she raced across the courtyard.

"What do you need, Sister?" the knight demanded when she stood before him.

He raked his gaze over Eve quickly, but then his eyes widened a bit. He frowned, looking her over in a much slower fashion. The gypsy woman tried to jerk out of his grip, but he yanked her back so hard she yelped.

Eve ground her teeth. "You should not treat a lady so," she said, struggling to keep her tone civil.

"This is no lady, Sister." The man's dark eyes bore into Eve. "Have you taken your vows? Seems a shame for one as young and pretty as you to give her life to God."

Eve's skin crawled at his words. She normally tried to avoid outright lying, but in this case, she would make an exception. "I am indeed a nun," she fibbed, "and I can assure you that God will condemn you for treating this woman so roughly—as would King Edward, I'm certain."

The knights all laughed. The one standing before her said, "The king gives us freedom to deal with Scottish townspeople as we see fit. And if God disliked how I was treating this woman, he would have incited one of the cowardly men over there to stop me." The knight waved a negligent hand in the direction of the square.

"God incited *me* to stop you," Eve said, clutching her hidden dagger more tightly as the men laughed at her. The gypsy's eyes grew large. To Eve's right, a traveling bard began to sing a story that, to her dismay, featured a young nun with lavender eyes and bold claims. Eve shot a glare at the bard, who grinned at her.

"How could you possibly stop me, Sister?" the same knight asked, amusement underlying his words.

Eve surveyed the man carefully. He was bigger than

her, but that alone did not frighten her. She'd long ago befriended the gypsies, known as the Summer Walkers, who traveled by the convent every summer, and they'd taught her to be quick with a sword and a dagger. She had spent the years in hiding training her mind and body so that she'd never again feel helpless the way she had the night she'd been taken. But she did not have her sword with her now, and the dagger could only do so much against a group of men. She could likely defeat this one man, but then his comrades would simply seize her if she did. This battle called for strategy.

"I'm quite good with a dagger," she finally answered, allowing her tone to become slightly boastful as she withdrew her hidden blade.

The knights' laughter immediately died when the sun caught on the sharp, gleaming edge of her weapon. The one before her cocked his eyebrow as he shoved the now-quiet gypsy woman to one of his comrades. "Where did a nun come by such a thing?"

Eve shrugged. "From the hand of a thief who tried to rob me."

"You disarmed the man of his dagger?" the knight asked, his disbelief clear.

"I assure you," Eve said evenly, "it is not as unlikely as it seems. I'll wager you that I can disarm you, too."

The man scoffed at her, but when she simply stared at him, he frowned. "All right," he replied, his tone taking on a manipulative edge that she recognized. The abbess of the convent always sounded that way when she was bartering in the markets. Sister Mary Margaret was a cunning woman with a huge heart, but she was unyielding when it came to getting what she desired. If Eve could be half the leader of her father's men that Sister Mary Margaret was of the nuns, then she would be a good ruler.

"You've nothing to offer me," the man growled, then leered at her. "Now, if you weren't a nun..." His gaze trailed slowly along her habit.

When his eyes returned to hers, Eve simply gave a half smile and a shrug. "If you're fearful I'll best you, simply say so."

"Come on, Darius," one of his comrades spoke up. "You cannot let a nun goad you like that. If you won't fight her, I will!" All the men standing with Darius laughed, and the knight's face turned red.

Darius look at her. "When I best you, I'll take your dagger as my prize."

"All right," Eve said, struggling not to smirk. "But when *I* win, you'll set the gypsy free and vow to let her go without harm."

"As you wish, Sister...?"

"Mary," Eve replied, using her sister's name on a whim. She certainly could not give her own, and it seemed fitting somehow to remember Mary when rescuing this woman, as Eve had failed to rescue her sister.

Darius pointed to Eve's dagger. "I suggest you sheathe your weapon for the fight."

"Ye kinnae really mean to fight the nun?" someone asked from behind her.

Eve whirled around to find the man who had refused to help the gypsy standing there. Behind him a small crowd from the market looked on from a safe distance.

The knight shrugged. "It was the nun's idea. But if you'd rather not, Sister Mary..."

Eve faced Darius once more. The man had brawn but little brains. "The winner is the first to disarm the other," she announced. "And you will take a care not to cut me."

She added the last line for his benefit, to make him think she was fearful.

"Of course," he replied, motioning to one of his comrades for his sword.

Eve eyed the sword, taking in the length, shape, and type of metal used to forge it. It was very similar to the one she secretly had made in town the previous year, in preparation for returning home. When Darius held the weapon out to her, she let it tip to the ground and then made a show of struggling to lift it upright. "It's very heavy," she huffed, inwardly rolling her eyes.

The pompous man snickered as she lifted the weapon with several well-timed grunts. When it was hip height, she said, "I believe I'm ready."

The knight nodded and swiveled his sword forward, gently tapping his blade to hers. She gasped and feigned nearly dropping it while he laughed. His blade was directly in front of her, mid-waist, exactly where she wanted it. This was too easy. "Sister, that was a warning tap," Darius said. "You're certain that—"

Eve shoved her sword upward and to the left, clanging against his. His jaw dropped. He tensed and began to react, but it was too late. The momentum of her hit had driven his blade far to the right. When he turned awkwardly in order to correct his hold, she dipped her sword down and into a full arc, bringing it back up to slam into the other side of his blade. His weapon went flying out of his hands, and she sent the tip of her sword toward his chest, directly over his heart.

"Hold still," she commanded, "or the point may slip and plunge into your heart. I am only a woman, after all, too weak to hold up this great big sword."

The knight turned nearly purple as his comrades guffawed. Eve smiled at Darius. "You will keep your word, yes, and allow the gypsy her freedom?"

Darius nodded. "Unhand the wench," he ordered his comrade, who immediately did so.

The gypsy woman staggered away from the man and turned to run, but then she glanced over her shoulder. "Ye have my eternal gratitude, Sister Mary," the woman said.

Eve inclined her head in acceptance. "Flee now, madam."

"Marianna," the gypsy supplied.

"Marianna, only God knows how long a promise, once given, truly lasts."

The woman nodded, turned, and ran down the same side street the knight had intended to drag her down. Eve focused her attention once more on Darius. "I'll lower my blade now, but if you think to harm me, I vow God will strike you down."

With that, she threw the sword at the man's feet and made the sign of the cross while narrowing her gaze upon him. Darius's face twisted with his rage. Eve bit her lip on the desire to laugh, and clutching her skirts, she stalked around the knight, and strode back toward the market and the road that led to the nunnery. As she passed the crowd that had gathered, they cheered for her. Grinning, she exited the market, the sweet, high-pitched voice of the bard singing about the dangerous, violet-eyed nun floating on the wind.

She laughed as she rounded the corner to the dirt road, but when the convent came into sight a few minutes later, her grin faded. Clara was going to be so upset when she heard of the day's event. Eve slowed her steps as she considered what to say. Clara worried because she loved her, Eve knew that. So she would simply tell Clara that there was no need to fret that their enemies might hear the story of a nun named Mary with strange-colored eyes and associate it with Eve. Besides, her uncle had explained carefully in his letters that he'd allowed everyone to think she and Clara had drowned on that fateful day eight years earlier. Clara worried unnecessarily, but even if Clara's caution was not unfounded, Eve would soon be gone from this place.

Eve entered the convent and hurried down the corridor toward the nuns' small bedchambers. She paused in front of Clara's door and inhaled a deep breath to steady her mind. It was time for them to return to Linlithian, and Clara needed to see that, too, because Eve could never leave the woman behind. She was like a mother to Eve.

Eve knocked and waited, but when Clara did not answer, Eve opened the door to the tiny, windowless bedchamber and went inside. The room was only large enough for a small bed, table, and chair, so Eve pulled out the chair and sat, determined to wait. Papers strewed the desk, and as Clara was the tidiest person Eve knew, her old lady's maid must have been called to help in the convent and had not had time to straighten up. Considering that she wanted Clara's undivided attention when she returned to the bedchamber, Eve began to gather papers and stack them, but as she did so, she spotted the letter she had given Clara to send to Frederick a sennight ago.

Eve picked up the parchment and ran her finger over her signature and seal, frowning. Clara must have forgotten to send someone with the letter. Eve stood and made her way out of the room, and to the abbess's chambers. She would ask Sister Mary Margaret to send someone with her letter today, as her uncle needed to know she was returning to her home.

Before she could even knock on the abbess's door, it

swung open, and the tiny, spritely woman blinked in surprise. Her gray eyes, which matched the color of her short hair, crinkled affectionately at the corners. "Eve, what can I do for you?"

Eve held the letter out to the abbess, glad she could speak plainly with Sister Mary Margaret. The woman had known the truth about Eve and Clara since the day they had come to the convent seeking shelter.

"Clara forgot to give you my regular letter to my uncle to be taken to Linlithian."

Sister Mary Margaret's silver eyebrows dipped together, and two extra lines appeared on her wrinkled forehead. "I know I'm aging, but I don't know what you are talking about. In all the years you and Clara have been here, she's never given me a letter to take to anyone, from you or her."

"Never?" Eve said, her breath hitching. An odd hollow feeling filled her stomach. That was impossible! She had been writing to her uncle for years—and he'd responded!

Sister Mary Margaret shook her head. "Child, I'm happy to have our man ride the letter there, but I must ask… Is this prudent? I know you have reached eighteen summers, but you need to pick a husband. Last I spoke with Clara, she believed another year was needed for you to make a wise choice of a husband. And then, of course, we will need to discreetly make inquiries of candidates and—"

Eve held up a hand, and the abbess stopped mid-sentence. The two of them stood facing each other in silence. The corridor seemed to grow smaller, the space more confined, hotter. Sweat beaded on Eve's lip, and her underarms grew damp. "Where—" The word cracked under the weight of her trepidation, and she had to swallow before forcing the rest of the question out. "Where *is* Clara?"

"She's in the chapel," the abbess responded, giving Eve a concerned look.

Eve nodded absently, her mind whirling with questions. Surely, the abbess was wrong and confused. She was old. Eve's stomach roiled as she took in Sister Mary Margaret's paper-thin skin, the lines around her eyes, her sagging neck, and weathered hands. She was very old. *That's all it is. Forgetfulness.*

Eve would speak with Clara the moment the woman was finished in chapel. "If you'll excuse me," she said, her head fairly spinning. She did not wait for a reply. She turned on her heel and made her way back to Clara's bedchamber to wait. She sat at the desk once more, Sister Mary Margaret's words playing repeatedly in her mind.

Wise choice of a husband… Never given me a letter…

A horrible suspicion began to niggle at Eve, and she found herself scanning Clara's bedchamber. If Clara was going to hide Eve's letters—assuming they'd been hidden and not destroyed—where would she do so? Eve looked to the cluttered desk as a numbness settled over her. Trembling, she started to sift through papers and open the desk drawers. With each one she opened, her stomach grew tighter and her heart pounded harder. When she came to the last drawer, she had trouble grasping the handle because she was shaking so terribly. The tiny drawer opened with the scrape of wood upon wood, revealing nothing more than green hair ribbons that Eve was positive must be a gift for her from Clara, likely for Eve's birthday. Clara never wore ribbons, and green was Eve's favorite color.

Eve touched the silky edge of the ribbon, and a wave of guilt flushed her. She hurriedly closed the drawer and sucked in a deep breath. She had no right snooping through Clara's private things. There had to be a simple explanation.

Eve shoved up from the desk, deciding it was best to simply go speak with Clara. Eve hated to interrupt her in chapel, but the sooner this could be sorted out, the better.

She started toward the door, but the tip of her slipper caught the edge of a small rug, and she lurched forward, catching herself on her hands as she fell to her knees with a painful thud. Rolling to her side, tears blurred her vision and her knees throbbed. She lay huddled that way for a long moment before putting her palms down to push herself into an upright position. When she did, the wood beneath her fingers gave a loud creak, and it felt as if the boards were bending forward slightly. Eve frowned and looked down at her hands, then at the spot where the rug had been pulled back. She gave the wood a hard push. The board was loose.

That same terrible suspicion overwhelmed her. Scrambling to her knees, she hooked her fingernails under the rough edge of the plank and pulled. The board moved easily, and she peered into the hole, her lips parting with a sharp intake of breath. Pain stabbed at her chest as her gaze traveled over a bundle of letters. A choked, desperate cry escaped her, and she reached for the letters as tremors of betrayal and rage coursed through her.

Slowly, she brought out the bundle, some of the paper yellowed from years of being hidden, and hot tears trickled down her cheeks. Nauseating, sinking despair threatened to engulf her, but she made herself open the letter on top, just to be certain they were hers. She had only to read the first line for the confirmation she did not want:

My dearest Uncle Frederick,

A bellow burst from her, and she slammed the letters onto the wood and beat her fists on top of them. Her lungs burned, her stomach ached, and her head pounded as she beat at the paper, trying to obliterate the betrayal which was impossible to destroy.

She stilled at the sound of the door opening and clutched at the letters scattered in front of her until she had a bundle in both her hands.

"Oh, Eve!" Clara cried out, the dismay evident in her voice.

Eve raised her head, shoving her hair away from her eyes with the back of her hand. "You've been lying to me!" Eve shook the letters at Clara, the woman who had long ago saved her, the woman who had taken her mother's place after her mother had been killed.

Eve expected tears, or denials, or pleas of forgiveness, and she clenched her teeth, prepared to ignore it all. But Clara merely folded her hands in front of her, and a determined look settled on the older woman's soft, wrinkled face and hardened her gaze. "Yes, I have. To protect you."

"Protect me?" Eve shouted, still waving the letters about as she rose to her feet. "Protect me from whom? My uncle? He is my kin, my blood!"

"Yes," Clara said with a nod. "Because I cannot say for certain that he was not the one to betray your father…"

It was too much. Eve could not listen. Going home was all she had wanted, all she had to look forward to. If she could not even trust her uncle, she had nowhere to go. No home. "I don't believe you!" Eve sobbed and threw the letters at Clara. "I won't believe you! You're a liar!" With that, she shoved past Clara and fled.

Chapter Three

The buzz of the distant crowd gathered around London Bridge hummed in Grant's ears as he and Ross crouched behind some trees in the woods. He skimmed the throng of people, looking for guards surrounding a prisoner. For two days, Grant and Ross had tracked Simon from where they'd left him in Scotland to here, and the last English knight they had come upon and coerced into giving them information told them that Simon had been taken to London to be tried as a traitor.

They had to hurry, to get to Simon before it was too late. But time was Grant's enemy. It had always been his enemy. He'd not had enough time to rescue his mother, nor enough time to say goodbye to his father. He could not let time best him again.

Where the devil was Simon?

Grant rose slightly from his crouched position to get a better view, but Ross's hand came to Grant's shoulder and pulled him back down. Ross motioned to two Englishmen walking nearby, whom Grant had not noticed in his distracted state.

He nodded to Ross in understanding. As the two strangers drew closer, he and Ross both moved backward, deeper into the underbrush.

"I always said Simon Fraser was a spy for the damned

Scots," one man said.

Was. The word hit Grant in the gut, making him wince. The distinct sound of someone relieving himself filled the momentary lapse in conversation.

"Well, King Edward having the MacDougalls behead the traitor should send a message to any Scots thinking to rise against our king." The man had the gall to chuckle.

Grant fisted his hands in the cold dirt as his stomach twisted. His head pounded, and the ground seemed to tilt underneath him for moment. Ross's hand came to his shoulder again, gripping him. Grant could not even acknowledge his friend. He had to direct all his concentration to not rising to kill the men urinating in front of him. Such an act would not only get himself killed but get Ross killed, too, surrounded as they were by the English.

Dead. The word was heavy, final, and suffocating. Disbelief stopped the world around him. Simon could not be dead. But as the men departed, Grant forced himself to rise until he could see the crowd once more. English knights were marching toward the end of London Bridge with the MacDougalls by their side. At the front of the line was Laird MacDougall and fisted in his right hand was Simon's head.

Grant leaned to the right and retched, then fell to the ground to press his forehead into the cold dirt. *It was not Simon. It was not Simon.* He kept repeating the mantra, but the truth of what he'd seen hammered at him. He gulped in deep breaths and pushed his hands against the soil to shove back to his feet. Ross's hand came to his arm, but Grant shoved him off.

"Dunnae look," Ross said in a pained whisper.

Grant felt as if he might retch again, but he swallowed until the feeling faded, and then he peered out from their cover and stared at his brother's decapitated head now impaled on a spike on London Bridge. Bile rose from his stomach, burning his throat, but he did not turn his gaze. He looked so that he would never forget what the MacDougalls and the English had done. He looked so that he would never again forget that time was not his friend. He looked so that he would remember how he had failed his brother. He would need the image to carry him through the battle, he was certain.

Rage coursed through his veins. He was going to hunt down the MacDougall laird and everyone who had aided him in killing Simon. He was going to behead them, just as they had beheaded Simon.

The treachery of the MacDougalls singed Grant's soul so that he felt it wither under the blaze of his fierce hatred. Many Scots had betrayed their homeland since the war with the King of England had started. Men had betrayed Scotland out of fear for their lives, their homes, the well-being of their wives and children. Those men he could never trust again, but he could understand their decisions. He could even forgive the weakness. But the MacDougalls had betrayed Scotland, had betrayed the sworn oath of allegiance to Simon as the laird of the Fraser clan, because of their greed and consuming thirst for power.

"What do ye want to do?" Ross asked.

Grant just continued to stare at his brother's head. His face was gray, his mouth hung open, and his eyes bulged. Grant's throat tightened with the need to scream—for the loss of his brother, for the fact that he had died alone, for not returning in time to save him.

Finally, he inhaled the putrid London air and turned to Ross. Their eyes locked. "I want to kill Laird MacDougall, his son, and all the men who aided in murdering my brother," Grant said. "I want to hunt them down and put their heads on spikes along the trail to my home so any who dare to cross a Fraser again will ken the revenge that will be exacted upon them. Any man who dares to kill a Fraser will die in the very manner they inflicted."

Ross nodded. "Bruce would surely agree with this."

"Ye should return to Bruce," Grant said, thinking of the fledgling king, who at this moment was fleeing toward the Atholl mountains to find more forces and gather support.

"Nay," Ross said, setting a hand on Grant's shoulder and squeezing it. "Ye heard the king yerself. He ordered me to aid ye in ensuring Simon made it back to Scotland alive, and we failed. The king would wish me to aid ye in taking vengeance upon the MacDougalls."

Grant opened his mouth to protest, but Ross's words were true. Bruce had ordered it, as well as insisted that Thomas and Allisdair make their way to the safety of the Fraser holding instead of accompanying Grant and Ross to aid Simon. The young boys had sputtered their protests about being sent away, but they had obeyed with a look of warning from Bruce. He was a truly good man and king. He strove to put Scotland and its people above himself always, which was why many nobles did not like him. He put more stock in ruling for the common people than the lairds. That was the heart of why the MacDougalls had turned against Bruce when he'd seized his rightful throne and killed John Comyn—the man who had tried to murder Bruce to gain a throne that was not his.

MacDougall was supporting King Edward over Bruce not because MacDougall was related by marriage to Comyn, but because the man wanted all the power and land in the Highlands, and he could not have that if Bruce became king. Bruce would rule Scotland fairly and give power and lands equally, not just to the rich.

Grant stared toward the now-dispersing crowd as he tried to focus enough to consider what to do. It was hard, so very hard. Disbelief pounded relentlessly at him and sorrow muddled his thoughts. His insides tightened into a hard ball.

"Grant, words are nae enough to tell ye my sorrow."

The pain in Ross's voice cut through Grant's haze. "Dunnae be sorry." He took one long last look at his brother's head before he faced Ross and formed a plan even as he spoke. "Be like a shadow. We will capture the MacDougall and take him to my home for his reckoning. I am certain Aros will follow once he kens we have his father. Are ye with me? It will be dangerous."

"Fear of danger is for the weak," Ross said, quoting words Simon had taught them both. Grant turned his head when his eyes watered, blinked several times, and faced Ross once more. The time to grieve would have to come later. Now was the time for vengeance.

Grant focused his gaze on the men who had departed the bridge and come near the woods to urinate. They stood not so very far from the woods and were set far enough away from the bridge that Grant and Ross could likely relieve them of their clothing without drawing notice. "We must become Englishmen and move through the darkness to take my enemy."

"*Our* enemy," Ross corrected. "We are brothers in our fight for Scotland's freedom."

Grant answered by motioning to the two English knights. They were laughing and talking like fools, heedless of the dangers that awaited them. "They kinnae make a sound," Grant warned.

Ross grinned, his teeth flashing white in the rapidly growing darkness. "Mine will nae," he vowed, his tone ominous. And then, as if in mutual, unspoken agreement,

Grant and Ross moved through the shadows, careful to keep to the edge of the woods, until the two knights were within arm's reach. The thuds of their dagger hilts meeting the knights' skulls blended into the night and the not-too-distant sounds coming from the taverns beyond the bridge. Before the knights even fell fully to the ground, Grant and Ross were dragging the men back into the edge of the woods that faced London Bridge.

Grant wiped his hands on his braies as he and Ross stood over the knights. "We'll don their clothing."

Ross nodded, already reaching to undress his captive. "God's bones," he swore under his breath. "I heartily wish there was another course. Seeing an Englishman naked turns my stomach."

"Aye," Grant agreed. He peeled off his own plaid and braies to don the armor of the knight he'd just disrobed. "They smell like dead fish."

"They look like fish, too, scrawny as they are," Ross said, facing Grant as he tugged on the last of the knight's armor.

Grant raised his bow and arrow to ensure he could maneuver well in the armor. He'd be able to kill a man, and that was all he needed to know. "Can ye shoot and swing?" he asked Ross.

Ross scowled at him and quickly bound the two knights' hands and feet, and stuffed cloth in their mouths. "That's like inquiring if I can please a wench. Dunnae ask such foolish questions."

Grant shoved his clothing into the sporran attached to his horse, Tintreach. "Tintreach, quiet," he instructed his beloved destrier before he gave a yank on the rope to make sure the beast was secure. The stallion dipped his head as if in understanding, to which Grant reluctantly smiled. It felt wrong to experience even a fleeting hint of lightness with Simon's death weighing so heavily on him. He patted the horse, which had been a gift from his father years before and had been with him through more battles than he could even remember. "I'll return." To Ross, he said, "Are ye ready?"

"Since the day I first walked," Ross assured him.

With that, they stepped out from the woods and moved toward the bridge.

There were commoners and knights alike crossing the bridge from both directions. Grant walked among the English, his footfalls on the wooden bridge thudding in time with his heart. When he got to the spike that held Simon's head, Grant's progress faltered and his grip tightened on the hilt of his dagger.

"Grant," Ross hissed low in his ear. "Dunnae be foolish. If ye act now, we'll nae make it out alive."

"It's quite a sight, is it not?" came a nasally voice from behind Grant.

He clenched his teeth until his jaw ached and then slowly turned toward the voice. Ice-blue eyes stared levelly at him. Grant inclined his head to the blond-haired man, who looked to be a nobleman based on the rich cloth of his cape and his neatly shaved face. The man was built like a warrior, but his armor gleamed in the glow of the torches and the moonlight above them. His armor appeared unmarred, as if it had never been worn in battle.

The man motioned to Simon's head. "Clearly, I speak of the decapitated Scot, Laird Simon Fraser," the stranger said, exasperation tingeing his tone. Then he chuckled, and it took every ounce of restraint Grant possessed not to plunge his sword into the Englishman's heart. "I suppose I should say the *former* laird. He is quite dead now."

"Yes," Grant answered, taking on the English accent his brother had made him practice nightly since they'd been reunited. Simon had insisted it might one day save Grant's life, and it appeared today might be that day.

"Did you happen to see the beheading?" the man asked. "I myself was detained and missed it."

Grant swallowed the rage clawing to get out of him. His fingertips throbbed where he clutched his dagger. "No, Lord...?"

"De Beauchamp," the man replied, flourishing his hand and offering a mock bow. "I'm Guy de Beauchamp. You may call me Lord de Beauchamp."

How typical of the English to be so pompous that they don't bother learning to whom they are speaking to ensure it is not an enemy. De Beauchamp waved a hand at Ross. "It that your man gaping at me?"

Grant stole a glance over his shoulder at Ross, who was, indeed, gaping. "Yes, my lord. He's mute. Fool got his tongue cut out by a Scot." Ross's lips pressed together in distaste at Grant's lie.

"That is quite foolish. Scots are cunning liars, though. No doubt they took your friend unaware."

"Indeed," Grant responded simply. The less he spoke the better. His English accent was passable but not perfect.

"Well, I'm headed to the tavern to hear the details from the MacDougall's own mouth. The king may trust the Scot, but I personally trust no Scot ever. They've proven in my personal experience to be treacherous." Grant grunted in return, hoping that would suffice, which apparently it did, the fool Englishman. De Beauchamp moved in front of Grant and motioned him to follow.

Grant fell in step behind the English lord and met Ross's gaze. *Stay to the shadows,* Grant mouthed, exhaling with relief at Ross's nod. MacDougall and Aros would both recognize Grant and Ross, so it would not do for the men to see them.

Men lined up outside of Straton Tavern, waiting to enter the establishment. But as de Beauchamp neared the doors, the men hastily moved out of the way. Grant stayed close enough to the man to enter the tavern on his heels but not so close that Grant and Ross could not fade away once inside. The throng of men filling the pub made it easy enough to lose de Beauchamp, and the thick smoke from the fires and poor lighting aided their task.

Grant swept his gaze over the crowd as he weaved in and out of knights swigging ale and singing bawdy tunes, searching for MacDougall and his warriors. It did not take long to spot the laird. He was an unusually tall man, standing a good head above almost all others in the crowd. MacDougall stood face-to-face with another man whom Grant did not recognize, but by the rich cloth of his robes, which carried the symbol of a serpent rising out of fire, and the heavy gold rings upon his fingers, Grant assumed he was another English nobleman. And when de Beauchamp stopped beside the two men and they all exchanged greetings, it seemed Grant's assumption was correct.

The man with the serpent crest waved yet another man over, but this stranger was assuredly not a nobleman. He wore a simple wool robe and no jewelry. After brief introductions, Grant watched the man take a deep breath, and to Grant's surprise, he began to sing. Grant caught the faint notes in the air, though at first, he could not make out all the words.

"Stay here," he instructed Ross. "I'm going to move closer to figure out what story the bard is telling."

Ross nodded, and Grant edged closer along the wall,

careful to stay behind the men who had started to gather around the bard, MacDougall, de Beauchamp, and the man standing with them.

"Never had I seen such a sight as a novice who could fight," the bard sang. "Graceful as a doe was she who felled the pompous knight, as pretty as you please, and all with a look that would render a man helpless when her violet eyes were upon you."

"Bard, where is it ye saw this novice?" MacDougall demanded, interrupting the song.

"At market in Hawick-upon-Tweed. She is a frequent visitor there from the Sisters of Saint Cecilia Convent."

Grant frowned. Why the devil did MacDougall care about a novice about whom a bard sang?

"And ye're certain of her eyes?" MacDougall demanded.

"Yes, my lord."

"By God!" MacDougall exclaimed and then burst out into hearty laughter. "Aros!" he boomed, and Grant's one-time friend, whom he had once trained with, strode up to his father. "Son." MacDougall clapped Aros on the shoulder. "Take all but five of our men and ride to Hawick-upon-Tweed. Bring the novice the bard sang of to our stronghold."

"Father, is she—"

"Shut yer trap," MacDougall thundered, to which Aros considerably reddened but nodded.

This was perfect. There was no way for Ross and Grant to take both men when they had their warriors with them, but they could concentrate on MacDougall. When Aros returned, he'd learn that Grant had taken his father to Dithorn Castle, Grant's stronghold in the Highlands. Aros would attempt to rescue him, the fool. Everyone knew Dithorn was virtually impenetrable. But Aros was just cocksure enough to ignore that fact. He'd join his father in death.

Aros gave a nod to his father, and with a shrill whistle, the man departed, along with a good portion of the men who had surrounded MacDougall. Grant smiled to himself. Aros was like his father. They both thought themselves invincible, but they would soon discover just how wrong they were.

As the laird exchanged words with the bard and de Beauchamp, Grant moved back along the wall the way he had come and found Ross. "We'll await MacDougall outside and take him unawares."

Ross arched an eyebrow at Grant. "What of his son and their warriors? They far outnumber us."

Grant quickly told Ross of MacDougall's instructions to Aros. Ross gave a long, hearty chuckle. "I do so love how foolish some men are."

"Aye," Grant agreed, feeling a grim smile stretch his lips. "Come. Let us get in place to capture our quarry."

Chapter Four

"Eve!" Clara pounded at Eve's bedchamber door. "Eve, your silence toward me has continued long enough. I know well that you're avoiding me, and it has to stop!"

Glaring at the door, Eve shoved the remainder of her clothes in her satchel, sheathed her sword and her dagger, took one last look around the small, sparse space that had been her home for the last eight years, and turning, she strode to the door and opened it.

"I'm glad to see you've got your good sense back," Clara said, reaching for Eve.

"My good sense is intact," Eve said. "I have not forgiven your deception."

"You opened the door," Clara pointed out.

"Yes," Eve replied, refusing to offer more. Clara was a liar. Eve tried to step around Clara, but the woman moved swiftly to block Eve in the small passage.

"If you opened the door knowing I was on the other side, surely that means you are ready to listen to me. It's been six days since you discovered those letters."

Eve snorted. "Is six days the allotted time for forgiving someone for lying?" When Clara opened her mouth as if to answer, Eve shook her head. "Never mind! I don't want to hear whatever lies you will spew." Eve inhaled a shaky breath. "I opened the door because I'm leaving." She sidestepped Clara, but before she could take another step, Clara was gripping her arm. Eve could jerk herself free; she was stronger than Clara. Yet, despite the fact that the woman had lied to her for years, Eve could not bring herself to do something that might cause Clara harm. Clara still held a piece of her heart, though Eve tried to ignore the tug.

"What do you mean, you're leaving? You cannot be so foolish as to venture to market after the fiasco last time?"

Eve whirled to face Clara, incensed that the woman was lecturing her. "No, I'm not going to market." She watched in satisfaction as the woman's face drained of color. No doubt, Clara was realizing that Eve was truly leaving. "I'm going home," she said, delivering the blow intended to hurt, yet when Clara's fingers tightened on Eve's arm, Eve was dismayed at the niggle of guilt she felt and pity.

"Eve, no! How would you even get there?"

"I have my ways," Eve said, refusing to tell Clara that she'd arranged to ride with Summer Walkers who were traveling to the Lowlands. It was none of the woman's concern, not anymore. "Now, if you'll excuse me, I wish to say goodbye to the nuns." She swiveled on her heel, but before she could take more than two steps, Clara was calling to her to stop. Instead, Eve rushed ahead, practically running toward the chapel. The desperation in Clara's voice made Eve want to halt and listen to what Clara had to say. But if she did that, her silly heart may wish to believe, and she could not be such a trusting fool again.

She burst into the chapel, panting. As Sister Mary Margaret turned to her from the altar with a look of surprise on her face, Clara barreled in behind Eve, her nun habit swishing around her ankles. A peaceful look was upon Clara's face, until the door clicked shut, and then irritation swept her friend's features. Clara had a unique ability to disguise her emotions that Eve had always been impressed with. She played the part of a serene nun perfectly, and sometimes Eve almost forgot Clara was not a nun. "Eve Decres! I have cared for you for all your life! When you had fever, I tended you. When you cried yourself to sleep for months after your parents died, I dried your tears. I rocked you. I told you stories. When you had bad dreams, I held you close. You will at least let me explain why I lied to you."

Eve bit down hard on her lip as guilt washed over her. Clara had indeed done all of those things and more. She had baked Eve treats to remind her of home. She had told her stories of her father, her mother, and her sister, so even though they were dead, they would never be forgotten. Indecision warred within her, but when her gaze caught that of Sister Mary Margaret, who nodded encouragingly to her, Eve felt herself give. Slowly, she turned to Clara, who now stood by the door to the courtyard, misery etched upon her face as she twisted her hands.

"You could not rule the castle and choose a husband in your own right until this week," Clara rushed out.

"Yes," Eve confirmed. She already knew these things.

Clara let out a long sigh. "I could not allow you to venture home without knowing if your uncle betrayed your father or not. He could have forced you to wed a man of his choosing and simply taken the castle from you! At the very least, you should find a husband first."

"I intend to do so when I return home," Eve said, not bothering to gentle the tone of irritation she felt. She had long ago decided she'd rather be dead than forced to wed a man for her castle.

Clara looked stricken. "But Eve—"

"I trust my uncle," Eve said, punctuating each word.

"*Scots* kidnapped us. *Scots* invaded my home. Not Englishmen, like Uncle Frederick. My uncle will guard me judiciously until I have chosen the man I will marry. My uncle will know to have extra guards at the castle upon my return."

Sister Mary Margaret cleared her throat. "I believe the point Clara is trying to make is that your uncle very well could have been plotting with those Scots to take the castle and you from your father, and if that is the case—"

"My uncle would have never done that," Eve interrupted, recalling memories of sitting on her uncle's lap by the fire listening to his stories. Her uncle had given her first dagger to her. It could not be true. She refused to believe it. He was the only family she had left!

"Eve," Clara started gently. "I—"

The chapel door swung open with a bang, and a man loomed in the doorway. His brown hair was tightly pulled back at the nape of his neck to display a handsome face. He had a sword in one hand and daggers sheathed at both hips. Footsteps sounded behind him, and suddenly, more men appeared, all big, burly, and wearing plaids.

Eve took an instinctive step back, and when she did, the man's dark gaze locked on her from the doorway. He studied her eyes for a moment and then strode straight for her.

She reached for her sword and even as she unsheathed it, the man grasped Clara and held a sword to her neck. "Unless ye wish to see the nun die, I suggest ye hand me yer sword."

Fear swirled in Eve's mind, and before she could decide what to do, Sister Mary Margaret screamed from behind Eve and ran past her, a chalice grasped in her hands. Before the abbess neared the man holding Clara, one of the other men stepped forward and knocked the chalice away from her, then clutched the nun by the shoulder while raising his hand as if to strike her.

"No!" Eve and Clara shouted in unison.

"Hold!" the apparent leader bellowed, glaring at his man.

Eve gripped her sword tightly as relief poured through her.

The man offered her a courteous smile as he held out his hand. "Ye will nae get more than a swing in before ye are taken down, and I'd rather nae see ye injured."

"Considering that you have stormed into a convent and are holding a nun against her will, I'm sure you can understand that your words don't provide me much comfort," Eve said.

"Aye, I ken how ye would feel thusly." He nodded. "Be that as it may, I still require yer sword."

"And if I refuse?" Eve asked, sweeping her eyes over the stranger and his men. Hopelessness rushed through her. She was vastly outnumbered.

He offered a courteous smile. "Ye would force me to hurt the nun, which I dunnae care to do." The statement was delivered in such a matter-of-fact way that Eve was left with a certainty that the man would do whatever he must to get what he wanted, and she suspected he had come for her—led here, no doubt, by her own foolishness with the English knight in the market. Damn the bard. He must have spread her story, and the words of his song had given some hint of who she was. It had to be her eyes; she could think of no other characteristics she possessed that were so unique.

Her heart hammered as she raised her sword to the man.

"Eve, no!" Clara cried.

Eve winced at Clara's use of her given name. The woman's eyes widened as the man holding her chuckled. "Thank ye, Sister. Ye have just made things much simpler than I feared they might be." With that, he shoved Clara to the side, grasped Eve's sword, and threw it to the ground, well away from them. "Yer daggers, as well, Lady Decres."

Eve's fingers fluttered to her daggers sheathed at her hips, but she hesitated when she brushed the hilts. She would be weaponless, helpless, if she gave them up, just as she had been the night her family had been killed.

The man in front of her sighed. "Perhaps I was nae clear enough. Ye *will* be coming with us, and I'd rather it be without having to hurt ye or the nuns. Dunnae be foolish and cause one of them to be gravely injured." His warning was not even slightly veiled.

Reluctantly, Eve handed over the daggers. The man took them and sheathed them on his hips beside his own daggers. Then he closed the distance between them and reached toward her. He grasped her right arm and turned it so her wrist was facing him.

"Don't you dare defile her!" Clara screamed, starting for Eve and the stranger, but she was abruptly stopped with a hand to her shoulder by one of the other men.

The stranger in front of Eve did not spare a glance for Clara. Fear and anger knotted inside her as he yanked up the sleeve of Eve's gown and set his forefinger to the small, half-moon birthmark on her wrist. He thought of his own mark on his wrist, which he'd long ago seared into his skin himself. The branding had been meant to match the one that his brother and his closest friends, the Circle of Renegades, which included King Robert, all bore. His lips tugged into a smile as his gaze met hers. "I had a moment of doubt that ye were really Lady Decres, though it is unlikely that there is another lass with eyes the color of summer heather and hair the color of flames in the place the bard sang of. I'm a thorough man, however…" He shrugged as he traced her birthmark once more. "Eyes like heather, hair like flames, and marked on her wrist, my father told me."

She jerked her hand out of his grasp and glared at him. "What do you want with me?" It was hopeless to deny her identity now.

He raised his fingers to her face and when she pulled away, his hand snaked around her neck and stilled her. Her blood rushed in her ears as his fingers tightened around her neck. "What do I want with ye?" he murmured, looking thoughtful as if he were truly contemplating her question. "I want yer castle. And so, lass, I will take ye and wed ye."

She sucked in a sharp breath as panic rioted within her.

"Dunnae be scairt, Lady Decres," he said, his tone low and lethal. "If ye always do as I bid, ye will please me and yer life will be well."

"And if I don't?" she asked, though she knew the answer. Men just like this one were the reason Clara had hidden Eve away in the first place.

"Dunnae make me clip yer wings, little bird. It will surely hurt." With that, he released her to his men. "Bring her."

"What do ye mean Thomas and Allisdair are nae here?" Grant demanded of his cousin as he and Ross stormed into the great hall passing the clanspeople lined up to the right to make requests and complaints of the laird as was customary every Sunday.

Bryden, who'd been sitting in the laird's chair at the dais fulfilling the duties of the Fraser laird in Simon's absence, looked warily between Grant and Ross. They probably looked as exhausted as they felt. They had ridden hard and fast for a sennight from London to Dithorn, stopping only to steal a few hours of rest. Simon's death had plagued him in the short times he should have been resting, so that his respite was fitful. Combining that with taking on the added burden of carrying his captive, Laird MacDougall, before him on his horse, Grant felt he would soon drop like a stone released from a great height, fast and hard.

The numbing weariness was well worth it to obtain vengeance for Simon, of course, but Grant was so tired now his lids felt heavy, his eyes burned, and his vision had taken on a blurriness that he could not blink away. Still, rest would have to wait. At least he did not have to think about MacDougall at the moment. He had handed off the laird to one of the guards the minute they had ridden into the courtyard at Dithorn. The devil should now be sitting in the Thief's Hole.

Besides a guard unlocking the door to the cave, the only way out of the stone hole that was used to house those who'd killed a member of the clan was to jump from the open side of the cave, and that jump only led to death. It was more than a 200-foot drop to the rocks and rough sea below, and no man had ever made the jump and lived to tell of it. If MacDougall chose to end his life in that manner, then so be it. It would bring further shame to the man's legacy than what he had already heaped upon himself by being careless and getting himself captured and six of his guards killed. Ross and Grant had followed the men after they'd left the pub and had taken them by surprise the next night when MacDougall had made camp. It had been easy, for the man and his warriors were too certain of themselves.

Grant blew out a long breath, shoving his thoughts of MacDougall aside. He motioned to the clanspeople who were still lined up in the great hall to make complaints or ask a request, as was the weekly custom. "Leave us," he said.

"Where is Laird Fraser?" one of the clansmen shouted.

The typically unremarkable question was like a dagger in Grant's heart. His throat immediately tightened. He had to tell the clan, but not before he told his brother, sister, and cousin. He motioned to one of the men standing nearest the exit. "Gather the clan in the courtyard. I will be there before the nooning meal to speak with everyone."

The man frowned. "What of our requests and complaints?"

Grant's head throbbed with the effort not to get choked up. "I'll hear them after the nooning meal. All of you—" he swept a hand to the people in line "—may return then. I have pressing business right now."

The clansmen nodded and began to file out, accustomed to Grant giving orders to them from the time Simon had been absent when he'd been a spy at the English court. They likely assumed Simon was on another mission. Grief rose in him as it did every day, coming in waves like the ocean. Sometimes they were high, sometimes low, yet there always.

"Cousin," Bryden protested, "I can finish listening to our people after the nooning meal."

"Nay, 'tis my duty," Grant said, as it was when Simon was absent and now forever. Desolation was the beat of his heart.

Bryden scowled. "Aye, but ye clearly need rest. Ye look—"

"Hold yer tongue," Grant snapped, irritated that Bryden would announce to the clan how tired he appeared. Lairds could never show weakness, for the minute they did, an enemy would take advantage. And like it or not, he was now laird. Grant had been taught to always show a strong face by his father, and it had been reinforced by Simon.

"I am nae ever too tired to do my duties," he assured his clanspeople as they moved slowly toward the door to exit the great hall. Once Grant, Bryden, and Ross were alone in the great hall, Grant turned to Bryden to express his irritation.

"I'm sorry," Bryden said before Grant could get a word out. "I spoke out of concern for ye. It's clear by yer and Ross's faces that ye are both exhausted, but I should have held my tongue."

"Aye," Grant said, "ye should have. But realizing yer mistake and admitting it is sufficient."

Bryden's shoulders sagged. Grant's cousin was a good man, just a young and impetuous one. Grant remembered being impetuous himself not long ago, before his strain with Simon when he'd thought Simon a traitor. Grant's life had become fully about duty to his clan after that. It was a heavy weight to carry but not one he had begrudged. The weight felt heavier now, as well it should. It was his own damn failure to rescue Simon that was the reason he now stood here as laird. Simon should be here. Simon should be laird. In this moment, Grant hated himself, yet he could not even allow self-disgust or pity to linger. Too many people counted on him to keep them safe. He could never again afford to be impetuous or even think of himself. His life was about duty and responsibility to the clan.

And now it was about vengeance, as well.

Ross met his gaze. "Grant—"

"Aye, I ken yer concern for yer brother," he interrupted. He was just as concerned about Thomas's whereabouts. The two lads were impetuous alone, but together, they were trouble. Still, he'd not thought his brother would defy King Robert's command to return to safety. God only knew what scheme the two may have hatched and where it may have led them. Or at least he hoped it was just the two of them getting delayed. The Frasers had many enemies, and what if…?

"The lads did nae arrive here?" he asked again, arching his eyebrows at his cousin. He wanted to make sure he had the details correct before he sent out a search party.

"Nay, Cousin. We've nae seen Thomas since he rode out after ye and Simon. Speaking of Simon… Where is he?"

Grant's throat constricted as he tried to speak. He had to swallow, and when his tongue still would not form the dreaded words, he stalked to the dais, poured a mug of mead, and swiftly gulped it down. He set the mug down with a thud and turned back to Bryden. "He's dead," he finally managed to force out, rage burning in him as Simon's face appeared in his mind.

"Dead?" a choked cry came from the door.

Grant stifled a curse as he turned to see his sister, Esme, standing in the entrance to the great hall. Tears welled in her blue eyes, but she swiped them away, defiance of her own weakness apparent on her face. Hurt for his sister, and all the loss they'd endured, streaked through him. "Esme—"

"Nay!" she said, holding up a hand as he started toward her. "I dunnae need sympathy any more than Bryden does."

That was not true, but Grant would not embarrass her by arguing the point. His fair and fragile sister liked to consider herself a warrior, but he'd learned long ago the importance of protecting those he loved, even if from themselves.

"What happened?" Bryden asked, sounding oddly detached, which Grant knew had to be from shock.

Grant glanced toward Esme, not wanting her to hear the gruesome details. "Esme—"

"I wish to ken it, too," she cut in, her tone defensive but her words laced with emotion.

Sighing, Grant jerked a hand through his hair in frustration. If he denied her request, he knew she'd be embarrassed and hurt. She had enough to endure today without one more lecture from him on why a lass should wear a gown and not hear the tale of how her brother lost his head. Grant's chest squeezed, but he forced out the words, "So be it," and then quickly relayed the MacDougall clan's betrayal. "I brought the MacDougall here to lure his son to us. Then we can serve them the justice they deserve. Meanwhile, it will send a message to our enemies."

"Let us kill him now!" Esme clumsily withdrew the sword that had once been their mother's.

He shook his head at her, eyeing the sword with the same regret he always felt when he saw it. Their mother had died because Grant had secretly taught her how to wield that very sword, despite knowing his father would not like it. And she'd become overly confident when she should not have been. He'd thought to destroy the damnable sword after her death, but Esme had begged him to let her have it, and he'd finally agreed with the strict orders that no one ever teach her how to wield it. He'd thought having their mother's great cumbersome sword would show Esme that she was not meant to be a warrior, but to his everlasting frustration, it had made her all the more determined.

"Nay," Grant said. "Sheathe yer sword, Esme. Ye'll nae have a part in this. I want ye overseeing the kitchens as

Simon told ye before we left." When she opened her mouth to no doubt protest, he glared her into silence and then spoke. "I want the MacDougall dead more than any man or woman," he added for Esme's sake. "But first we will use him to get his son, as well. When we are done with the MacDougall clan, there will nae be a clan left to oppose King Robert or betray Scotland—or us—again."

"Let me be the one to guard the MacDougall," Bryden offered.

Grant shook his head. "Nay. I want ye to take a party of men out to search for Thomas and Allisdair immediately after I tell the clan of Simon."

"I'll go on the search as well," Ross said.

Grant nodded, not surprised that Ross had spoken up. Ross was as close to his brothers as Grant was to his. He stilled. He could not lose Thomas. His family, his blood was being taken from him all too soon. He had to protect Esme and Thomas, and his cousin. "Ye two take a small party and search the roads from the woods to Tyndrum. And be careful. If ye are spotted by the English…"

"Our heads will likely end up beside Simon's," Ross finished.

Grant nodded, already thinking where he would search. He'd scour the woods and the lands from his borders to those of all his enemies around him, but he'd have to do it by day. If Aros came to rescue his father, Grant had little doubt the man would try to storm the castle by night. It had always been that way, though it was a foolish decision. The cliffs to Dithorn were steep, and night provided little visibility, though it did offer cover.

"Leave at daylight," he said, glancing first to Ross and then Bryden. "Cousin, have one of the upstairs servants show Ross to a bedchamber so he can get some rest before ye depart." He started past them toward the door, but stopped at Esme, giving her a fierce hug. She tremored in his arms for a moment, then pushed away.

"I have work to do," she said, her voice a shaky whisper.

He nodded, understanding as Esme rushed from the room. Later, he would go to her. Now, he realized, she needed to be alone. She was in shock, and she would not allow herself to break down in front of any of them. Once Esme had fled, Grant turned to leave as well.

"Grant!" Ross called. "Where are ye going?"

"To start the search for our brothers," he replied not turning back. "I'll be back in time to speak with the clan in the courtyard."

"Ye need rest, as well," Ross shouted to Grant's back.

Grant raised a hand in farewell. "Lairds rest when they're dead," he said, smiling to himself as he recalled Simon and their father telling him the same thing many times. He was laird now, and he had much to live up to. He would not disappoint his father and brother.

Chapter Five

When the flap of Eve's tent was thrown open and the man who'd told her his name was Aros loomed in the doorway, Eve cursed herself for the fear that shot through her and caused gooseflesh to cover her body. They had ridden for four days, stopping only to water the horses and allow them brief periods of rest, but Eve had not been untied at all during that time until moments ago.

She was so sore that she could barely stand, but she jumped to her feet now and scuttled backward to put distance between her and the Highlander, who had not spoken more than two words to her since he had taken her. Her fingers fluttered to her wrists where the tightly tied ropes had cut deep into her skin. Without a word, Aros stalked into the tent. His gaze swept over her and then lingered on her wrists for a moment before he strode to her and yanked her hands up to look at her wounds.

With a curse, he released her hands, stomped out of the tent, and shouted, "Bring Tyrion to me."

The flap of the tent was flung back once more, and Aros stalked back in and pointed to the ground where a pallet had been placed for her. "Sit. I'm certain ye must be exhausted, and we have two more nights before we reach the Highlands. My father will wish us wed that night."

Eve did not move. Instead, she inhaled a long breath

and folded her hands in front of her. "I will not wed you."

"Ye will," he replied. He sounded so sure about it that fear trickled through her.

"I won't," she repeated. "I will never wed you and grant you control of my castle."

Eyes as dark as obsidian narrowed on her. He opened his mouth, but a voice came from outside of the tent before he could speak.

"Aros, ye called for me?"

"Enter," Aros commanded, his tone cold.

The warrior who had tied her wrists entered the chamber and stopped in front of Aros. "Ye've need of me?" the man, Tyrion, asked, a hint of wariness in his voice.

"Aye," Aros replied, motioning at Eve. "If ye ever tie her wrists so tightly that the ropes injure her again, I'll cut off yer hands. Do ye ken me?" The man flinched but nodded, and Aros waved a dismissive hand. "Leave us." As Tyrion departed, Aros moved close to Eve and took hold of her chin in a viselike grip. "As my wife, ye will be protected."

She shuddered that his first response would be to maim the man. Never would she bind herself to such a person. Eve swallowed. "As your wife, I would be caged and ruled by you."

"Everyone is controlled by someone, Lady Decres."

Her parents had been partners in governing her father's castle. Eve knew it was unusual, but that was what she had hoped to have one day. "Well, you will not control me, because I will never wed you. Not this night, nor any other."

"Then we will wed in the day," Aros said with a mocking smile, "or we will both face my father's wrath."

Eve tensed, but she was saved responding by a man

calling from outside the tent. "Aros! Ye're needed at once."

Aros frowned and started for the exit. When he reached the flap, he turned toward her. "Sleep, little bird. We ride early tomorrow for our destinies. And ye can rest easy kenning a guard is outside of yer tent."

The flap fluttered closed behind him, and Eve moved toward it to listen. Several voices talked urgently and all at once, but they were too far away for her to make out the words. Sighing, she scanned the tent, contemplating if she could somehow escape from another side of it, but when she moved to the back and lifted an edge, dismay coiled in her stomach. Men guarded her tent from all sides.

Hopelessness threatened to overwhelm her, possibly as much as her weariness did. She lowered herself to the ground and hugged her knees to her chest. She needed sleep. Her mind would be clearer with it. Clara had always said a proper rest cured much.

Oh, Clara.

Eve's throat constricted with remorse that the last words she'd said to Clara were harsh ones. Yes, she had lied to Eve, but she could now see why, even if the woman was wrong about Uncle Frederick. Clara had simply feared for her.

Lying on her back, Eve squeezed her eyes shut, as warm tears seeped out and rolled across the sides of her temples. In the morning, she would have a clearer head, and she would escape.

"Get up!"

The shouted command jerked Eve from sleep. Hands clutched her arms, and she was dragged to her feet before her vision had even focused. Early-morning light and cool air hit her at once, making her squint and shiver as she was pushed through the tent flap and into the day.

"Please!" came a boy's cry.

Eve blinked and focused on the scene coming rapidly close to her as she was propelled forward by the guard who'd awoken her. Aros stood in the center of the MacDougall camp brandishing a whip. Two ragged boys, not yet men but no longer children, knelt before him. They did not wail, but one hissed in pain and the other moaned when he moved. Eve's heart squeezed in her chest and outrage filled her breast. She instinctively reached for her sword, only to remember it had been taken from her. Aros's whip whistled through the air to crack against the back of one of the boys. He yelped so loud that a moan escaped Eve. When she was pushed closer to Aros and the boys, and she saw their bloody backs, nausea roiled her stomach.

"Stop it!" she shouted when Aros lashed one of the boys again.

A tall man with blond hair stood beside Aros and frowned at Eve when she spoke. "Silence, woman," the man said. "Ye have nae been given permission to speak."

Aros glanced at her then, rage twisting his features. "Dunnae fash yerself for these lads, Eve. They are our enemies. That one," he said, kicking the back of the smaller boy who had curly red hair, "is a worthless MacLorh. And this one—" he pointed to the bigger lad with wavy brown hair who had just been lashed "—is a Fraser. His traitor brother has captured my father."

The Fraser lad appeared to be no more than thirteen or fourteen summers, and he looked over his shoulder to glare at Aros. The glare was not as effective as it might have otherwise been, given the unshed tears that filled the boy's eyes. "My brother is nae a traitor! He's loyal to the King of Scotland. Ye're the traitor, ye filthy coward."

"Ye squeal just like yer older brother did before his head was lopped from his body," Aros taunted.

She tried not to gasp. He raised the whip to lash the boy once more. This time, the lad did not utter a sound, but his face went white, whether from rage, pain, surprise, or a combination of the three, Eve was uncertain. All she knew was the lads would likely be killed if she did not think of some way to stop Aros.

"My liege," she said, forcing herself to take on a placating tone. "Could you not trade these boys for your father?"

Aros did not spare a glance for her but continued to whip the boys. "I dunnae need boys to aid me in getting my father back. I'll storm the damn Fraser castle, kill Grant Fraser, and secure my father's freedom," Aros roared, almost in a frenzy now.

Bile rose in Eve's throat at the exhibition of such hatred. She swallowed, feeling shaky. When the redheaded lad suddenly slumped forward and went limp, she knew she had to do something drastic to make Aros listen to her. A glance around at his gathered men, who looked too fearful to speak to their leader at all, told her that none of these cowards had the courage to utter a protest on behalf of these lads.

"Aros, please," she begged, but he ignored her and continued to lash the Fraser lad, whose back was looking more horrid by the breath. What could she say? What would get Aros's attention? Suddenly, she knew, and she blurted, "I will willingly wed you if you will but stop lashing the lad! I cannot stand it!"

Immediately, Aros drew the whip down and turned to

her. "The lass has a gentle heart."

She nodded, even as thoughts of killing this man before her ran through her mind. It was a very good thing he could not see into her heart at the moment. "I cannot abide others being hurt—even ones loyal to the wrong king," she added as an afterthought. She did not know enough about the political happenings of Scotland and England to make an informed decision on whom she believed should sit upon the Scottish throne, but it seemed to her that a Scot should rule his own country and not King Edward, who had all of England with which to content himself. Needing to reign over both Scotland and England seemed greedy to her. Still, she would withhold her decision as to where she would align her men and her castle, until she was well-versed on the political landscape and honor of both men.

"I appreciate yer kind heart, lass," Aros said, swiping his hand across the perspiration on his brow, which the wretch had gotten from his efforts in lashing the lads, "but it's best to kill one's enemies so they kinnae conspire against ye, as my father always says."

Eve wanted to snap at Aros and tell him to think for himself. He was like an obedient dog to his father, it seemed, but she bit her cheek on the urge. "I will not ever willingly wed you if you kill these lads or harm them any more. I cannot in good conscience bind myself to a man who would harm innocent young boys. They cannot help the crimes of their families any more than you can help the evils done by yours," she finished, daring to speak so close to her inner thoughts. He looked thoughtful for a moment, as if contemplating her words. She needed to press the seeming advantage while she still could. "This castle your father is being held at—"

"Dithorn," Aros supplied.

"Is it well fortified? Situated in a way that would make it easy to breach?" She could tell from the uneasy looks exchanged by his men that the castle must be very difficult to attack successfully.

"I will spare the filth," he said, motioning to the boys. "But only because it pleases ye, and I wish to content my soon-to-be wife."

What a liar this man was. He spared the boys because he finally saw the wisdom in using them to trade for his father. She forced a smile, though it made her face feel as if it would crack in two. She had saved the lads and doomed herself. She prayed she would find a way to escape.

"Truss the boys like the pigs they are," Aros demanded, and then to her grim astonishment, he held his hand out to her. "Ye shall ride with me today."

Left with little recourse but to agree, she inclined her head and soon found herself upon Aros's destrier with the man pressed firmly against her. He captured the reins with one hand while slipping the other tightly about her waist. "Little bird, ye have made me happy this day."

"I'm glad," she lied through gritted teeth.

"Soon, I will rule yer castle, and ye will give me sons."

"And if I were to give you only daughters?" she asked, thinking of her and her sister, and then recalling her mother telling her of the grand feasts her father had ordered on the days they each had been born. Her father had not cared a whit that her mother had not given him sons. He was simply thrilled to have children of his blood with her mother.

"Daughters are good for gaining me more land, but I require sons, so you *will* give me sons. And if you cannot, I'll take another to my bed who will."

"You would have a bastard?" She was surprised that

he'd suffice with a child not of wedlock, though she was not surprised to hear he'd take another to his bed.

"Nay, I'd nae have a bastard."

She frowned. "But you just said..." Her words trailed off as she realized what he was implying. He would kill her if she did not give him sons. Never, never would she wed this man. "'Tis good to understand the value you place on a wife," she snapped.

"I place the same as any man, Lady Eve. Ye will come to ken that, the more ye see of the world."

Was he right? Had her father been the exception in how he had loved her mother and truly valued her? Eve squeezed her eyes shut as the horses began to gallop, and fuzzy, long-forgotten memories of her parents played through her head. She had known since the day she'd been named heir that men would want her for her inheritance, but she'd believed that one day, she would meet a man who would want her more for her than her castle. Perhaps it had been a foolish hope. Perhaps, she would be better served to hope to find a man who would be honorable and strong enough and cunning enough, to defend her castle. The thought of having to give up on love left her feeling bleak, but when she heard a whimper to her left and opened her eyes to see the smaller of the two lads groaning upon his horse, she buried her ebbing despair.

She was an heiress with responsibilities. She needed to escape, and then she needed to secure a strong, honorable husband, who, God willing, wanted her more than the castle. A desperate ache to hear Clara's counsel, to feel her warm, comforting arms around her shoulders, pierced Eve. Thank God above, it had not occurred to Aros to take Clara with them to use her to get Eve to acquiesce to whatever he demanded. For now, Clara was safe, and Eve would do whatever it took to ensure her friend remained that way.

Eve reached out in the dark for the lads who had just been shoved to the ground beside her. No one had tents this night. They'd galloped across the countryside all day, and Aros had ordered his men not to make camp, as they would be riding again in a few hours. Eve and the lads had been left by a tree with a guard close enough to see them if they tried to flee but not so close that he could hear them if they whispered. In the distance, a fire flickered, and Eve could just barely make out silhouettes of men huddled around it. Aros had claimed he was thoughtful, but his supposed thoughtfulness did not extend to warmth this night for her or the boys. For herself, she did not care, but one of the lads was violently trembling while the other hissed when he breathed.

She scooted across the damp grass and tree roots toward the boys, her heart aching for them. "Shh," she said, patting one of their shoulders.

"I'm nae weeping," came a stubborn young voice. "That's Allisdair. He's younger than me."

"I'm nae weeping, either," protested the other boy. "I'm sucking air in slowly. 'Tis different. 'Tis manly."

Eve had to smile at the bravery the two were determined to display.

"Lean against me, both of you," Eve instructed, knowing they must be exhausted and in pain.

Immediately a head came to her left shoulder and a solid weight settled against her. The smell of sweat and dirt filled her nose, as well as the scent of blood. She frowned, wishing she had something to ease the pain the lads were likely in. She didn't have to wonder long which boy had laid his head against her because Allisdair gulped in air.

"I'm nae weeping," he assured her again. "But my back does ache."

"Aye," the Fraser lad said. "Allisdair is nae a cry baby, or I'd nae be his friend. But ye do need to quit sucking in air like that as if ye *are* going to cry," the Fraser lad chided.

"I was hit longer and harder than ye were, Thomas," Allisdair objected.

Thomas shook his head. "Ye were nae. I simply dunnae suck air because Fraser men dunnae show weakness."

Eve bit her lip on the desire to laugh at the exchange between the two boys. "Who told you that, Thomas? Your laird?"

"His brother Simon always said that," Allisdair supplied between sniffles.

"Simon's dead," Thomas said numbly. But Eve heard the boy shift several times beside her, and she suspected he was working very hard to hold in his emotions so that neither she nor his friend would see him upset.

"Thomas, won't you rest your head on my shoulder?" she asked.

"Ye're a Sassenach," Thomas replied, as if that one sentence explained everything.

Eve frowned into the darkness. "And you don't like the English?" She considered her own long-held opinion that Highlanders were barbarians. Aros surely was, but these two lads seemed nice.

"Yer king just killed my brother," Thomas supplied in that same emotionless tone.

"Aros told us that the king ordered Simon's head removed," Allisdair bit out, his voice rising with emotion.

"Not so loud," Eve cautioned them in a fierce whisper.

So Thomas had just learned his brother had been killed. "How did you two come to be in the woods outside your clans' borders?"

"We disobeyed the king," Allisdair whispered. "King Robert ordered us to go straight to the Fraser holding, but we wanted to help save Simon."

She nodded slowly. "To help whom save your brother?"

"My other brother...Grant," Thomas said, his voice hitching as if he'd shoved past great emotion that he was holding in. "Grant insisted we were too young to aid him and that we would hinder him and Ross."

"Who is Ross?" Eve asked, trying to keep up.

"Ross is *my* elder brother," Allisdair supplied, pride clear in his tone. "He's going to be livid when he sees me."

"For disobeying?" Eve asked.

"Aye, and for getting caught. And he'll kill Aros for whipping me."

"If we ever *see* our family again," Thomas muttered. "I dunnae trust Aros. He's worse than an Englishman; he's a traitor to all Scots."

Eve pressed her fingers to her temples. She had a pounding ache in her head. "You will see your family. I vow it. Aros wants very much to wed me, and he understands I will not willingly say the vows if he harms you."

"He loves ye verra much?" Allisdair asked.

"No," she said, sighing. "He—" She stopped. She'd spent her life avoiding telling people who she really was so that evil men would not try to capture her and force her to wed them, but it no longer mattered. She had been captured by an evil man, and unless she could get free, she would be forced to wed him or she'd be killed. She did not want to die, and she did not want to wed Aros. Somehow she'd have to escape, but she could tell these lads who she was. She'd never see them again. They'd be traded, and she'd hopefully be far away soon after ensuring they were safe. And then she would make her way to her uncle in the borderlands. "He wishes to wed me so that he may gain Linlithian Castle, to which I'm the heiress."

"Why did ye say ye would wed him, then?" Allisdair asked, bemused.

"Ye're such a clot-heid sometimes, Allisdair. She said she'd wed him to save us. Did ye nae?" Thomas asked, turning to her.

"I did, but don't you worry for me. I will escape somehow, once I know you two have safely been returned to your brothers."

Beside her, Allisdair yawned loudly and leaned more fully into her. Eve started humming a tune that Clara had always hummed for her, and soon, the boy became limp against her. Eve lowered his head to her lap and brushed her hands through his locks. It was not long before she could feel the rise and fall of his chest and then heard his snoring.

"You must be tired, as well," she said to Thomas, who was staring up at the sky, silent.

"Nay, I'm a Fraser man."

She smiled at that. Thomas was hardly yet a man, but she would not be the one to tell him so. "Fraser men don't get tired?" she asked, teasing him just a bit in hopes to ease his pain.

"We do, but we dunnae show it."

"What do Fraser men show?" She was truly curious as to what principles this boy had been raised to embrace.

"Honor. Allegiance. Courage. *Je suis prest.*"

She had to admit, those first three codes were good ones. She tried to adhere to them, as well. "What does '*Je suis prest*' mean?"

"I am ready," he replied. The wobble in his voice betrayed doubt that he was certain that he was indeed prepared.

"What are you ready for, Thomas?" she asked softly.

"Vengeance... I'm certain my brother Grant will avenge Simon, and I will aid him, as will all the warriors in my clan. I—" He paused, and she heard him audibly swallow, but the grief that she imagined had been rising in him since he'd learned of his brother's death could not be held back. Very quietly he sniffled, and she suspected, he was quietly crying.

She touched his leg and squeezed it, offering silent support. After a moment, the sniffling ceased and he drew a shuddering breath. "I should nae have done that," he said solemnly.

She pressed her lips together on responding right away. It was obviously very important to him to appear unaffected. She understood that. Still, she asked, "You should nae have done what?" She hoped he understood that she would never tell a soul, though he hardly needed to worry since they would soon be parted.

"Cried," he said. "I'm sorry I judged ye, too. Ye may be Sassenach, but ye're verra honorable. Like a Highlander."

"That's quite all right," she said, wincing as she thought of the judgments she'd made about Highlanders. So far, they'd proven to be correct, except for Thomas and Allisdair. But they were only lads and had not yet had time to be made into unscrupulous savages.

"Ye dunnae like Highlanders?" he asked carefully.

"I like you and Allisdair," she reassured him.

"Aye, I ken, but why do ye dislike Highlanders?"

She told him of her parents and her sister being killed, and how she had been kidnapped herself but had escaped. She also told him of her time in the convent.

When she finished, he said, "Just because the men who took ye had Scottish accents dunnae mean they were Highlanders. They could have been Lowlanders."

"Well, Clara seemed to think their accent sounded of a Highland bent. It's of no matter. I should not have judged a whole group of people based on that. You're a Highlander, and you seem to be a very honorable, brave lad."

"I'm nearly a man," he boasted.

"Yes, of course," she said as solemnly as she could. "But even men need sleep. Why not rest your eyes?"

"I..." He hesitated, and she heard him audibly swallow once more. "I'm scairt," he whispered so softly it took her a moment to process what he'd said.

"I promise not to let anything happen to you so long as I draw breath. You have my vow as a Decres."

His face scrunched up. "Women give vows?"

His astonishment made her laugh. "Yes, we do." Though her knowledge of the rest of the world was admittedly limited, she felt certain there were other women out there who made vows to protect others.

He held out his hand to her. "I dunnae have my dagger, because Aros took it, but clasp my hand?" She did as he asked because his tone had become serious. "My brothers always said that when ye form an alliance ye must offer something in return."

"I see," she said slowly. His brothers certainly did sound like honorable men. Her heart broke thinking one of them had been killed.

"Ye are giving me yer protection this night, so I vow ye have mine."

"Thank you," she said, leaning toward him and giving him a quick hug. The lad would soon be gone and forget all about her, no doubt, but she appreciated this moment. If she could only meet a man who had the same true heart as this lad, one not yet corrupted by greed, then maybe love could be hers.

Chapter Six

"They could be dead," Bryden said.

"Nay," Grant and Ross answered in unison, then looked at each other as an unspoken agreement passed between them.

Thomas and Allisdair had been missing for a fortnight. The countryside had been scoured, the path to London had been searched, and there was no sign of them. Yet neither man was willing to count their younger brothers as dead until their bodies were cold before them. The mere thought filled Grant with terror. He could not lose Thomas, too.

Grant stared at the map on the table in the great hall, trying to decide where they should look next. The weariness pressing on him made it hard to concentrate, and as he stared down at the maps, the door swung open with a bang and Kade rushed in.

Grant glared at his commander of the watch. Kade had been instructed to train the men in Grant's absence. "Unless someone has died in training, I dunnae wish to be disturbed."

"Aros is here, and he has yer brothers."

For a moment, shock held Grant still, but then rage flooded him. He withdrew his sword, the blade singing from its sheath in harmony with Ross's. Grant looked to his friend. "He's mine to kill."

"Only since we are on yer land, but if ye fail—"

Grant nodded. "Finish the deed, cut off his head, and set it on a spike upon the long path to Dithorn."

"They've come by horse upon the steep mountainside trail," Kade clarified, "and they are flying a truce flag."

Grant made a derisive sound at those words. "Aros dunnae wish for a truce."

Kade nodded, stepped toward Grant, and handed him a folded note. "I agree, but that is the game he plays for now. He sent a rider ahead for ye. He told me what the letter contained so I'd ken the urgency."

Just then, the door to the great hall flew open once more and Esme raced through the entrance, long blond hair flapping behind her. "Does nae anybody knock?" Grant asked, frowning at Esme's attire. He'd told her a thousand times it wasn't proper for a lass to wear braies, but the hellion refused to wear gowns, just as she'd so far refused to consider marriage, though at eighteen summers, she was plenty old enough.

Esme set her hands on her hips and glared at Grant. "I was on the rampart, and I saw the MacDougalls approach. I want to fight!"

"Ye can help by staying in the safety of the castle," he snapped. "I've told ye a thousand times nae to go up to the ramparts." For one thing, she distracted the men up there. Esme was a beautiful lass, though she did not appear to realize it. But his men did. They would stare at his sister when they should be concentrating on the narrow passage below that led to the castle. One thing Grant had learned while he led the clan when Simon had been playing the traitor in England was that no matter how seasoned a man was, the one thing above all else that could make him weak was a beguiling lass.

Esme's face took on a very familiar, stubborn look. Devil take her. She intended to argue, and he simply did not have the time to be as patient with her as he always tried to be. Esme's life had been hard. Losing both their parents when Esme was so young. And now Simon's death clearly had shaken Esme to her core, as it had him.

"I dunnae wish to be kept in a safe place like a valuable," she said. "I wish to fight by yer side."

"And I wish ye wed to a man who can take ye in hand. If ye refuse to leave this room now, I'll write to the laird of the MacPherson clan and tell him I accept his offer to wed ye to his son, and then I'll see that the wedding takes place in the next sennight."

She gasped. "Ye would nae!"

"I would, and I likely should have done just that when ye first refused the offer."

Esme bit her lip. "At least let me stay and hear what's transpiring."

With a sigh, he waved her to a chair. "Nae a word from yer mouth, ye ken?"

"I ken ye," she muttered. "I'm nae deaf nor dumb." She strode to the chair closest to them and sat, a mutinous look settling on her face.

Grant frowned, refocused his attention on Kade, and reaching out, he took the paper from his commander. He unfolded it and read the letter aloud:

"Laird Fraser,

I will give ye until the striking of the next bell to release my father. If ye do this, I will release yer brother and the MacLorh lad. If nae, I will slit their throats and attack yer home, take my father, and kill ye as I killed yer brother Simon. If ye try to attack me and my men, I assure ye, yer brother will die before I do.

Aros MacDougall"

Grant crumpled up the note and threw it in the fire, his anger swirling within.

"Grant," Ross began, his worry evident by his tight tone.

"Dunnae fash yerself, Ross. I will send the MacDougall, but at the same time, Aros must send us our brothers. We will nae release the MacDougall before then."

"Cousin, what is yer plan?" Bryden asked. "Let me be the one to accompany MacDougall to his son for ye. I fear Aros will try to kill ye."

"Dunnae fash yerself about me. I ken how to protect myself. And if Aros attempts to kill me, our men can attack with one simple signal," Grant said. "Aros is in a desperate situation, and he kens it. Dithorn is impregnable unless someone on the inside turns traitor."

"I'd kill any man who did such a thing," Kade growled.

"As would I," Bryden added.

Grant acknowledged both men's comments with a nod, even as he thought upon the likelihood of a traitor in their midst. It was never out of the realm of possibility, which was why he was always checking in with the guards, speaking with them, and taking their measure. There was one entrance route to the castle, and it was a plunging nightmare, a narrowed path carved into the rock from the seashore to the land at the top of the cliff upon which Dithorn sat. Whoever dared to venture onto that pathway risked their lives. The path twisted narrowly, purposely, so that the would-be attacker would be blind to the archers lying in wait. And they did wait, day after day, night after night, frequently rotating the guard duty, for only the men he considered the best shots with the truest character could be given the responsibility.

"I ken Aros crows like a rooster about breaching Dithorn, but I also ken he will nae hesitate to kill Thomas and Allisdair if I dunnae send him his father. I will nae sacrifice the boys for vengeance. Vengeance will come for Simon another way, so help me God." Grant felt as if a fire had been lit in his heart, which sparked flames through his body. "I will hunt Aros and his father down until both their heads are on spikes."

"I will aid ye," Ross and Kade declared as one.

"Ye ken ye always have my sword arm," Kade said.

"And mine as well," Bryden added. "We are as brothers!"

"Aye," Grant agreed, looking to Bryden. His cousin had been raised more like a brother than a cousin after his father, Grant's uncle, had been killed ten summers earlier by an English knight. Grant's father had become laird after his elder brother had died, and he'd raised Bryden as one of their brothers, honoring him by making him head of all the guards, since he was no longer in line to be laird of the clan. Bryden had always been loyal.

"Bryden, bring me some parchment," Grant said.

Bryden rushed to the end of the table and came back with parchment and a quill. Grant took them and quickly penned his response, reading it aloud as he did:

> "I will bring yer father to ye. I will meet ye at the entrance."

Grant paused to think. If they met there, Aros, his father, and whatever man Aros brought would have to get their horses up the other side of the mountain to the woods before they found cover from arrows in the dense forest. If Grant worded things just so, perhaps Aros would not realize what Grant intended.

> *"Ye may bring one man and nae more. Bid yer other men to stay at the path to the other side of the mountain. My warriors will be ready, so dunnae think to cross me. Once the exchange is made, I will hold the temporary truce until ye are off Dithorn Cliff. Then the peace is over.*
>
> *Laird Fraser"*

Only the cliff carved into the land upon which Dithorn actually sat was known as Dithorn Cliff. The other side of the mountain, the side they'd need to climb to reach the woods, was simply called Fraser Mountain. The only trail up that mountain to the woods was a narrow one that had several drops to the sea below.

He trembled as he stared down at the title he'd just signed, a potent reminder that Simon was gone.

Ross arched an eyebrow at Grant. "Ye mean to have the archers kill the men as they traverse Fraser Mountain?"

Grant grinned. "Aye. The righteous shall prevail," he said, reciting the motto that Simon had long ago told him by which Bruce's closest confidants, known as the Circle of Renegades, lived. He handed the letter to Kade. "Take this to Aros personally. If his answer is aye, hold yer sword high above yer head and I'll bring the MacDougall down."

"I should be the one to take the offer," Ross said.

"Nay. It would be far too tempting for Aros to have the laird of the Frasers *and* the brother of the laird of the MacLorhs at his fingertips. Ye must remain, and if anything should go amiss, take control and care for Esme."

"Move yer arse," Grant said not long later as he pushed Laird MacDougall along the path around the mountain and through the tunnel that led to the sandy shore and water. Up ahead, the sunlight streamed in, so he knew they were close to the entrance. He nodded to another set of his warriors as he passed them. Each man had been informed of what was occurring, from the guard on the wall above, to the warriors in the tunnel, to the archers situated upon the cliffs of the mountain passage, their arrows aimed toward the men on the shore. They understood their roles: protect the lads, guard the tunnel, kill the MacDougalls.

When he came out of the tunnel, he increased his grip on his sword and on the rope that bound the MacDougall's hands behind his back.

"Grant!" Thomas shouted, his dirt-smudged face cracking into a wide, relieved smile. He tried to surge forward, but the guard holding him jerked him back.

Grant ground his teeth. "Send over my brother and Allisdair."

"I will. At the same time ye release my father," Aros responded.

Kade came immediately to Grant's side as Grant released his hold on the MacDougall when Aros motioned for his guard to release Thomas and Allisdair. The boys started toward Grant as MacDougall started toward Aros, but when the laird passed the boys, he made a grab for Thomas. Grant sprang forward at the same time Aros did. Aros yanked his father toward him as Grant tugged both the boys to him. His heartbeat thudded in his ears. MacDougall twisted in Aros's arms to glare at Grant. "Ye're lucky my son stopped me. I'd have snapped yer brother's neck."

Before Grant could respond to the devil, Thomas tugged on Grant. "Brother!"

Grant glanced at Thomas, and his heart squeezed tight with relief and an overwhelming flood of gratitude for getting the two boys back alive.

"Brother, I—"

"Silence," Grant interrupted, turning his gaze back to his enemies. Later, he would listen to Thomas beg forgiveness for disobeying orders, as he assumed Thomas was trying to now do, though Grant kept his gaze trained on Aros. Grant could not be distracted from his enemy. "For keeping yer word," Grant said to Aros, "I will kill ye swiftly."

Aros smirked. "If ye get close enough to kill me, though I appreciate the sentiment."

Grant nodded. "Yer father I will kill breath by breath, as if he had a thousand days to live in pain."

"I'd expect no less from one bent on avenging his brother," Aros said, offering a mock bow. When the MacDougall went to grab a dagger from the guard, Aros took hold of his father's arm. "Save yer strength and yer anger. We'll need both." He turned away, still gripping his father, and motioned to his guard.

Grant watched them stride toward his other men, who were mounted in the distance. Five more steps and his enemies would be off the land known as Dithorn Cliff, and his word would have been kept. His body hummed in anticipation.

Four steps. Three.

He slowly started to raise his hand to give the signal.

Two.

Aros turned suddenly, glanced up toward the archers who were visible, smiled, and then leveled his gaze on

Grant before saying, "Demaskas, bring forth the woman!"

Grant frowned at Aros and then toward Thomas, who was frantically pulling on Grant's arm. Suddenly, a man rode toward the front of the line, and as he did, he pulled down the hood of the cape upon the rider mounted in front of him. Grant felt his jaw slip open as waves of shiny red tresses spilled in vivid contrast against the dark cape the woman wore. Her thick hair blew around her with a gust of sudden wind. She raised her hand and grasped the edges of her hair to twine it into a knot at the nape of her neck. His gut tightened at the sight of the willowy creature with ramrod posture, a proud and stunning face, and eyes the color of heather. He blinked, sure he was imagining it, but her cat-shaped, heather-colored eyes narrowed on him with obvious mistrust.

"Grant, Grant!" Thomas cried.

Grant flicked his gaze to his brother, who looked up at him desperately, but then Aros spoke, drawing Grant's attention once more. "If ye shoot at us, the lass will die." The guard Demaskas, who sat behind the lass on the steed, brought a sharp, gleaming dagger to the pale, slender column of her neck. Grant half expected her to cry out in fear, but the only noticeable reaction she had was to fist her hands.

Christ. Disbelief rendered him speechless for a moment. Was the lass a pawn or a willing participant in keeping MacDougall and Aros alive? "What do I care if the lass lives or dies?" Grant asked, choosing his words carefully to try to discern what was really occurring. "She dunnae mean anything to me."

"Grant," Thomas practically yelled, but Grant ignored his brother as Aros smiled slowly.

"I'd thought ye more honorable than to kill a lass," Aros

said.

"Ye're mistaken," Grant lied. "Any lass who is friend to ye is foe to me."

"I'm not—" the lass started to say, but Demaskas drew a drop of blood from her neck. She gasped and fell silent immediately, and Grant's fingers curled reflexively around the hilt of his sword with the instinct to protect her, but did she need it?

"She's a rather special lass," Aros said, a smug smile on his face. "She's agreed to wed me in exchange for allowing yer pups to be returned to ye unharmed."

"A convenient lie to keep ye safe," Grant replied, though doubt niggled at him.

Aros arched his eyebrows. "Can ye live with her death if I'm being truthful?"

Grant's eyes met hers, and for a breath, he saw them flash with fear before she averted her gaze. It was either real or she was excellent at portraying a false face. But if it was real...

"Away with ye, then," he growled. "I vow my men will nae shoot at ye."

"We ride!" Aros ordered.

The MacDougall, who'd been unusually silent, chuckled. "Bested again, Fraser!"

With that, the men quickly mounted the destriers being held for them and started toward the path that would lead them across the mountain to the woods.

"Grant, ye must listen to me!" Thomas hissed to him.

"Aye, ye must!" Allisdair seconded.

"Silence!" Grant commanded, his mind racing as his eyes skimmed the terrain as he sought out a way to kill his enemies and rescue the woman, if she indeed needed rescuing. He raised his right hand, giving the call for his men to sound the war horn and come to aid him, and then he turned to Kade. They had few precious moments before the MacDougalls would enter the forest, which would make it much harder to find them. And once the MacDougalls reached their land, which was not that far from his own, nothing short of war would get the lass back, and he could not risk his clan by rushing blindly into such a thing. That would take preparation. "I'll get the lass; ye go after the MacDougalls. Kill who ye can."

"Aye, laird," Kade answered, already turning to run toward the mountain path.

Grant swung toward his brother and Allisdair. "Make yer way inside the castle to safety, and dunnae even think of defying me."

"We'll nae," they both assured him.

"Grant," Thomas wailed, tears flooding the lad's eyes.

Grant stared in shock. Thomas had not cried since their father had died.

"The lady is called Eve. 'Tis as Aros said. She saved our lives," Thomas went on. "She traded herself for our safety."

"Christ," Grant whispered fiercely. Then seeing the fear in his brother's eyes, he said, "Dunnae fash yerself. I'll rescue her." He did not wait for his brother to reply, but instead, he took off toward the mountain path as the war horn sounded from above. His men would be coming, but it would be too late. Even the warriors stationed on the cliff path were not close enough to aid him.

He raced across the rock, scaling upward past the path upon which the MacDougalls were treading and Kade was following. He'd cut them off by going high when they had to wind about, and then what?

He caught the sharp rocks with his fingertips and found his footing, then climbed at a dizzying speed, higher and higher. The wind blew hard, setting a rushing sound in his ears and mingling with his breath, which was coming in sharp, desperate intakes as his heart pounded.

To his left was nothing but blue sea and jagged rock, except where the waves tumbled white when they met the rocky shore. The path the MacDougalls rode would take them over a deep section of the sea. Grant glanced down to get his bearings as to where they were, but his foot slipped from the ledge he'd just stepped onto, and for a moment, he clung to the rock with his hands and a single foot, searching for purchase once more. Finding it, he located the woman, and the guard Demaskas whom she rode with. Demaskas led the fleeing party. Grant had but one choice: drop straight down in front of them, get hold of the lady, and then they'd both jump into the waters below. If God was feeling merciful, they'd live. If not, he'd see Simon sooner than he had thought he would. A grim smile stretched his lips, and then, with a prayer, he released the ledge and dropped.

He landed with a hard thud as the horse holding the lass and MacDougall reared up. The lass screamed, and Demaskas tried to withdraw his weapon, but Grant squeezed between the beast and the rock and plunged his sword into his enemy's gut. The guard fell sideways off the horse and down to the water below. Grant did not have time to ensure the man had met his maker, but he prayed he had.

"Dunnae shoot the Decres wench!" Aros barked, and an arrow flew at Grant, skimming his shoulder.

"What's your plan?" the lass demanded, her eyes flashing impatience. She did not wait for his answer but slid off the horse and moved to stand in front of Grant, holding her arms out to either of his sides.

What the devil?

He frowned as realization struck: she was trying to protect him. He gaped at her but shook off his surprise as his enemies quickly approached.

"We jump," he said simply, sure he'd have to force her, but she nodded and launched herself without hesitation toward the water below. Once again, the heather-eyed lass had rendered him frozen in place. Her hair flew up behind her as she fell at a rapid pace to the turning sea. He'd never met a more reckless lass in his life, he thought as he followed her off the cliff.

Chapter Seven

"Why was Aros trying to force ye to wed him?" Grant asked Eve. It was the same question he'd posed since the moment his feet had hit dry land, and she had refused to answer the inquiry, nor would she tell him her last name. In fact, all the lass had shared was that she was not injured and that she needed a horse immediately.

Grant stared at the drenched woman standing before him in the great hall. Her long, flaming hair clung to her neck in wet strands and her gown molded to her chest, the lush outline of her breasts clearly visible. She crossed her arms over her chest, but instead of covering her cleavage, her crossed arms had only lifted the orbs, which looked like two ripe melons. This was the most inopportune time to lust after her, but lust cared little for convenience.

Grant's loins tightened as he jerked his gaze away from the woman's breasts and met her eyes. Their startling, exceptional color sent another shaft of astonishment through him, and then irritation as she lowered her lashes, no doubt so he could not determine what she was thinking.

The water dripping from her gown hit the floor with a pattering sound that made Grant clench his teeth. He never lost control, but at the moment, his hold on his temper was by a lone silk strand as thin as a spider's web. Since he and the lass had swum in from the sea and made their way to the great hall, he'd received nothing but bad tidings. He checked them off in his mind as he decided how to proceed with Eve and the MacDougalls. First, Kade had managed to catch up to the MacDougalls and kill three of them; unfortunately, neither Aros nor his father could be counted among the felled. Grant still had every intention of obtaining vengeance for Simon, but now it was a matter of how and when.

Second, Thomas and Allisdair had not gone to the castle and sought shelter as they had been instructed. Those two muleheaded clot-heids had tried to steal horses from the stables to join in the fight, but Ross had intercepted them and had sent them to the thief's hole to put the fear of God in them. He'd learned all of this from Bryden and Ross in the time it had taken for him and Eve to walk from the courtyard to the great hall. What to do with Allisdair and Thomas was simple, at least. As soon as Ross returned from the thief's hole with the two troublemakers, they would be ordered to work in the stables shoveling horse manure, just as his own father had ordered him to do when he'd been an unruly lad. Then they'd spend their days bringing water to the guards who trained, and their nights emptying chamber pots.

The lass with the rosy, bow-shaped mouth that sullenly turned down at the corners was his biggest problem. He hoped Thomas and Allisdair knew why Aros had wanted to wed her because asking her directly wasn't working. Trying a new tactic, he cleared his throat, aware Bryden was staring at him expectantly, as if he ought to force the answers out of the lass. But Grant was not the sort to raise a hand to a woman. "I'd like an answer, Eve, but if ye dunnae wish to tell me, at least give me yer last name."

She snapped her eyes to his. For a moment he thought

she looked afraid, possibly of him, but on closer inspection, the emotion he saw was smugness. She smirked at him. "Do you think I'm a fool?" she asked, her voice low and husky. Her voice stirred his desire just as much as her appearance. She plunked her hands on her hips. "If I give you my last name, you will learn things that are none of your concern."

He fixed her with the glare he often used on his siblings, and her smirk wavered, much to his satisfaction. Her pretty lips formed an O. "Ye are on my land, in my home, under my protection," he said, "and I just saved yer arse, so everything about ye is my concern."

"Well, Lord Fr—"

"Laird," he corrected. She did not know much about Scots if she did not even realize his people used *laird* instead of *lord*.

"Laird," she said, drawing the word out and eliciting a snicker from Bryden, which died on his lips when Grant scowled at him. "I did not ask to be dragged from the sea, brought onto your land, and into your home, and I certainly do not want your protection."

He arched his eyebrows at her, and much to his surprise and a bit of amusement, she matched the gesture by cocking up her own red brows. She may be English, but she looked like a Scottish lass—and she sure as the devil acted like one. She had to have some Scot in her with that blazing hair and fiery attitude.

He crossed his arms over his chest, mimicking her stance, and her mouth slipped open. Without hesitation, he took advantage of the discomfiture he'd caused her. "Ye did, in fact, ask me of my plan," he reminded her, almost laughing at the dismay that swept across her face.

She quirked her mouth and appeared to be considering what he'd said. After a moment, she spoke. "When I asked your plan, I was clearly inquiring about the one to get away from the MacDougalls." She tossed her hair over her shoulder, and her wet, heavy tresses smacked against her back. "I assumed you knew the best chance we had, considering this is *your* home. I told you in the water that I needed to depart immediately, if you would but loan me a horse. I have to get to someone before Aros does."

Before Grant could respond, the door flung open and Ross prodded Thomas and Allisdair through. The boys both had stubborn looks on their faces, but the minute Thomas saw Eve, he grinned and ran to her, launching himself into her arms. "Thank God, ye're alive!"

When Thomas pulled away from Eve, Grant saw the bemused look of adoration on his brother's face, and no wonder. Thomas was a lad on the verge of manhood and before him stood a beautiful lass who'd risked herself to save him. She'd clearly won Thomas's affection.

Her rich, hearty laugh set a peculiar warmth in the upper region of Grant's chest. "I can say the same about you," Eve replied, ruffling Thomas's hair as if they had known each other forever. Thomas's cheeks turned pink at her attention.

"I'm glad ye're alive, too," Allisdair said, then came to Eve's side and gave her an awkward hug and the same look of adoration that Thomas wore.

Grant and Ross exchanged a knowing look. Thomas and Allisdair were most definitely smitten with Eve.

Grant cleared his throat, having not the time for niceties at the moment. "Thomas, tell me how ye ended up in Aros's clutches," he asked, figuring his brother would let Eve's identity slip in the process of answering.

Thomas flushed guiltily. At least the lad had the good sense to feel bad about disobeying orders. "We wanted to help ye," Thomas said.

"Explain, please," Grant replied, determined to stay patient.

"Well, we decided to follow ye to help ye aid Simon." For one moment, Thomas looked as if he would break down, and Grant felt as if someone had punched him in the gut. His grief twisted within him, as Thomas struggled with his and finally mastered it. His shoulders went back and determination set his mouth into a thin line.

Allisdair glanced at Thomas with a look of understanding. "We wanted to help ye, but we got lost."

"We ended up in England but nae where we intended. Then we saw Aros at the head of a party of his men, and we kenned God had granted us a boon," Thomas finished.

Grant rolled his eyes at his brother's naivete. "God did nae grant ye a boon, ye clot-heid!"

A *tsk* came from Eve. "God works in mysterious ways, Lord—errr, Laird Fraser. Do not presume to know his mind."

He frowned at the lady. It was true her bravery and boldness had impressed him, but it would not do for her to think she could chastise him in front of his brother and men. "When I wish ye to speak, lass, ye'll ken it."

"Barbarian Highlander," she muttered under her breath as she turned her head away. But she'd not spoken so low that he had not heard it.

"What did ye say?" he demanded, sure she'd be too fearful to repeat it in a louder tone.

She faced him once more, her eyes sparking with ire. "I said, you are a barbarian Highlander."

He swept his hand toward his brother and Allisdair. "Am I to assume ye consider all Highlanders barbarians?"

She opened and closed her mouth several times, looking

much like a fish struggling for breath. "Highlanders killed my parents and my sister," she said, her voice cold.

Grant frowned. "Why do ye believe that?"

"Because I—Just because," she finished, looking uncomfortable.

"Do ye hate all Highlanders, Eve?" Grant demanded, motioning to the lads.

Eve looked stricken then quickly shook her head as she focused on Thomas and Allisdair. "No! Thomas, you know I don't! We spoke of this. Allisdair, the two of you are still lads with pure hearts. See that you keep them that way." She gifted each of the boys with the loveliest smile Grant had ever seen, and they nodded like puppies, joyful for her attention. Her face was radiant, as if a beam of sunshine came from within her.

"How generous of ye," Grant said, feeling his lips curl into a smirk.

Her response was to scowl at him. Though, God's truth, the banter with the woman did amuse him in a way that was very surprising. Still, he did not have time to indulge in it. He needed answers. He gave Thomas a stern look. "Am I to ken that ye saw Aros, recognized him, and thought to attack him?"

"Thomas did not say that!" Eve protested, clearly offended on Thomas's behalf that Grant would think his brother would make such a foolish decision. Her loyalty to a lad she hardly knew touched something deep within him. His mother had been like that—a woman prone to trust people easily. In the end, it had cost both her and his father their lives.

Thomas's cheeks splotched ruby red with his embarrassment, and he shuffled his feet back and forth. "Thomas," Grant said in a prodding tone, "my patience is becoming thin."

Thomas hung his head forward. "Aye. We tried to sneak into their camp to attack, and we were caught." He raised his head and eyed Allisdair. "'Twas nae my fault we were caught," Thomas said, his tone accusing and sullen.

"Are ye saying it was mine?" Allisdair asked, his eyes now narrowed on Thomas.

Thomas matched Allisdair's expression. "I did nae say it, but 'tis telling, dunnae ye think, that ye immediately thought that. As if ye feel guilt."

Allisdair curled his hands into fists and raised them. "I'll punch ye for accusing me of—"

"Boys," Eve said in a stern tone before Grant could get any words out. "Fighting amongst yourselves helps nothing. I suggest you put the matter behind you and work together to train to be better warriors all-around."

Grant watched in fascination as the boys both immediately offered nods of agreement. "Will ye train us, Eve?" Thomas asked.

"Ah, she kinnae," Grant, seizing his chance to get the information he had been after. "Eve must leave today to go to someone else's aid."

Eve nodded her head, and Thomas said, "We must accompany her, Grant. She would nae be safe traveling alone, and we formed an alliance."

Eve paled. "Oh, that won't be necessary. I—"

"It will!" both boys said in unison.

Thomas nodded vigorously. "Aros will nae stop trying to wed ye since ye're the—"

"Thomas!" Eve's voice echoed in the room. "Your brother has more important matters to attend to than listening to my life story."

"Nae at this moment," Grant said pleasantly, to which

Eve twisted her hands and scowled. When an uncertain look crossed Thomas's face, Grant added, "Ye would nae wish to send Eve into danger, would ye?"

"Oh," Eve moaned. "That's very manipulative."

Grant grinned at her as Thomas started to talk again. "Lady Eve is the heiress to Linlithian Castle."

"Oh, Thomas!" Eve paled, clearly distraught that he had announced her identity.

Grant locked gazes with Ross and Bryden, and they all turned to Eve, who took a step back, looking like a rabbit being hunted by a fox. Suddenly, Grant remembered the story of Linlithian, a strategically located castle that sat on the border between England and Scotland in the Valley of Blood. Whoever held that castle could well decide who passed through the valley, be them Scots or Englishmen, because whoever wished to pass through the valley could not do so without passing the castle guards. The King of England had given the castle to a Lord Decres, an Englishman who had been friend to both the Scottish and English. For what, Grant could not recall at the moment, but it made no real difference now.

What mattered, what could aid the Scottish in winning the war against the English, would be possessing that castle. King Edward himself had declared that should Decres's heir be a girl, she could rule the castle in her own right upon reaching eighteen summers until the day she was wed. Then the castle would become the property of her husband. But the two young Decres daughters had disappeared when her father's castle had been invaded, and Lord and Lady Decres murdered. Lord Decres's men and the girls' uncle had searched for them but had never found them, according to what Grant had heard. None seemed to know anything for certain, however, except that the heiress of Linlithian was gone and her uncle ruled her castle in her place. Whoever wed Eve Decres would inherit her castle, and if they had the mettle and Eve's aid, they could command the loyalty of the men who protected Linlithian, as they had been Lord Decres's men.

Grant understood perfectly now why Aros wanted to wed Eve. Grant shifted his stance as his thoughts turned. There was an opportunity here to turn the tide of war for Bruce and the Scottish cause and to get the justice he wished for against the MacDougalls. If he commanded his men and Eve's, Aros and his father would never escape justice, and Grant could aid Bruce in keeping his throne. Grant allowed his gaze to wander over Eve. He'd honestly not given any thought to wedding anyone. The only time he'd ever considered taking a wife had been when he'd met Lillianna de Burgh, who had married Ross's eldest brother, Angus. And the only reason he'd thought of it had been because she was in desperate need. He had not pondered wedding beyond that. But now he was. He did not know Eve, but it mattered little. He'd wed the devil himself to avenge Simon's death and keep Scotland free from the king of England's rule, and Eve was much lovelier than any imaginings he'd ever had of the devil.

But he had to know without a doubt that she was the lost heiress. He started humming to himself, trying to recall the songs he'd heard about her. Her brow wrinkled as she stared at him. Then he started to sing. *"And the wee lass with eyes the color of heather, she was so fair it would make a man weep."* Eve gasped and started to take another step back, but Grant grasped her wrist as more of the old song came to him. *"And the wee lass shone bright, she did, she did, sparked by the mark of the moon on her wrist."*

Eve tugged at her wrist, but Grant held her firmly. He

tried to keep his grip gentle, not wanting to scare her more than she likely already was, as he tugged up the sleeve of her gown and turned her delicate arm over to see the thin skin of her inner wrist. There, in the center of her wrist, was the mark of a half-moon. He drew his eyes to her face, surprised to see not a trace of fear there, only depths of bitterness.

Before he could speak, Eve said, "I will never utter the words of consent you need to wed me. You cannot force me." Her tone was strong up until the very last word, which trembled.

It was that slight revelation that the lass was fearful and determined that filled him with regret for what must be done, but regret could not deter him. Still, he would rather not be enemies with a woman he would take to wife. "I would nae ever force a lass to wed me, Eve." He'd chosen his words carefully, well aware he *would* be manipulating her into wedding him, but there was no help for it. He'd made a vow to avenge his brother and a vow to Bruce to do all in his power to aid the Scottish cause. He meant to see both vows through, as was his duty not only as laird but as a man of honor. "When we wed, it will be because ye willingly consent to be my wife."

Her response was quick as her open palm smacked his cheek with a *whack* that seemed to resound in the complete silence of the room. She hit surprisingly hard for such a petite lass. His cheek stung with her effort.

He sighed inwardly. This was not a good start to getting her on his side, and he'd need her there eventually to help sway her father's men. Funnily, he wasn't angry at her for hitting him; he understood how she must feel. But she'd not want to hear that, so he said, "It's good to ken ye're a braw lass. Ye'll need to be as my wife."

"Do you mean to hold me prisoner until I agree?" she demanded, her tone vibrating with anger.

"I'm nae the sort of man to hold a woman prisoner." And he meant it. He was not Aros. He would treat Eve with respect and care as his wife and protect her always. He motioned to the door. "Ye're free to leave."

"Grant!" Ross protested at once, but Grant held his palm up to his friend.

Eve whirled toward the door, and he let her get all the way to it and start to open it before he spoke. "Ye'll want to keep to the woods. I'm certain Aros will be sending men to wait along the border of my land for any sight of ye. And watch for the wolves at night." The door stilled in mid-opening, and she stopped but did not turn toward him. "I dunnae ken where exactly ye're going, but if Aros found ye and recognized ye, other men will, as well. Do ye have a weapon? Oh, that's right, ye dunnae."

Her shoulders rose, her tenseness clearly increasing.

"Grant, I gave my vow to protect Eve," Thomas said, to which Grant waved him silent.

"I imagine," Grant continued, sensing that Eve might now truly be understanding and accepting the peril she was in, "that ye are headed to retrieve yer sister."

She swiveled toward him, the heavy lashes that framed her glorious eyes flying wide open. "My sister?" She frowned. "Mary is dead."

It was Grant's turn to be surprised. "Dead? Did she die in hiding, then? I presume someone took the two of ye to safety after yer father's castle was attacked and thought to keep ye hidden until ye could claim yer inheritance, aye?"

Eve bit her lip. "Why would you think Mary died in hiding? She was killed the day of the attack. I saw her trampled by a horse."

"Ah, I'm sorry, lass. I did nae ken. The bards all sing of the missing heir of Linlithian Castle and her missing sister."

"My God," Eve muttered, all the color draining from her face. She swayed and reached for the door, but then Grant was in front of her, gripping her by the arm, afraid she might fall.

"Bring Eve some wine," he said, looking to Thomas, who scrambled to do so. "Come sit, lass," Grant said gently. He thought she might argue, but she nodded and followed him to the chair, muttering to herself as they went.

Once she was sitting and Thomas had handed her the wine, Grant had to put the cup to her lips and urge her to drink after she simply stared at it, dazed. She looked toward Grant but through him, as if perhaps replaying the last day she'd seen her sister. "Could it be that my sister lived?"

"If ye did nae see her truly dead," Grant said carefully, "then aye."

When a single tear trickled out of Eve's eye, a crushing tightness gripped his chest, surprising him. The tear had rolled almost to her chin before she wiped it away with the back of her hand, and her lavender eyes cleared and locked on him. "You must aid me." Her voice was a desperate plea that made his gut clench.

Devil take it! He'd aid her, no matter if she wed him or not. He could not honorably do otherwise. But Eve did not need to know that yet.

"Find yer sister?" he asked, assuming that's what she meant.

She wrung her hands in front of her and shook her head. "No. I've no notion where to even begin to look, but Clara—"

"Who's Clara?"

Eve bit her lip, indecision clear upon her lovely face.

"I kinnae aid ye if I dunnae ken the truth, lass."

"How do I know you won't simply use whatever I tell you against me? That's what I'm trying to prevent with Aros!"

"Ye dunnae ken that I will nae, but I give ye my word I'll nae." She snorted at that, which caused guilt to settle in his gut when he realized that he would feel the same way in her situation. "I ken yer feelings," he said slowly, "but when we are wed, I will do all in my power to protect ye, and those ye love, who dunnae wish me and my clan harm," he added, thinking it necessary considering her uncle was an English lord.

Looking forlorn, she rubbed her temples for a moment. "If we were closer to Linlithian, I'd risk trying to reach my uncle," she said, her tone acerbic.

"Well ye're nae close to the borderland here," Grant said, matter-of-fact, "and if ye need aid immediately, the only way ye'll get it is to wed me."

The glare she shot him could have frozen Hell. "What do you want with my castle anyway?" she demanded.

"Peace," he said. And then because honor would not allow him to lie to her, he added, "And revenge."

She stood, the top of her head coming only to his chin, and she tilted her head back to look at him. Gold rimmed the lavender of her eyes, which seemed to burn with an inner fire. "Revenge and peace," she said, her voice soft, her gaze speculative. "The very things I wish for, as well. I pray that we don't destroy each other trying to achieve our hearts' desires."

"Does this mean ye willingly agree to wed me?"

She frowned. "*Willing* is a funny word, wouldn't you say?"

He was fascinated by the way her emotions showed so

vividly in her eyes. He'd never seen the likes of it, or the likes of her. Her sharp gaze assessed him, taking his measure, likely plotting how to rid herself of him at the first available moment. He was well aware a marriage could easily be dissolved by her king if it was not sealed by a bedding, so he'd see to that immediately.

"Thomas, go fetch Father Tavish," he said.

Thomas nodded but surprised Grant when he walked to Eve instead of to the door. He surprised Grant again when he hugged Eve. "I'm glad ye'll be part of our family, Eve."

She bit her lip again, revealing her distress, but managed a tremulous smile and patted him on the shoulder. With a nod, Thomas, with Allisdair falling in behind him, left the great hall.

"Father Tavish is old and slow, so it could be a bit. Would ye care to wash before the wedding?" It seemed strange to be speaking of his impending marriage, one that he had no notion of this morning.

She nodded. "We cannot tarry, though. We must set out today."

"Who are we setting out for and where?"

"Hawick-upon-Tweed. It's the convent I was hiding in with my old lady's maid, Clara. She is the one we are going to retrieve. I'm afraid Aros will search for her once he and his father have time to consider how to force me to wed him. They will use her."

"Ye're likely correct. We'll ride once the wedding is over." He did not tell her that by *we* he meant himself and some of his men. Eve would slow him down and give him one more thing to be concerned about. He picked up a bell and rang it, expecting the great hall servant, Lydia, to appear, but his sister breezed through the door and plunked her hand on her hips. She scowled at him before sweeping her gaze over Eve.

"Is this the lass that slapped ye?" Esme demanded.

Grant rolled his eyes heavenward with exasperation. It seemed some of the servant women had been standing with their ears pressed to the door. He'd have to talk to them. But now was not the time. He needed a private moment with Ross, Kade, and Bryden.

"Aye," he answered Esme. "Meet my soon-to-be wife, Eve."

Esme tilted her head and stared at Eve for a long, silent moment. Most women squirmed under Esme's scrutiny, but Eve stared back, making Grant want to grin. Finally, Esme shook her head. "I dunnae ken why ye'd wish to wed my brother. He'll give ye precious little freedom."

"Esme," Grant said in warning.

His sister scowled at him again.

"I don't wish to wed him," Eve said, also scowling at him. "But he'll not aid me unless I do, and I need help immediately."

Esme snorted. "Well that explains it. Men!"

"Yes," Eve agreed too wholeheartedly for Grant's liking. "Men."

"Come on, then," Esme said, linking her arm through Eve's. "I'll get ye cleaned up before ye stand as the sacrificial lamb."

Eve shot a petulant look over her shoulder at him as she turned to exit the great hall. The minute the women disappeared from sight, Bryden turned to him. "Grant, ye would sacrifice yerself by wedding that English lass?"

Anger stirred in Grant's chest. "What do ye mean by 'that English lass'? Are ye implying that Eve is nae bonny?"

"Of course nae. He kinnae be," Kade answered, cuffing Bryden on the shoulder. "Lady Eve is surely one of the loveliest lasses I've ever seen."

"Aye," Ross agreed.

"I want to bury my face in her hair," Kade said, to which he and Ross chuckled while Bryden stood scowling.

Grant felt his brows pull forward in his own scowl. He recognized jealousy, but it was ridiculous to feel it for a woman he didn't even know, had no feelings for. Yet jealousy was burning inside him now.

"I can think of better places to bury my face in a lass as luscious as the Decres wench," Ross said.

"Dunnae," Grant said as his jaw tensing, "*ever* speak so of Eve again, even in jest." He stared at Ross until the man gave a quick nod, and when he turned his focus on Kade, Kade threw up his hands.

"Ye dunnae have to repeat yerself, laird. I hear ye and will nae ever be such a clot-heid again. I did nae think ye'd care, nae kenning the lass and all."

Grant clenched his teeth. True, Eve was a stranger to him, but she would be his wife. Though the wedding had nothing to do with love. He was not a man inclined to soft feelings. He ruled his emotions with iron control, just as he'd been taught, thankfully. He'd made too many near-fatal errors allowing emotions to cloud his mind in the past. This was a tactical marriage, but that did not mean he would not be a good husband, and that included ensuring Eve had the respect of his men and family, as well as his protection. And in turn, she would bring him her castle and, one day, hopefully sons and daughters. That was all he needed.

"I dunnae think ye should wed her without speaking to King Robert," Bryden said, his words drawing Grant from his thoughts. "What if he has someone else to whom he wishes to wed the wen—lass. Ye may incur his disfavor."

"Did ye get hit on the head, Bryden?" Ross demanded.

"Nay," Bryden bit out.

"Well, ye certainly seem to have lost yer sense. How could Bruce have anyone in mind to wed Lady Eve when he dunnae even ken she's alive?" Ross glanced at Grant. "I agree ye should wed her. It will gain us the border castle and may help sway other Scots on that border to switch their allegiance to Bruce. And if she remains unwed and nae bedded, someone else—Aros and his father for two—will try to take her and wed her."

Grant nodded. "I thought of that, as well. She must be wed." *And bedded.* "And then when we go to her castle, I will have the right to claim it, as the English king himself declared."

"What makes ye think he'll nae simply be untrue to his word?" Kade asked.

"He might," Grant replied, "but Decres's warriors have always been kenned as honorable. I think they'd pledge their loyalty to Eve as the rightful heir, and then to me, her rightful husband, especially once they see I have her loyalty."

"How do ye intend to get the lass's loyalty?" Ross asked. "She appears to hate ye."

"She seems to hate all of us," Kade added. "Except the lads."

Could they blame her? She thought Highlanders had killed her parents, and she knew for sure that she'd recently been kidnapped by Highlanders, then rescued by him, another devilish Highlander, only to be informed he'd not aid her without her wedding him. Guilt niggled at him again.

"I'll do what I must," he said.

"Ah, seduction!" Ross chortled, to which all the men

except Grant began to laugh. His mind immediately went to the lavender-eyed, creamy-skinned lovely lass. It would not be a hardship to seduce her, and he'd not feel bad about the eagerness that fired his blood when he thought of it. She'd soon be his wife, and he'd give her not only his protection and care but all of his desire.

Chapter Eight

With her emotions careening between anger and lingering shock over learning Mary could possibly be alive, Eve stomped up the stairs after Grant's sister, Esme, who kept shooting her sympathetic looks over her shoulder. Eve forced a smile for Esme's benefit. Eve may not like her brother, or any Highlander men for that matter, but Esme seemed quite nice. She also appeared to be as equally appalled by the conversation they had just eavesdropped on among Grant and his men as Eve was. Plus, she liked that Esme had offered the idea and chance for Eve to listen at the door of the great hall. Eve had no notion why the woman would wish to aid her, but she'd take the woman's sympathy and help. Eve was going to need it if she was going to succeed with the plan that had formed in her mind before she'd ever verbally agreed to be Grant Fraser's wife.

Seduction, indeed! She ground her teeth as she recalled the most inappropriate part of his conversation with his men. The devil thought to wed her, take her castle, and apparently claim her loyalty, all through seduction! The Highlander surely thought highly of himself and his appeal to women. An image of the man's blue eyes and thick, wavy, shoulder-length brown hair appeared in her mind. Oh, he was handsome. There was no point denying it. He was compelling, too, with his dimples and half smile. And a bit intimidating being so tall and, well, solid. She'd never seen shoulders so broad or a chest and stomach so riddled with muscles. There was not a bit of fat on Grant Fraser. He had the look of a man who'd honed his body through constant rigorous training and battle, and—

With a sharp intake of breath, she stopped herself. What was she doing, dwelling on the Highland devil's pleasing looks? He may be a feast for the eyes, but he was manipulative, unbending, and greedy. She paused on the steps, and Esme immediately turned to look at her.

"Why'd ye stop?" Esme huffed.

"Sorry," Eve muttered and kept going. She supposed Grant might not be greedy. He had said he wanted her castle for peace, after all. She did not know much about the political mechanisms between England and Scotland, but she did know that whoever ruled her home had control over who passed through the Valley of Blood with ease and who risked their lives to get through. Grant, naturally, would want her castle so he could aid his king in getting his soldiers into England. She scrunched her nose in thought. Perhaps Grant wanted her castle so he could simply stop more English soldiers from invading his homeland. She'd have to ask him.

No, she would not do that. She may have agreed to wed the Highlander, but it would be a temporary union. She grinned to herself at her cleverness but then bit her lip with worry. Her plan for her marriage to be temporary hinged upon Grant treating her with honor and not forcing her to join with him until she was ready, which, if her plan went correctly, would be never. Clara had long ago told her that if anyone ever succeeded in kidnapping her to wed her, the king could dissolve the marriage if she managed to stay chaste until she was rescued or freed. She had every intention of employing that tactic now. She may not have any choice but to wed Grant in order to rescue Clara, but she had no intention of staying married to the man.

She would choose her true husband wisely. He'd be a man whom she could love and who could love her, and he would be honorable and capable of helping her find her sister, if she lived, and gain and hold her inheritance, though she was certain her uncle would also aid her in that regard. Once she had her castle, she would decide which side in this war she was going to take.

When they reached Esme's bedchamber, Esme opened the door, and they both entered. The chamber was lovely with feminine touches of tapestries hanging on the walls, a plush animal skin on the ground where one would step out of the bed, and bright-yellow flowers in a large vase. But beside the flowers was an enormous gleaming sword.

Eve immediately went to it. "Is this yours?" she asked, awed. Esme came up beside her, and Eve looked over at her.

She nodded and grinned. "Aye. This is Fate."

"It's beautiful," Eve said, thinking of the weapon her own father had given to her that she had lost. "Did your father give it to you?"

"Nay," Esme said with a bitter laugh. "My father would nae allow such a thing. He had verra strong notions that a woman was to be protected by the man always."

"I see," Eve said. "And what happens to the woman when the man is not around to protect her?"

Sadness filled Esme's eyes. "Exactly..."

For the first time since meeting Esme, Eve really assessed her. The woman was stunning with her golden hair, eyes the color of the ocean, and heart-shaped face. She looked delicate with her tiny stature, yet she stood ramrod straight and, Eve realized with shock, was wearing braies and a léine with a rope tied around the waist. Eve looked between the sword and the woman before her. Esme was staring at the sword with obvious pride.

"You wish to take up arms with the men?" Eve asked, though she was certain she knew the answer.

Esme's gaze alighted on her. "Aye! Like ye!"

Eve shook her head. "I never dreamed of taking up arms and becoming like the famed shieldmaidens of old Viking legends. I was forced into this role when my father was betrayed and my family slaughtered."

"My parents were killed, as well," Esme said softly. "My mother trusted an enemy's wife, who had come to her under the guise of needing a healer for her ailing bairn. My mother went to them to heal the bairn, and they took her captive in order to draw my father to them."

Eve sucked in a sharp breath, fearing what was to come since Esme had just told her that her father had never taught her or her mother how to defend themselves.

"My mother had secretly had a sword made, this sword. *Fate.* She persuaded Grant to teach her how to wield it. She wanted to show my father her skill—I think to make him see that women could do such things—so she felt comfortable going to our enemies, though she'd only had a few lessons from Grant. Ye see, he was banished shortly after he started teaching Mother how to use *Fate.*"

"And your father found out?"

Esme shook her head. "Nay. Grant missed too many training sessions, spoke disrespectfully to our da, drank too much mead, and took too many women to his bed. Da, I think, was at his end with him, so he banished him and told him he could only return when he was a changed man."

Eve's heart squeezed for Grant, imagining what it must have felt like to be banished. He sounded as if he'd been irresponsible, yes, but had that required banishment?

"Anyway," Esme continued, "Mother took Fate with her when she went to see the sick bairn." She ran a finger down the shiny blade of her sword. "My father risked his life to save my mother, but they still killed her…and then him."

Eyes brimming with pain and helplessness met Eve's. "I could nae help. My brother Simon was in England at the time, and Grant had nae yet returned. I was useless. My da and his men rode off to get my mother, and all I could do was stand and watch him go. I did nae have any skills. So we are alike, ye see." Esme reached out and grabbed Eve's hand. "I did nae dream of taking up arms with the men, either, but 'tis all I dream of now. I will nae ever be helpless again."

"How did you get Fate back?" Eve asked.

Esme smiled sadly. "Word of what had occurred reached Grant. He returned to us at the same time as Simon. When Grant heard that Mother had gone on her own to the enemy armed with her sword, he blamed himself, I think. He and Simon killed them all, and Grant brought back the sword. I begged him to let me have it, and he did, but with a threat of banishment to any man who dared show me how to use it."

"May I?" Eve held her hand out, and Esme set Fate in it. The sword had a good heft to it. "You could learn to wield this with the right teacher."

"Maybe ye could teach me?"

Eve's chest tightened. She didn't plan on staying. "Esme, I—"

Suddenly, Esme pressed her finger to her lips and motioned to the door that had not quite closed. It swung open and Ross gave them a long look.

"Is it time already?" Eve squeaked, her pulse spiking.

The man grinned, his eyes shining with friendliness, and then he chuckled. It made Eve feel as if she could like him, but that was foolish. She needed to keep her guard up. "Nay," he said. Eve blew out a relieved breath, which earned another chuckle from the man.

Esme set her hands on her hips and scowled at the man in the doorway. "If it's nae time for Eve to return to the great hall, why are ye here lurking outside my door, Ross MacLorh?"

His brows pulled together in an affronted frown. "I dunnae *lurk*. Nae any woman has ever said that about me."

"Bah!" Esme said, waving her hand at him. "There has nae been a woman who has ever been braw enough to call ye a lurker, 'tis all."

"I assure ye, Esme," he said, his gaze sliding over Grant's sister in a slow fashion that made Eve's breath catch, "the lasses beg me to lurk." Eve had no doubt about that. The man was compelling, but not as compelling as Grant.

A flush turned Esme's porcelain skin deep red, but she did not turn away to conceal it. "I dunnae wish to hear about yer depraved life. Again, why are ye standing at my bedchamber door?"

"Nae for ye," Ross snapped.

A hurt look crossed Esme's face, and Eve stared pointedly at Ross, willing him to apologize, but he simply glared at Esme. Eve looked between the two, trying to decide if they liked each other or despised each other. If Ross did have a tendre for Esme, Eve doubted he'd get far with this tactic. Highland men were clearly obstinate fools. Eve cleared her throat, feeling compelled to alleviate the tension. "Surely, if Esme wished for your attention, you would be only too happy to give it. Isn't that so, sir?"

She could see his lips forming a *no*, so she cleared her throat again and glowered at him, until he said, "Aye. Of course."

Eve was breathing out a sigh of relief when a slow, devilish smile turned up the corners of the Highlander's mouth, and his gaze locked on Esme. "Do ye need particular attention from me, Esme?"

She gasped and so did Eve. The man had not said anything improper, but it was *the way* he had said it. The tone in which he'd said it had been like water sliding over one's skin. It made her wonder if Grant had such a tone. Her cheeks heated at the thought.

Ross swept his gaze over both of them with a laugh, and then he said, "Grant sent me to guard the door."

The nerve of the man! There was not a chance Grant feared anyone getting in his castle. It seemed practically impossible to her. "You tell your lord—"

"Laird," Ross corrected, to which she stuck her tongue out at the man, feeling extremely childish the moment she did it. He cocked his eyebrows at her, and she growled at him.

"You tell your *laird*—"

"He's nae *my* laird," Ross said with a wink. "He's my friend."

"Bah!" Eve bellowed, stealing Esme's word as it seemed to perfectly fit how the man was making her feel. She marched toward Esme's door and slammed it in his face. Satisfaction poured over her, and then she turned to Esme and both women broke out into hearty gales of laughter.

Esme took Eve by the hand and led her to the bed. Once they stopped laughing, Esme padded over to a table, picked up a brush, and indicated toward Eve's hair with a sweep of her hand. "I ken the marriage is being forced upon ye, but I'm certain ye dunnae wish to attend yer own wedding looking as if a bevy of bees made a hive in yer hair."

Esme's words gave Eve an idea. "As a matter of fact, I do. The more unappealing I appear, the better."

"Oh, aye?" Esme tilted her head. "Why?"

Eve's lips parted automatically to tell the woman who felt like a newfound friend, but she pressed them back together and shrugged. "I really should not say."

Esme's smile faltered a bit, but then she nodded. "'Tis smart. I am Grant's sister, after all."

"Yes, there is that," Eve said apologetically.

"So we shall leave yer hair?"

"Yes," Eve replied, then turned to look up at Esme. "You don't happen to have spare braies that I can wear do you?"

Esme offered an impish smile. "I do, but that will irritate Grant something fierce. He dunnae care for even me wearing braies. He says I look like a man and nae a woman."

Eve grinned. "That's perfect! I shall live in braies henceforth."

A frown knitted Esme's brow for a moment, but then awareness swept her face. "Ye dunnae wish my brother to find ye attractive?" It was not truly a question but a statement. Eve nodded, feeling it was all right to share that secret. "I'd ask why, but…"

"It's best you don't know," Eve stated. "I'd hate for your brother to place blame on you if my plan works."

Esme nibbled on her lip for a moment. "Does yer plan include ye nae living here with us as Grant's wife?" Eve opened and closed her mouth, knowing she should deny it, but she did not wish to lie to Esme. Esme waved a hand at her. "Ye dunnae need to answer. I'll keep yer secret. Grant has threatened to marry me off, and I fear he eventually will do so to make the clan stronger. If that happens, I've every intention of running off."

"I'm sorry, Esme. If my plan comes to fruition, know you can always come to me and I will give you shelter."

Esme grinned, then frowned again. "I like ye. I wish ye were staying."

Eve impulsively stood and hugged Esme. "I like you, too, but I cannot stay."

"What if ye fall in love with Grant? Would ye stay then?"

"I'll never fall in love with your brother," Eve said with a laugh, then slapped her hand over her mouth as she realized how rude she was being. "I'm so sorry. He's handsome enough. Very handsome, but I wish for a husband who does not want me for my castle."

"But how will ye have that when ye'll be wed to Grant?"

Eve was spared having to remind the woman she did not wish to tell her by a banging at the door. "I've received word that Father Tavish is ready for ye," Ross bellowed.

All the air seemed to leave Eve's lungs as Esme stomped to her door, slung it open, and snapped, "Ye go tell my brother and Father Tavish that Eve is changing, and she'll be there when she's good and ready. Grant can wait a spell. After all, Eve will be his wife for the rest of his life." With that, Esme shut the door with a bang and turned to face Eve.

Eve saw Esme's lips moving, but she could not hear what the woman was saying. Her ears were ringing with

Esme's words about Eve being Grant's wife for life. All her bravado, all her surety that she could undo what was about to be done wavered. What if he insisted on a joining? What if he forced himself upon her? She did not think he was that sort of man, but what did she really know about men? She began to tremble violently.

"Eve?" Esme was by her side in an instant, gripping her elbow. "What is it? What's wrong?"

Eve's throat constricted as memories of her parents and how happy they had been together flooded her mind. Fear knotted her belly, rushed through her veins, pounded her temples, and left her freezing. She wrapped her arms around her midriff to stave off the shaking, but it would not stop. Her eyes burned as panic welled in the chambers of her heart and flooded her with poisonous fear. She had to go through with the marriage for Clara's sake.

"Eve? Eve? Ye're scaring me. Should I get Grant?"

Tears began to leak out of her eyes. She let them flow and promised herself it would be the only time she permitted herself the weakness. "I'm afraid," she choked out. "I...I always thought I'd wed for love. What if this is it?"

Her eyes locked with Esme's. She patted Eve's hand. "If this is it for ye, then rest easy in the knowledge that my brother is a good, honorable man."

"Good and honorable do not equal love," Eve muttered.

"Nay, they dunnae," Esme said with a sigh, "but better tied to life with my brother than with Aros MacDougall."

Eve shuddered, recalling how Aros had lashed the boys. "Yes, I suppose there is that," she whispered. Still, it was precious little comfort for the possible loss of all the hopes and dreams she had clung to all those years in hiding, the ones that had kept her spirit alive.

Grant turned from speaking with Father Tavish and looked at the door to the great hall as it squeaked open. He frowned when Ross strolled through the door alone. "Where are my sister and my bride?"

Ross pointed over his shoulder. "In yer sister's bedchamber. Esme said ye can wait, and yer *bride* slammed the door in my face after bellowing at me."

"Are ye trying to tell me ye could nae manage to get two women to follow ye down the stairs?"

"That is exactly what I'm telling ye," Ross snapped. He flopped into a chair, kicked his feet out in front of him, crossed them at the ankles, and then folded his arms over his chest. "That English lass is going to cause ye trouble, ye mark my words."

"I'm certain I can handle one wee little lass. I—" Grant's words ground to a halt at the sight of Eve standing in the doorway. She had on braies exactly like the ones Esme wore, a léine, with a rope tied around the waist, and her hair was in wild disarray, tumbling over her shoulders in fiery red waves. She set her hands on her hips, and the motion caused the léine to slide down over one perfectly creamy shoulder and droop just enough that he got a glimpse of the top of her rounded breasts. His mouth went dry at the enticing picture. Eve Decres had to be the only woman alive who could make men's clothing look alluring. But why the devil was she in them?

"Why are ye dressed like a man?" he demanded.

"A man?" she asked, giving him a ridiculous confused look. He did not know the woman, but any lass capable of persuading a man like Aros not to kill two relatives of his enemies was not a simple lass.

"Aye," he said, striding toward her and stopping a hairsbreadth away. "Why. Are. Ye. Dressed. Like. A. Man?"

She pursed her lips. "Don't speak to me like I'm simple."

"Then dunnae pretend to be," he said.

Her eyes widened at that, as if she'd only just realized her error. "Braies will be easier to ride in for our journey to the convent," she said, motioning to the braies that hugged her hips rather nicely. He stared at her long and hard. He'd learned the trick from his own brother using it on him whenever he'd wanted to see if Grant was telling the truth. Eve began to fidget with her hands, and she motioned to the braies again. "They won't allow me to be chafed," she said, the inflection of her voice pitching ever so slightly. Most people would never notice it, but Simon had trained Grant to detect the changes in people's tone when they were attempting to hide the truth.

She was lying. He'd not embarrass her by stating so. Did her voice always go slightly higher when she lied? It was too enticing and would be too useful not to find out. He cocked his head. "So ye're nae wearing yer gown because ye will be chafed."

"Yes," she murmured, the inflection so slight but there again.

"That makes sense," Grant fibbed. "I suppose it's nae of import. After all, this wedding is one of necessity, so it dunnae matter what ye wear, does it?"

"No," Eve said, her tone low and husky once again and laced with an odd sadness that made him want to ask her what was wrong. "It is of no import."

He had the sudden, distinct feeling it very much mattered to her, but he doubted she'd speak freely with him if he asked her. Even if she did, it would not change the truth of their marriage, though he did wish her to know he would be true to her and treat her with kindness.

The great hall door creaked open once more, and Thomas poked his head in. "I wish to attend the wedding."

"Ye may," Grant said without turning to look at his brother. Instead, he caught Eve's frightened gaze, and his chest squeezed. "But wait outside in the corridor for a moment. I wish to speak to Eve alone." He'd thought to get the wedding and the bedding over quickly, but he could see by Eve's tense posture and pale face that she was very nervous. The least he could do was take a moment to put her at ease.

"All of ye, out," he commanded, sweeping his gaze around the room.

The men, including Father Tavish, started to file out immediately, but Esme hesitated. He shook his head slowly at his sister. "I'm nae in the mood to tolerate yer obstinance, Esme. Time is of the essence for Eve's companion, so out ye go. I wish to speak to Eve alone."

He didn't know whether to be glad or irritated when Esme glanced at Eve questioningly and Eve gave an almost imperceptible nod. Eve had not even been at his home a full day and his brother and sister had already taken to her. He was, he realized, immensely pleased.

When the great hall door closed behind Esme, Grant turned to Eve. She looked up at him with a shy, vulnerable expression that made him want to gather her close and ease her fears. It was strange to feel protective of the lass, but he supposed it was because she would be his wife. He tugged a hand through his hair, thinking of what to say and where to start. "I thought it would be good if we had a moment alone since we are about to wed."

Her frown surprised him. He had thought she'd be relieved, even grateful, that he was trying to be considerate. "Why do you wish to be alone with me?" she asked, her tone oddly suspicious.

He frowned now. "I wanted to tell ye—" It was much more difficult to speak plainly with the lass than he'd imagined. "Well, I wanted to tell ye that ye need nae be scairt."

"I'm not—"

He pressed a finger to her lips, and her eyes grew large. "Dunnae lie," he chastised.

She shoved his hand away from her face, anger overtaking her features and somehow making her even more beautiful. Her lavender eyes narrowed. "I do not lie."

"Nay?" He arched his eyebrows at her as a dare for her to continue.

"No. I'm a very truthful person," she said, the tone of her voice changing almost imperceptibly but just enough that he heard it.

A smile tugged at his lips. He ought to keep it a secret that her voice changed when she was not telling the truth, but it was too irresistible to prove her wrong now. Plus, if she ever came in front of an enemy and her life depended on concealing the truth, she needed to be aware she wasn't any good at it. "Yer voice goes up ever so slightly when ye are nae telling the truth." Her lips parted, and her hands came together, her fingers twisting. He chuckled. "And ye fidget."

She immediately unlaced her fingers. "Bah! My voice does not go up, and I will henceforth never fidget."

He chuckled at that. "Most men would nae ever notice the change in yer tone, but I've been trained to detect such things, and a man who had been trained as I have, might take note as well, so take a care."

She bit her lip but nodded. "Thank you," she said. "You could have used that weakness against me."

"Aye, I could have, but as I was saying," he said in a gentler tone, "ye need nae fear me. Nay, we are nae wedding out of love, but I will be true, I will be kind, and I will protect ye always."

Some undefinable emotion seemed to spark in her eyes, and she bit her lower lip once more, looking as if she were considering something. "I'm not afraid of you," she said, her voice husky. "It's just, well, I wanted to wed someone who cared for me and not my castle. I wanted—" She looked toward the floor, and he stared at the top of her head. "I wanted to wed for love," she said in a suffocated whisper, "just as my parents did."

"Most marriages are nae made for love, lass," he said, thinking of his own parents who'd wed to bring peace between their clans. His parents had seemed happy enough to him. True, he did not know what his parents' marriage had been like in the beginning. He'd never spoken to either of them about it. Perhaps Esme knew, though. She had often sat with their mother, talking and knitting.

Eve huffed, drawing him back to the present. "No, I suppose they aren't, but I would think that when two people wed that they usually know each other for more than a few hours."

"Ye are likely correct," he conceded.

"And," she said slowly, twisting her hands once more but then stilling her actions, "I imagine when two people wed who have known each other for a longer period than we have, if they are not in love, they at least are attracted to each other."

Was that why she was fretting?

"Ah, lass," he said, stepping forward and clasping her body tightly to his. "I vow to ye, I desire ye."

"What?" Stark, vivid fear glittered suddenly in her gaze, confusing him. "How could you possibly desire me? I have on men's clothing. I'm unbathed. My hair is a mess. I have too many spots peppering my nose and cheeks. I'm too thin by far. I—" Her gaze darted wildly around the room.

Ah! He understood now. Though Eve was a beautiful woman, she did not see it. She feared he would not want her, perhaps be untrue because of it. He slid his hands up her back, feeling her shiver. He touched his fingers to the silky, fiery strands of her hair, and lust seized him in a harsh grip. "It dunnae matter if yer hair has been brushed," he said, his body strumming with desire. "It beckons to me with its warmth and softness." Her lips parted on a sharp intake of breath, and he continued, sure he could ease her fears. He ran his fingers over the perfect contour of her cheek, reveling in the smoothness of her skin. "And the spots on yer cheeks and nose make ye even lovelier."

"They...they cannot possibly!" she sputtered.

"They do," he assured her. They made her real. They showed she went into the sunshine and enjoyed life. When she tried to twist out of his arms, he increased his grip, acutely aware of her lush breasts pressing against his chest. "And ye are nae too thin. Ye are graceful, lithe, and have curves exactly where ye need them, where a man truly appreciates them."

"Oh," she groaned. "This is wrong."

"Wrong?" He frowned. "Do ye mean sinful?" She had lived in a convent for many years, after all. "I assure ye, a man desiring his wife is nae sinful."

Panic burned her gaze into his. "I...I am afraid!" she

blurted, turning a deep red. "I'm deathly afraid of you. Of...of...of the joining!"

God above, he'd been slow. She was afraid to join with him. "Eve, we must—"

"I would ask a courtesy," she said, her voice shaky and sounding fragile.

Her heart beat harshly against his chest. In that moment, he felt he would grant her anything if it would wipe away her fear of wedding him. "What is it?"

"I'd like to come to know you before we join," she said, her voice and her body both trembling even more now.

God's teeth. He should deny the request; it was unwise to relent to it. Foolhardy, even. If she was taken or captured, and the marriage had not been consummated, it could easily be dissolved. "Eve, I'm sorry—"

"Please," she whispered, tears springing to her eyes, making them turn even brighter. "I don't want to be fearful the first time we join. You're a stranger to me."

He could not deny her request. There was no possible way he could bring himself to do so, no matter how unwise. But then he could not leave her here when he went for her friend as he'd intended. He could not seduce her but also put her at ease if they were separated. He needed to launch a slow seduction. Starting *now*.

"I'll grant ye yer request on two conditions," he said, his mind turning.

Relief swept her face, and then she said in a wary voice, "What are they?"

"One," he said, holding up a finger, "ye will sleep with me in my tent when we travel." She bit her lip but nodded. "Two—" he held up another finger "—ye will allow me to touch ye and kiss ye." He could have said more, such as caress her, introduce her to passion and pleasure, but touching covered that, and there was no need to scare her further.

Her eyes widened. "But—"

He shook his head. "On this I'll nae relent, Eve. Ye will be my wife in all ways but the joining until ye are ready, or I kinnae grant yer request." After all, he could not very well seduce her if he could not even touch her. "I will have yer vow."

"Fine, you have my vow," she muttered, and he could not stop the laugh that rumbled from his chest. She frowned. "What's so amusing?"

"Well..." He tugged a hand through his hair, unsure how honest to be, but he decided to be totally truthful. He did not like deceit. "Ye're the only woman I've ever met that acted so forlorn about the prospect of me touching them. Usually the lasses are eager."

"Then, by all means, go touch one of them." She gave him a dismissive wave.

He purposely roved his gaze lazily from her eyes to the creamy expanse of her neck, and down lower to her chest before inching back up to her face and meeting her gaze again. "From this moment forward, *bean bhàsail*," he said in a low voice, "ye will be the only lass I ever touch again." He slid his hands to the base of her skull, his blood racing in anticipation of tasting her.

She licked her lips. *"Bean bhàsail?"*

Ah, he'd forgotten she would not know Gaelic, being English as she was. "It means *temptress*," he answered, making slow circles on the base of her skull with his fingertips. She leaned into his touch, he was certain, without even realizing what she was doing.

"I'm not a temptress," she said, her voice heavy and lazy, as if she was growing very relaxed.

"Ye surely are," he said. And because his body strummed and ached so harshly with the need to feel her lips on his, he leaned forward and brushed his mouth to hers. She stiffened at first, but when he traced his tongue over the crease of her soft mouth and ran a finger down her chin, she relaxed under his touch. "Open yer mouth for me," he whispered, and she did so with a whimper not of fear but of burgeoning desire. Triumph flared through him as he slid his tongue into the hot, welcoming recesses of her honeyed mouth and began his seduction.

Chapter Nine

Eve meant to stay utterly still and unresponsive during the kiss Grant had stolen, but what her mind planned and her body wanted were appallingly at odds. She'd never been kissed, so she'd had no notion what to expect, nor how it would make her feel. But as his tongue swirled in her mouth and his strong arms circled her protectively while his hands worked wonders upon her back, her heart pounded, her belly tightened, and a strange tingling ache filled her to her core. She found herself leaning toward him, giving freely to the passion of his kiss.

He tasted of mead and smoke, and he smelled of the grass and the sea. He'd called her a temptress, but she had to wonder now who was tempting whom.

Just as she was getting used to the feeling of his lips gently on hers, his tongue tenderly exploring her mouth, his kiss became hungry, his lips ravishing hers. Yet, her response both shocked and scared her by the mere fact that she was *not* afraid of what he was doing to her. Now she was fearful of how she was responding. The pit of her stomach swirled wildly, and gooseflesh covered her skin. His kiss sang through her veins and ignited an ache unlike anything she'd ever experienced. He was a stranger to her, yet when he kissed her, it felt as if she'd known him for a thousand years.

His lips left her mouth to trail a fiery path down her neck to her chest, and instead of pushing him away, she fisted her hand in his thick hair and shamefully pressed his head closer to her chest. She quivered beneath his magical lips as they descended with precision to the valley of her breast, which was exposed by the overly large léine. She had a vague awareness of his fingers parting the material farther until it gaped open, but it was not until cool air hit her breast and his wet tongue circled her nipple that she became fully aware of what she was allowing to happen.

Heaven above, it had to be a sin, but it felt so blessedly good. Hot desire gripped her in an unmerciful hold as astonishment slammed into her. She should push him away, her mind screaming at her to tell him to stop, but when she attempted to speak, a moan escaped her instead. Grant took her nipple fully into his mouth and suckled, causing shameful lust and need to pulse from her heart to between her legs. Clara had told her about what occurred when a man and a woman kissed, but she'd said it felt pleasant. *Pleasant.* Clearly, Clara had purposely left some details out. That or Clara had never been properly kissed.

This was beyond pleasant. This was robbing her of her good sense. She wanted nothing more than to press Grant closer, to give over to the ache consuming her, but if she did that, she'd join with him before they were even wed! Perhaps she was a harlot at heart. No, she could not join with a man she had no intention of staying married to. Lust was not love. Besides, he had already admitted that he wanted her for her castle.

She shoved at his chest until he broke the contact, and he raised his head, his compelling blue eyes meeting hers and pinning her to the spot. He was so appealing to all her senses that her breath caught in her throat, and she could do no more than stand agape as his fingers brushed gently over the bud he'd just suckled and then pulled up her léine until she was covered once more. Yet, even when his hand fell to his side and they were no longer touching, she felt something invisible reaching across the divide between them to circle her and bind him to her.

Her heart fluttered wildly as he smiled wickedly, possession gleaming in his eyes. "Ye see? Ye dunnae have anything to fear."

He was wrong. She had everything to fear. She knew he was trying to seduce her. She'd heard his plan when he had spoken with his men in the great hall. Yet, here she stood, perilously close to forgetting his true intention and giving in to the need he'd awoken. The man was a wolf, and she his prey. He was playing a game with her, and she'd almost lost. The minute he took her, bound her to him forever, she had no doubt the promises he'd made would be forgotten. She could not be so foolish or weak again. She had to be more cunning and more careful than this warrior before her, for if she was not, her dream of marrying for love would be lost forever.

"Come." Grant took her hand, and when she tried to pull away, his fingers curled more tightly around hers. "Ye gave yer vow, remember?"

"Bah," she groused, but she did not attempt to pull away from him. He raised her hand to his lips and pressed a featherlight kiss there that made her tremor. Then, with another wicked smile, he released his hold on her, though the warmth of his touch lingered on her skin, and the desire he'd stirred thoroughly heated her. She felt branded. He turned, strode to the great hall door, and cheerfully beckoned everyone in for their wedding. She studied his broad back that tapered to slim hips and strong legs. Heaven help her, he was handsome. She had given her word, and she was a woman who kept her promises. She'd simply have to find a way to avoid him and not break her word. Surely it could not be that hard?

Putting distance between her and her husband—*her husband for now*, Eve mentally corrected herself with a gulp—was proving much more difficult than she'd imagined. Grant was the most stubborn man she'd ever met. *Or wed*, she thought hysterically, nearly laughing at her horrible humor. Yet, it was either find humor in the situation or cry.

As Grant's stallion pounded over the uneven terrain toward the convent, Eve could do little more than sit rigidly and try not to lean into the man she'd wed. Her mind drifted to Clara and rescuing her, and then to her sister and finding her. But as the day and the distance wore on, she was finding it harder and harder to keep a stiff, straight spine. Grant's solid chest beckoned to her aching back. If only they would stop for a rest. Before they'd all set out for the convent, he'd said that they would halt at nightfall and sleep until daybreak, and Eve found herself looking hopefully at the sky, which had gone from sunny to lovely shades of purples and grays. Night was descending, and none too fast enough for her.

As the stallion raced across the countryside, Eve could not decide what pained her more: her aching bottom, back, or head. She was positive that if she'd been allowed to ride a horse by herself, she would have been much more comfortable, but Grant had flatly refused her request. He'd told her in front of all his men that he could not be bothered with worrying about her keeping pace, so she would ride with him.

Keeping pace! She was an excellent rider, and she would have had no trouble keeping pace if only he'd given her the opportunity. It infuriated her. She could never stay wed to a man who did not think women capable, and it seemed that was the sort of man Grant was—or guilt had made him into, at least. She could not help but recall the story Esme had told her of Grant teaching his mother how to wield a sword. Perhaps he felt such responsibility for his mother's death that he had taken the opposite views he'd once had on women. Eve's anger abated a little as the suspicion sank in that it was guilt and fear for the women under his care that led him to be overly protective.

Finally, Grant held up his hand and whistled for them to halt, and immediately, Kade and Ross slowed their destriers. Eve wanted to weep with relief, but she was determined not to show Grant how tired she was, especially when he didn't seem the least bit weary from the journey. He guided their horse into a clearing surrounded by trees and rocks, and he quickly dismounted. Then he reached up and before Eve even knew his intentions, his hands were about her waist and he was pulling her off the horse.

"I can dismount myself," she objected.

"It's been a long journey, Eve," he replied, setting her on the ground but not releasing his hold on her. Though his concern was touching, it was also irritating, and her lack of sleep and growling stomach did make her temper short.

She swatted at his hands. "I've been managing just fine for eighteen summers before I met you. I do not need, nor want, your help, so please release me."

Without a word, he did as she asked. She took a step away from him, and her legs promptly buckled. She fell to the grass with a thud that jarred her entire body and sent a spike of pain to her head. With a groan, she looked up just in time to see a torch flame to life and then Grant kneel in front of her. He had a distinctly amused look upon his face.

"You could have caught me!" she accused.

"Aye." Laughter underlay his tone, and snickers came from Ross and Kade behind him. "I could have," Grant confirmed. The flames flickered near his face, illuminating him. A half smirk stretched his lips and his eyebrows were arched. "Ye did say ye did nae want my help."

"It's not well done of you to point that out," she grumbled. "Clearly, I had no idea my legs would buckle."

"Clearly, ye did nae," he agreed, raising the torch above his head. Ross bent down to take it from Grant. Suddenly, his arms slid around her, and he pulled her to her feet so quickly that she gasped. One of his arms tightened around her waist and brought her closer to him while his fingers curled into her skin. He brought his other hand to her face and tucked her hair behind her ear. She sucked in a sharp breath as he said, "I kenned yer legs would likely buckle, but ye did nae wish to listen to me. It's important to ken yer limits."

They stood face-to-face, the length of his hard body pressed against hers, and her breath caught with the desire he stirred in her, desire she could not afford to feel. She cleared her throat and leaned away from him as much as his embrace would allow. "What are *your* weaknesses?"

A long silence stretched between them, and she decided he was not going to answer. But then he inhaled deeply and said, "Lairds dunnae have weaknesses."

She suspected sons of lairds were not supposed to have them, either, and at one time, Grant did not care for that. "That's a heavy weight to bear," she murmured.

"Aye," he said, releasing her. "It is. Now come. We'll

eat a bit and then sleep."

Grant found himself repeatedly glancing at Eve as she ate beside him. Flames and shadows flickered on her face, making her look at once fierce and fragile. A strong wave of protectiveness rolled inside him, making his heart thump against his ribs. Eve was now his responsibility, just as his family and clan were. He could never forget that, despite how independent his new wife was, she had to be shielded, even from herself and her own reckless impulses, as he'd failed to do with his mother. He had to control for her what she would not, as he'd failed to do with his mother. Not only that but Grant feared the trouble Eve and Esme might get into together. He'd have to speak with Esme when they returned to the keep. In truth, it was probably time to marry off Esme, but Grant had hoped she would reconcile herself to a woman's true lot before the time came. He worried she'd wed a man she could bend or manipulate to her will, just as his mother had bent Grant to her will when he'd been young and foolish, but he would choose her husband wisely, a man who would tolerate no disobedience to his command, just as Grant would not, could not. A weak man would not do for Esme, and he feared she'd end up like their mother if she was wed to a man who did not control Esme's desire to wield a sword and fight with the warriors.

"Wine?" Ross offered Eve and held out the wine skin to her.

When Eve bent forward to reach for it, her léine parted to reveal the upper swell of her breasts. Desire hardened Grant, and he instantly recalled the silky feel of her breasts against his hands and his mouth. His innocent wife, so fearful of their joining that she'd begged him to wait, had a great deal of lust in her that he eagerly anticipated unleashing. He had to bite his cheek to keep from grinning. He considered it a definite boon that he was so attracted to her. With a little care tonight, he fully intended to show her more passion, and before they reached his home again, he was certain they would be joined.

Just as Eve's fingers touched the wine skin, Ross jerked it away with a laugh. Eve sprang up quicker than he'd ever seen someone move and snatched the wine skin back before he had a chance to bring it close. Kade burst out laughing, and Grant assessed his wife, who was drinking greedily from the wine skin while smiling.

"Ye're verra fast," Ross said, finally recovering.

"Thank you." Eve beamed. "Every summer for eight years I trained with the Summer Walkers, and before that, my father had taught me to wield a sword and a dagger."

Grant could not stop the groan that escaped him, and Eve turned to him with a frown. "You don't think a woman should be taught how to defend herself?" Her gentle tone surprised him. He would have expected her to be angry, but she sounded less irked and more understanding. Then it dawned on him that Esme must have spoken of his past to Eve. He had to work to unclench his teeth to respond to her.

"If a woman could be taught to defend herself *only* when trouble came to her and there was no one to help her, then aye, I'd be wholeheartedly in favor of women learning to protect themselves. The problem is," he said, purposely eyeing her, "that women are reckless and impulsive. They act afore they think, and once they feel adept with weapons, they falsely believe themselves invincible."

She surprised him again by setting a hand on his bicep. The innocent touch stirred his desire for her dangerously. Her slender fingers curled gently around his arm, and her eyes, brimming with tenderness, met his. "I'm certain that is not what your mother thought."

He stiffened at the confirmation that Esme had, indeed, been speaking of that which she ought not to have. "Ye kinnae ken that, Eve. Ye did nae even ken my mother."

"No," she said softly, "I did not. But I am a woman who has been taught to wield a weapon, and in no way does it make me think I'm invincible. It makes me feel less helpless, but I'm very aware of the fragility of life. I watched my father be butchered before my eyes. I saw my mother lying in a pool of her own blood. My mother had no skills with weapons. If she had…"

"If she had," Grant finished for her, "she likely would have died anyway. My mother did have skills, which I showed her." He could hear the intensity in his own voice, and he paused. He had not meant to say so much, to offer such a glimpse into himself. "Those skills did nae do anything but make her think she could go to the aid of our enemy with nary a defense but her sword."

Eve withdrew her hand and settled it in her lap. "You cannot keep the women in your life protected at all times, Grant."

"I can try."

"Women should be in the kitchens," Ross piped up.

"Aye," Kade agreed, "where it's safe."

Color rose in Eve's cheeks, and she jolted to her feet. "My mother was supposedly safe in our castle, you stubborn, foolish men!" Eve plunked her hands on her hips and swept Grant, Ross, and Kade with a fiery gaze. "What if your women were attacked when you were not around? Or what if they were attacked when they were with you? Would you wish them helpless? Unable to defend themselves or help you?"

"I will protect what is mine," Grant said, feeling his own irritation rise, yet his vexation was not entirely aimed at Eve. She was asking the same questions Grant had long ago asked his father when his mother had first requested to learn how to use weapons. His father had made the same argument that Grant was now making to Eve, and Grant had ignored his father and aided his mother. Age-old torment twisted inside his chest. The doubts, the questions, the guilt came crashing back down upon him like a giant wave. He'd once believed just as Eve did, but his mother's death had taught him he should have listened to his father.

Grant stood, towering above Eve. He looked down at his new wife. He didn't know what skills she had, but whatever they were, he did not want them making her bold. He wanted her cautious, because a cautious woman was a living woman. "I forbid ye from ever using yer knowledge of weapons."

"You *forbid* me?"

He'd not particularly wanted to have this conversation in front of Kade and Ross, but have it, he would. "Aye, I forbid ye."

"Let me make certain I understand you… If someone attacked us this very night, you would want me to sit there cowering, or hide, or watch you get killed when I could pick up a sword or a dagger and save myself and you?"

Her snide tone was not lost on him, and neither were her well-raised points. He jerked his hand through his hair. Esme had been much easier to force obedience from for the last six years since their father's and mother's deaths than his new wife was proving to be in the two days since they had met. His fear of what trouble Eve could get herself into warred with his understanding that what she said made sense; yet, when he pictured his mother's and his father's bodies as they'd been laid shamefully on the road up to Dithorn Castle, fear won out. "You will not cower. Ever. You are a Fraser now. There is a difference between cowering and being safe."

Eve scoffed, then poked him in the chest. "There is little difference if choosing not to pick up arms means being killed. Listen to me, *Grant Fraser.* If your sister was about to be ravaged, and all that stood between her and defilement was a dagger, you would want her to pick up that dagger and plunge it into her attacker's heart."

Devil take the woman! He *would* want that. "Fine," he growled. "If ever ye are under attack and I kinnae come to yer aid, pick up arms, but dunnae go courting trouble."

She grinned up at him, and the upper region of his chest, near his heart, squeezed into a tight ball. "I'm pleased to see you can be reasonable. Might I have a dagger or a sword?"

"Nay!" he snapped, keenly aware he'd just fought a battle with his new wife and lost.

She nodded. "All in due time, I suppose." Eve plunked back down, but before she got all the way settled, she yelped, and in the flash of light from the fire, Grant saw why.

Without hesitation, he lunged for the snake that was coiled to strike Eve and smacked it in midair. Fangs sank into his arm like a well-placed blade and sliced open his flesh with a sharp sting that instantly made his arm feel as if someone was bludgeoning it with a large rock.

He flung the snake up into the air, and with his good hand, he grasped his dagger and sliced the head off the serpent. It fell to the ground with a *thunk*. Grant looked to the grass, trying to focus on the unmoving snake, but the ground tilted and his stomach roiled, and then he was sitting in the dirt with no idea how he'd gotten there. Eve kneeled beside him, worry etched on her face.

"You've been bitten," she said, her concern clear in her tone, as well.

"Aye," he replied, the word seeming to draw out for an eternity. "I feel it."

Eve grabbed his arm as Kade and Ross kneeled alongside her. She set his now-numb hand against her knees and ripped at the material of her léine, growling her frustration.

"What are ye trying to do?" he asked, though God's truth, it was hard to form the words with how sick he felt. He swallowed repeatedly to keep the contents of his stomach in place as sweat trickled down his brow and back.

"I'm trying to help you, you daft man. You may count your blessings that I'm not a helpless woman." With that, she turned to Ross and snapped, "Rip my léine," before focusing on Grant again.

Grant somehow found a way to chuckle at the irony of her claiming not to be helpless and then demanding Ross rip her léine. He forced his eyes to narrow as he met Ross's.

"Grant?" Ross asked.

"If ye tear my wife's clothing, I'll rip out yer heart," Grant growled.

"Do not listen to him, Ross," she ordered. "I need the strip of cloth to stop the spread of the venom. And I need it *now*."

"Venom?" he repeated, surprised at her knowledge.

She nodded, pointing at the body of the snake. Ross still hadn't made a move to help her. "If you are not going to tear a strip from my léine," she said firmly, "then you must take one from your plaid."

The ripping of material filled the air as Eve focused once more on Grant. "'Tis an adder, which is venomous, but you won't die."

"Hold in yer disappointment, aye, lass?" he managed to joke despite the throbbing pain.

She smiled at him as she started to wind a strip of Ross's plaid around Grant's arm. "I certainly would not be pleased if you died," she said, tying the material so tightly around his bicep that he hissed. She frowned. "Just because I do not wish to be your wife does not mean I want you dead. Especially since you just took a snakebite for me."

"Dunnae that at least make ye like me a little more?" he teased, trying to flex his fingers and failing on a wave of pain. "I'm going to toss all my food," he grumbled.

"Ross, Kade, do either of you have any wine?"

"Aye," both men answered at once, and they each thrust their wine skins toward her. Eve took one of the skins and pressed it gently to his lips. "Drink this for the pain."

He was only too happy to do as he was bid. When the last drop of wine was emptied from the skin, Eve took it. Then, much to his surprise, she bent forward and sealed her mouth over his wound. "What the devil are ye doing?" he demanded, reaching for her shoulder. Without coming up, she smacked his hand away. After a moment, she came to a seated position, then turned and spit.

When she faced him again, she wiped the back of her hand across her lips. "I had to suck out the venom," she said, matter-of-fact.

Out of the corner of his eye, Grant saw Ross and Kade staring dumbfounded at Eve. Likely, he looked the same way. "How did ye learn to do that?" he asked.

"The Summer Walkers," she replied. "Ross, might I see

your wine skin?"

"Do ye wish a drink now, too?" Ross asked.

"Don't be daft," Eve said, then snatched the flask Ross held out to her and dumped the contents over Grant's arm, ignoring Ross's protests. Eve scowled at him. "Grant needs his wound cleaned. Would you rather have wine than your friend keep his arm?"

"Well, that *was* awfully good wine," Ross teased, winking at Grant when Eve was not looking. She gasped, which only served to prompt Ross to continue. "I suppose," he went on, catching Grant's eye, "if ye only had one good arm, ye'd be a bigger pain in my arse."

"That's a horrid thing to say!" Eve bellowed. "Grant—" she leaned close to him, the smell of freesia surrounding him "—you need to find better friends."

He had to rip his gaze from her enticing curves, and when he saw her angry scowl directed at Ross, Grant smiled, pleased that his wife was the sort of woman who was loyal to her husband. "He's only teasing ye, *bean bhàsail.*"

"I told you," she said, huffing as she situated herself beside him and then, with a gentle pull on his shoulder, indicated her lap, "I'm no temptress."

He eyed her lap. "Ye wish me to lay my head in yer lap?" She nodded. "And ye claim yer nae a temptress," he teased. Kade and Ross chuckled.

"Oh, do hush. You need sleep so your body can properly fight the venom." With that, she shoved his head in her soft lap and trailed her fingers lightly over his shoulder. He was certain she did not even realize what she was doing, because if she knew and understood how his body was responding, he was certain her fear of joining would make her stop. To his surprise, after a few moments, lust loosened its grip on him and was quickly replaced with grogginess.

"Sing to me, lass," he said, closing his eyes, reminded suddenly of long ago and how his mother would sing to him whenever he had trouble sleeping.

Eve began to sing, her voice flowing over him with its richness as her fingers ran through his hair. His last thought before he drifted to sleep was that she was his to protect and he could not fail in the duty. Yet, the certainty that the greatest threat to Eve was his stubborn wife herself would not release him from its grip.

Chapter Ten

"How did ye do that?" Ross whispered to Eve. She looked down at Grant's relaxed face nestled in her lap, and her heart tugged unexpectedly. She sucked in a breath, but because she felt Ross's keen gaze on her, she forced her thoughts away from the surge of emotion for Grant and concentrated on the Highlander staring at her. "It was not truly me that did it. The poison attacks the body, and now his body is fighting off any lingering traces of the venom that I could not remove. That leaves him exhausted."

"Ah," Kade said, nodding. "That explains it. I dunnae think I've ever seen Grant sleep when duty calls."

"But that's impossible," Eve protested. "No man can go without sleep."

"I've seen him sleep," Ross said in a low, confident tone as he lay on his plaid and faced them. "In the middle of battle, he sleeps sitting up. Ye kinnae even whisper beside him without him awakening. He is always at the ready to put himself in peril, to do what he must for the good of the clan."

All three of them looked at Grant, and his response was a loud snore, which made Eve giggle. She slapped a hand over her mouth. What was wrong with her? Her brain must have been addled on the jarring ride here. Grant Fraser had wed her to use her. He just wanted her help in swaying the knights who guarded Linlithian Castle and getting them to pledge their loyalty him. He was obstinate. He was overbearing. He would expect her, as his wife, to bend to his will. A will that included her never taking up arms unless she had no choice, because a threat could not be avoided.

Yet, she had discovered that he was so overly protective out of fear and guilt born from a tragedy in his past. He was honorable, she believed. She did not think many men would have waited to join with her and make their marriage true, yet Grant had agreed to wait. He was brave. He had risked his life for her without hesitation or thought. And he was a very good kisser. Or at least she thought he was. Since he was the only man she'd ever kissed, she supposed she did not know for certain, but she'd lost all her senses when he'd kissed her. All she'd wanted to do was kiss him back, the man she'd wed with no intention of remaining his wife. She wasn't supposed to like him, but she did. Yet, no amount of liking or desire changed the fact that he did not want her for her, but for her castle, and she wanted more from her marriage than that.

If she was smart, she would scoot out from under him, put a safe distance between them, and pray that she could somehow maintain that distance until she had Clara, and they could devise an escape plan. But as a scowl tugged Grant's brows together in his sleep, she found herself rubbing his forehead lightly until his frown disappeared. Desire to learn more about him began to gnaw at her.

"Has he always been so concerned with the clan's welfare?" she asked, turning to Ross. Guilt niggled her for the leading question, yet she left it floating in the air between them. She wanted to learn more about Grant, but she certainly did not want his friends to realize she wanted to learn more. It made her feel vulnerable, and there was nothing she disliked more than that. She mollified herself with the thought that just because she was not planning on staying married to the man, it did not mean she should not discover all she could about him.

Grant could someday be an ally. Or, she thought with a sense of dread, what if he was someday an enemy? She likely already should consider him her enemy since he was a Scot, and a Highlander at that. Her uncle was the King of England's man, according to Grant, and Highlanders had killed her family.

"He was raised to put the clan first and maintain discipline always, even as a child and young lad," Ross said. "Though when he was a young lad, he fought against the strictures his father demanded. He was nae to be carefree but restrained."

"He and Simon were to train every day with the warriors," Kade added, "then an extra two hours after the warriors quit for the day."

Ross nodded. "They were also nae to join with any lass but the ones they were promised to for the good of the clan."

"Grant was promised to another lass?" Eve asked, surprised to hear the news.

"Oh aye. But it dissolved when he openly chastised the lass for hitting her lady's maid. The wench took exception and persuaded her father to break the contract. The lass is Aros MacDougal's sister. She's wed to a Comyn now, and the Comyns are loyal to King Edward." Ross paused, and both men suddenly eyed her warily. She was certain they were wondering where her loyalties lay. She could not say, since she hardly knew herself. Ross cleared his throat. "The MacDougalls took the Comyns' side when John Comyn was killed by Bruce. The men were in an argument, and Comyn tried to stab Bruce, so Bruce defended himself. Anyway, Aros and his father sided with the Comyn family and against Bruce because of the connection to their family."

Ross eyed Eve for a long, silent minute, and she got the distinct feeling he was trying to convey something to her or expected her to make a connection, but she wasn't. "And?" she asked tentatively.

"And King Robert told Grant recently, after the king had to flee, that the MacDougalls would likely still be his allies if Grant had done his duty and ensured his wedding proceeded with the MacDougall lass, whether she was a heartless, immoral wench or nae." Ross ran a hand through his hair and stared silently into the dark night. "Bruce was angry, of course, at his own circumstances, and took it out on Grant, we all kenned that, but I think it's stayed in Grant's mind, like a splinter that's worked its way deep under the skin."

The connection finally formed in Eve's mind. This marriage to her was Grant's way of making up to the king and his father for his perceived failure when he did not marry a woman he'd seen as cruel. Sympathy coursed through her. She could not afford sympathy, understanding, and desire, but it was all blossoming nevertheless. She clenched her jaw and tried to will her heart to stay cold and still, but the blasted thing squeezed within her. If she fled him, his king would think Grant had once again failed him. Grant would believe it, as well.

"'Tis a heavy burden he carries," Kade said, "but his marriage to ye will help alleviate it. The king will be most pleased when Grant takes Linlithian Castle for him."

"Shut yer mouth," Ross snapped, but he was too late. Kade's words were potent reminders of what she already knew. Grant had wed her to ease his guilt and fulfill his duty. Love could not blossom from that.

"I'm very tired," she said, needing to put some distance between them now. "Could one of you help me ease Grant off my lap? I'd like to lie down."

Kade nodded and quickly aided her in sliding out from under Grant. He started to take off his plaid.

"What are you doing?" she asked.

Kade motioned to the ground. "Making a pallet for ye. Grant would nae wish ye to sleep on the dirt, and we dunnae travel with blankets."

She didn't particularly want to sleep on the ground, either, but she was not going to force Kade to do so in her stead. "Keep your plaid for yourself. The ground will not kill me." With that, she moved to the only empty space around the dying fire, lay down, and closed her eyes. The ground was cold and hard, and there was barely any heat coming from the fire anymore. The temperature had dropped, and the breeze had picked up. She was certain sleep would never come, but Grant's steady snoring was like a sleeping draught, and soon her eyelids grew heavy and oblivion claimed her.

The need to relieve herself dragged Eve from her slumber. As she struggled to come fully awake, she became aware of two things: someone had her wrapped in his very sturdy arms, and she was no longer lying on the ground. Well, she was on the ground, but something soft was under her and covering her. She blinked her eyes open and gasped. Grant's face was a hairsbreadth from hers, and there was just enough moonlight that she could clearly see that his eyes were wide open and intently upon her.

"How long have you been awake?" she asked, careful to keep a hushed tone, the sound of snoring coming at her from both Ross and Kade.

"Since ye fell asleep," he said in a low voice.

Eve frowned. "Were you awake when I was talking with Ross and Kade?"

"Nay. I suppose when ye quit talking, when I could nae hear ye any longer and ken ye were safe and near, it eventually woke me."

His words and what they meant struck her to her core. She didn't know what to say. She was touched—and confused. He'd wed her only because of Linlithian, but his actions kept showing honor and kindness, the sort of things she'd hoped to gain from a marriage of love. She swallowed, and her bladder reminded her of why she'd woken. "I need a private moment," she whispered, hoping he'd understand.

"I'll accompany ye," he said, unwinding his arms from her, but she grasped him by the hand before he broke all contact.

Her face heated, but she forced herself to try to be clearer. "I, er, would rather you did not. You see, I—"

"Dunnae fash yerself, lass," he said with a low chuckle. "I dunnae intend to watch ye. Just stand guard and be near should ye need me."

"Oh." She found herself smiling at him. "That's very considerate of you."

His fingers curled snugly around her hand, and he pulled her to her feet so fast that when she came up, she was propelled forward into his hard chest with an *oof*.

His arms circled her and his lips brushed her ear, making her shiver. His warm breath caressed her skin as he said,

"'Tis nae considerate. 'Tis my duty. Ye are my wife now."

Some of the warm feelings his actions had given her dissipated. *Duty.* Of course she was merely a duty. "You may release me," she said. "I can hardly walk with you clutching me so."

"That is likely true," he said with a chuckle and relinquished his hold on her waist, only to immediately take her hand. When she tried to tug her hand away, he simply increased his grip and started to walk around the fire toward the woods.

"Is it your duty to hold my hand, too?" she asked, feeling mulish. To her, holding someone's hand was an intimate gesture and not one of duty.

"Aye," he said, walking slightly ahead of her to lead her. "If ye trip and injure yerself, ye will slow us down. I'd rather nae contend with that."

She glared at his back as they walked, unsure why it bothered her so much that everything he did for her that indicated a degree of affection was, by his own admission, done out of duty. Suddenly it hit her that he was bare chested. "Did you cover me with your plaid?" she asked.

"Aye," he replied without stopping or looking back.

"Because of duty?" she surmised.

"Aye. Ye could have caught yer death, and I need ye alive."

"Of course," she muttered, clenching her teeth. "You require me alive in order to sway my men, the men of Linlithian Castle, to accept you and pledge their loyalty to you!" They were far enough away from Kade and Ross now, and into the thick of the woods, that she did not rein in the anger in her voice. She was seething, and she didn't care if he knew it. The only indication that the stubborn Scot even heard her was his fingers tightening ever so slightly around her hand. For some reason, it increased her vexation tenfold.

She dug in her heels, leaned away from the direction he was leading her, and threw her words at him like stones, wishing they'd whack him in the head like a big rock. "I'll have you know, if you intend to seduce a lady into doing your bidding, you might think not to tell her at *every* turn that she is nothing more to you than a duty!" She gasped at the sudden understanding that his words had hurt her, had injured her pride.

He stopped in his tracks, and she collided with his back, losing her breath and her footing in the same instant. She flailed her arms to gain balance, and just when she was certain she'd fall, he whipped toward her and clutched her by the wrists, pulling her body tightly to his. Then his hand skimmed up her midriff, over her breasts, and splayed across her chest. The shock of his touch, of the desire he ignited, caused her blood to course through her veins like a wild river.

"Ye were eavesdropping," he accused.

"I wasn't," she lied. She was a fool for letting her temper take control of her tongue.

His teeth flashed white and wolfish in the dark of the night. "Dunnae bother lying. The pitch of yer voice rose ever so slightly, as I've told ye, *and* I ken my sister's eavesdropping ways."

"Well, I know that you do not desire me at all! You simply want me to bend to your will, and you..." She poked him in the chest. "You are so dishonorable that you would...you would..." she sputtered, so angry that her words were jumbled in her head, "you would steal my innocence!"

"Ye are my wife," he said, exasperation tingeing his

words. "Yer innocence is mine to take. It would nae be stealing. And *when* I take it, it will be because ye gave it freely, willingly—"

"Never," she said, allowing the force of her anger to come through in the one word. She took a deep breath to blast him with more of her vexation, but she was suddenly lifted up, her feet dangling off the ground and her mouth brought directly to his. Before she could protest, his lips, hard and searching, sealed over hers for a demanding kiss. His tongue twined with hers and desire coiled in her belly.

Fear caused her to whimper, and immediately, her feet touched ground, he broke the kiss, and tremors surged through him so strong that she could feel them in his hands. "God's blood," he whispered, the regret in his voice undeniable.

She brought her own shaking hand to her tender lips, a coil of confusing emotions unraveling inside her. She hated him, but she didn't hate him at all. She'd been scared, but of her instantaneous lustful response to his ravishing kiss, not of him. For even laced with anger as it had been, she could feel that he'd been careful not to hurt her. She ought to let him think he had; perhaps then he'd keep his distance until she could escape him. Yet, she did not want him to have one more reason to punish himself. "Your kiss—"

His mouth claimed hers again, reverently, tenderly, begging forgiveness. His kiss shattered the last bit of control she possessed. This time, she lifted herself onto her tiptoes to match the hunger she tasted from him. His demanding lips caressed and cajoled her to part her own, and she did so with wanton eagerness, whimpering with desire when his tongue thrust into her mouth. Their tongues mingled, tempted, and danced until Grant growled and broke the kiss, only to bring his lips to the pulsing hollow at the base of her neck. She hissed with need as he blazed a fiery path across her collarbone to the valley between her breasts, which grew instantly tight in anticipation.

He stopped his onslaught of passion as quickly as he'd begun it, leaving her panting with yearning. As he moved away from her skin and gazed into her eyes, a knowing light glimmered there. "I wed ye for duty, aye, but I desire ye, and ye desire me, too."

Never had she felt so exposed, so vulnerable. "I don't." She shook her head for emphasis. Her words sounded utterly ridiculous after the way she'd responded to his kiss. She was no more than someone to sate his lust, and she'd not be that for him or any man.

He snorted. "Yer words dunnae match what yer body tells me."

She crossed her arms over her chest, determined not to let him make her lose her senses ever again. "My body—and my voice—is telling you *no*. Will you throw me on the forest floor here and now to satisfy your lust?" she taunted. She was playing a dangerous game, but it seemed the only way. "Will you ravage me?"

A disgusted look crossed his face. "I told ye I would nae, but ye will eventually yield, Eve, and we will truly be man and wife. Yer body will nae deny me for long, I vow it."

He was so arrogant that she wanted to throttle him, but mostly, she was fearful he was right. She was surely wanton, for she desired him with every fiber of her being, despite him admitting that he was using her. She couldn't stay wed to a man like that. Hope had kept her alive thus far, and that hope had been kept bright by two things: the desire to one day have a love like her parents had possessed, and the yearning for vengeance. Grant was not offering either, and she did not think he ever could, given his past. It was best for her if they parted ways, and soon.

Chapter Eleven

Grant shifted his focus from the abbess of the convent to Eve. The abbess had just informed them that Clara had been taken by Eve's uncle Frederick, and Grant winced at the hope he saw in Eve's lavender eyes. His wife believed that her uncle coming here was a good thing, but he did not see it that way. He steeled himself for the battle that was about to ensue. He may have been wed to the beguiling lass for only two days, but he knew by now she was stubborn to the core.

Eve looked from the abbess to him, and the grin that lit her face as bright as the sun faded as she studied him. "Why do you look troubled by the news that my uncle came for Clara?" she practically bellowed. Another thing Grant had learned about his wife was that despite the fact that she was a slip of a lass, she had a temper like a giant and she could voice herself louder than any man he'd ever met.

Grant inhaled a long breath for patience. He did not want to strain his relationship with Eve any more than it already had been, and not just because he needed her to help him take control of Linlithian. He did need her to do that, and he needed her to be willing to join with him so their marriage would be consummated, but he also wanted Eve as he'd never wanted another woman in his life. "I find it odd that yer uncle showed up here now, after Aros found ye. How did yer uncle ken where to find ye after all these years?"

Her eyes sparked with obvious ire. His wife was a stunning creature, but he'd been with many striking women in his life. It was not simply her beauty that called to the most primal part of him. He didn't know if it was because she was his wife or if it was because she was like a knot he had an itch to untangle. He could normally figure out a lass rather quickly, but Eve baffled him. He'd tried to make it clear that he was honorable and would always fulfill his duty to her, and it had seemed to only vex her. She'd made it clear that she wanted to return home, and he'd assumed it was because she felt a duty to her family, so he'd thought duty would mean as much to her as it did to him.

She waved an angry finger in his face. Kade and Ross both glanced at him with expectant looks. He supposed they thought he ought to put a stop to Eve's bold behavior now, and God's truth, they were probably correct. But he did not want to trample his wife's spirit if he did not need to. He rather liked it, as long as it could be controlled enough not to lead her into harm.

"You're a cynic," she accused.

"I'm realistic, not cynical," he said with as much restraint as he could muster. The woman could spark his temper faster than his sister could, and that said a great deal. "Be logical, Eve. The MacDougalls wanted ye for themselves. When they heard the song from the bard that I did, they came straight here for ye.

"Well, mayhap my uncle or one of his men was at that tavern," she said, "and heard the bard as well."

"Mayhap," Grant said, "but then why would yer uncle nae have come straight here as Aros obviously did. Why would yer uncle have waited until yesterday?"

Confusion, hurt, and then anger flashed across Eve's face in the most fascinating display of emotions he'd ever seen. "Perhaps my uncle had to return home for his men," she said with a stubborn lilt to her voice.

Ross snorted at that, and Grant shot a warning look at his friend. Her uncle was clearly important to her. Believing him good was also clearly important to her, and Grant understood why. Her uncle was all she had left. He was her only true family. Of course, she did not yet consider herself a Fraser. Grant would have to show her little by little that she was now part of the Fraser clan. "Ye have been missing for eight years, Eve. If my niece had been taken and missing for eight years, the Devil himself could nae slow me down from being reunited with her." He hoped his words showed her just how important family was to him, which meant she was now that important, as well. But when she frowned, he felt his own brow furrow.

"My uncle came for me. That's all that matters," she attested. "I was not here, and so, of course, he took Clara."

"Clara did not want to go," the abbess said.

"Clara is a suspicious old woman," Eve grumbled, but a fond smile pulled at her lips. "She ended up going willingly, yes?"

The abbess bit her lip, but then she nodded. "I assumed it was willing. Your uncle spoke with her privately in her room, and when they came out, she told me all was well and that she would see you soon. That we were not to worry."

"There! You see," Eve exclaimed. "Clara knows Uncle Frederick, and he set her mind at ease. She imagined things while we were in hiding that were never so. I'm not vexed anymore," Eve said, more to herself than Grant or anyone else.

"Were ye vexed at her, lass?" Grant asked.

Eve looked suddenly regretful. "Yes, but I will set it all to rights when I see her. We can go there at once. How long will it take us to journey from here to Linlithian? A sennight?"

Grant's jaw slipped open at Eve's lack of knowledge regarding where her home had been. But then, she had not been there since she was ten summers, so she likely would not know. Except he would have thought Clara would have told her. "Nay, lass. The Valley of Blood is but a half-day's ride from here."

She frowned, looking as if she were trying to puzzle something out. She finally said, "My uncle must have truly believed me dead."

Or he'd hoped, anyway, Grant thought to himself, clenching his jaw on the statement until he knew the truth.

Eve turned to the abbess. "I must leave at once. I'm sorry, Sister Mary Margaret. I would have liked to visit with you, but—"

"'Tis all right, Eve. I understand. I have a parting gift for you, though, if you will come with me to my room?"

Eve nodded, linked her arm through the nun's, and departed without a backward glance. Grant watched her walk away, his eyes drawn to the feminine sway of her hips. She'd demanded to know if he'd intended to satisfy his lust upon her in the forest, and it had taken all his restraint not to do just that. He wanted Eve with a fierceness that defied reason, but he wanted her willing.

He faced Ross and Kade, who both looked at him expectantly. He knew they wanted to hear what he planned to do. "We'll take Eve back to Dithorn, and then we will go to Linlithian with an army. I hope her uncle will peacefully relinquish the castle to me, since Eve is my wife—"

"He will likely want proof," Ross interrupted. "We should bring the lass with us."

Grant shook his head. "Nay. If he's nae honorable, as my gut tells me he's nae, then I kinnae chance Eve being near enough for him to take her."

"Do ye think he'd hurt his own niece?" Kade asked.

"I dunnae ken," Grant replied. "But until I ken the sort of man he is, I kinnae risk it. He likely will nae be happy she is wed to me, and as she is nae happy about it, either—" *not yet,* he thought, but he was hopeful Eve would come around, given her attraction to him—"it would be easy enough for them to have the marriage dissolved and Eve wed to another."

"They kinnae dissolve a marriage made true," Kade insisted.

Ross shook his head at Kade. "Ye clot-heid. 'Tis what Grant is trying to tell us. He has nae joined with his bride."

Kade's brows dipped together, and he regarded Grant quizzically. "Dunnae try to tell me ye dunnae find Eve bonny," Kade said slowly.

"Nay, I find her verra pleasing to look at. What I dunnae find pleasing is the thought of having to ravage her to make our marriage true."

"I always told ye that yer honor would cause ye problems with the lassies," Ross teased, but Grant knew by his friend not protesting Grant's decision that he wholeheartedly agreed with it.

Kade shifted back and forth, too well trained to question his laird aloud but not so well trained that he could hide that he was near bursting with the desire to do so. "Speak yer piece without fear," Grant ordered Kade.

"Laird," Kade began, "if ye should lose the lass—"

"I'll nae," Grant clipped. "If I were to lose her, I'd fail

the king, I'd fail the clan, and I'd fail my father and brother once again. Eve will stay my wife whether she likes it or nae." Though he could not deny that he would prefer her to like it, to like *him*. "I will secure the castle for Bruce and avenge my brother, and I will do so with honor." And it was not only dishonorable but repugnant for any man to take a woman, even a wife, without her consent. "Eve will return to Dithorn, and ye will personally guard her until I return," Grant went on. "I'll leave half the men to keep our castle safe, and I will bring the other half to Linlithian Castle. I'll take it if I must."

"I'd like to accompany ye to Linlithian," Ross said.

Grant locked gazes with his friend. "I was hoping ye'd say that, but what of Bruce? Should ye nae return to his side and aid his flight to safety?"

"And leave ye to fight the battle here alone while the English king gathers strength out of reach of his enemies? Nay. That is nae my way. I will stay by yer side as long as ye will have me."

"It's decided, then," Grant said by way of thanks. His father had always taught them to restrain their emotions, and though Grant had once rebelled against nearly everything his father had taught him, he was wiser now. "We will leave for Dithorn as soon as I collect Eve. I'll meet ye both in the courtyard."

Kade nodded, but Ross fell into step beside Grant as he exited the chapel to find Eve. Grant paused in the passageway outside the chapel and looked at Ross. "Ye've something to say?"

"Dunnae ye think Eve will balk at being taken back to Dithorn?" Ross asked, concern in his voice.

"Aye," Grant acknowledged, "I do. But Eve is my wife now, so she will do as I bid." When Ross burst into laughter, Grant quirked a brow. "What?"

"I dunnae claim to ken much about how a lass's mind works, but I can tell ye from observing my brother Angus with his wife, Lillianna, that just because Eve is yer wife dunnae mean she'll do as ye bid. In fact, as far as I can tell, it makes it more likely that she will nae, so prepare yerself."

"I can manage my wife," Grant said confidently. "Mark my words."

"I'll remind ye of that," Ross replied with a wink.

"What in God's name do ye mean she's gone?" Grant roared at the abbess, not feeling the least bit guilty about it. The woman had put him off for near to an hour, telling him that Eve had felt ill and had lain down, and now he knew it was because the conniving nun had been trying to give his wife a good head start on escaping him. He gritted his teeth as Ross smirked at him, and Grant recalled his earlier words about managing Eve. "Where has she gone?" he bit out, though he was almost certain that Eve was trying to make her way to Linlithian. The idea of her undertaking the journey alone set ice in his veins.

The abbess leveled him with an annoyingly calm look. "I could not say—"

He waved a silencing hand at her. He could see he would have to paint a clear picture for the unthinking woman, who had undoubtedly only been trying to aid Eve, who had probably talked the poor woman into abetting her. "Sister Mary Margaret, do you ken the type of men that travel the roads to the Valley of Blood?" Her instant frown told him the sheltered nun had no notion of the outside world. He did not wait for her to reply. "Bloodthirsty men,

Sister. Lonely men. Men separated from their wives or mistresses for months on end because of war. Men whose morals have been shattered by the killing of war."

The nun's face drained of all color, as did her lips, which pressed together in a thin line. "Men who come upon Eve alone would nae hesitate to take her and use her in the worst way ye could possibly imagine." Painting the picture for the nun had the unintended consequence of creating a clear, ugly scene in his mind of Eve being ravaged. He gripped the handle of his sword as his heart pounded viscously. "Sister, was she headed to Linlithian Castle? Which way did ye tell her go to?" He would have already left if not for the fact that there were several routes to Linlithian and taking the wrong one could mean Eve got too far ahead of them for them to catch her before nightfall. The thought of her alone in the dark make him suck in a ragged breath.

The nun bit her lip, a look of indecision skittering across her face. "Sister," he repeated, the urgency he was feeling making his voice shake, "Eve is my wife. I only wish to protect her."

"She does not wish to be your wife," the nun stated emphatically, making him clench his teeth so hard that pain shot along the edge of his jaw.

"Wish it or nae," he bit out, "she now is, and I would protect her with my life."

The abbess's lips parted, and her eyes widened. "She said you only wished to use her. That you do not care for her."

He winced at that revelation. "'Tis true we were nae wed for love, and 'tis also true I need her castle, but now that she is my wife, I *will* care for her."

The abbess frowned. "There is caring for someone's

welfare," she said, looking pointedly at him, "and then there is caring for someone's heart."

Grant growled, and the abbess jerked. He did not have time for this nonsense. "Her life is what concerns me at the moment, Sister, and 'tis what should concern ye. If I fail to care for her welfare, it will nae matter if her heart is injured for she could well be dead."

The abbess tilted her head and moved her lips side to side, clearly considering what he'd said. "You speak true. I cannot deny it."

"God's teeth," he bellowed, "tell me the path she's taken so I can catch up to her before men bent on ravaging her come upon her, or the man who took her before does. I can vow to ye that he would nae treat her with the respect and kindness I intend to."

The nun sucked in her lower lip. "Her uncle will protect her," she said stubbornly. "Eve is certain it is so."

"Mayhap. Or mayhap nae. Would ye have her death on yer mind, her blood on yer hands, if she is wrong?"

"Oh dear," she murmured. "Eve seemed so certain that her uncle is good." The nun nibbled on her lip. "But then, Clara did, at one point, seem certain he was evil." The sister quirked her mouth then took a long breath. "Eve thinks he'll be able to help her get her marriage to you dissolved since it has not been consummated."

He scowled at the abbess, whose tone had been very close to chastising. "I did nae deem it acceptable to ravage my wife to make the marriage true, would ye?" he demanded.

"Certainly not," she said, and then shocked him by smiling. "It pleases me to discover this about you, Laird Fraser. And since I believe you will eventually make Eve a worthy husband and learn to make her happy, I'll tell you she is taking the north pass. But you need not be terribly worried; I gave her a dagger to travel with."

"A dagger? Ye gave her a dagger?" he repeated, near to seething between the abbess dragging out the telling of which way Eve had gone and the discovery that not only had his wife fled him but she had every intention of getting her king to dissolve their marriage. She'd maneuvered him like a chess piece. It was shameful, and damned if it wasn't rather impressive, as well. "A dagger will nae save Eve if a group of men come upon her, Sister."

"Ha!" the abbess said. "You've never seen Eve wield a dagger. 'Tis quite impressive."

The nun's words sent memories of his past crashing down around him. "I thought the same of my mother's skills," he said. "She's dead now."

With that, he turned on his heel, intent on reaching Eve before the same could be said of her.

Sleep would not come. *And no wonder,* Eve thought, turning on her other side. Her heart was racing, the ground was cold and hard, and every blasted sound seemed exactly like the sound of someone coming for her. And even if her mind had not been busy conjuring all the scenarios of different men she might encounter who would wish her ill, guilt festered inside her, which was horribly irritating.

She flipped onto her back and stared up at the moon. Why should she feel guilty for fleeing Grant? True, he was her husband, but that had been forced upon her. He cared nothing for her or her wishes. He'd proven that when he made offering help to rescue Clara contingent upon Eve becoming his wife, and he'd proven it again with his constant talk of her being his duty. He'd proven it a third time at the convent when he'd been speaking to Kade and Ross, telling them that he was going to take her back to Dithorn because he would not risk her at Linlithian until he'd stormed her castle and taken it, if necessary, since risking her meant failing in his duty. The man really ought to learn to check if people were eavesdropping at doors, though the Highlander probably simply didn't care if Eve heard or not with what little regard he had for her.

Eve huffed out a breath. She did not want to be a man's duty. She wished to be a man's heart and soul as her mother had been her father's. Once she was reunited with her uncle, they would speak with the king, and the king would surely dissolve her marriage. Then Eve would find her sister and secure the husband that she wished. Together, they would rule her home and avenge her parents. She squeezed her eyes shut to picture it, but to her vexation, a very clear image of Grant filled her mind.

She tried to push the picture away, but the harder she tried, the more real it became, until she could hear his voice, velvet-edged and strong, *I desire ye, but ye desire me, too.* Devil take the man for being right. Even now, parted from him as she was, she could feel his strong arms as they'd circled her, taste his heat and passion when he'd kissed her, seen the blue of his eyes darken as his lust for her overcame him. She fanned her face, suddenly hot despite the breeze of the cool night air.

Why, with the spark between them, if only there had been a possibility of love to come, she might have considered staying wed to him. The errant consideration had her bolting upright and staring wide-eyed into the darkness. How could she have thought such a thing? He'd forced her to wed him! But then he'd allowed her leeway in the joining...

She bit her lip at that fact. He had taken a snakebite for her, proving his bravery and that he would willingly protect her. Of course, the willingness to protect her was not born from love or even a liking of her, but of the need to have her aid him with her castle.

Her stomach growled, and her head pounded. She'd not ever sleep this night. She glanced at the sky. The moon was high, full, and bright. She'd stopped for fear of going off the path, but now she considered it might be best to continue on. Yet, as she pressed her hands down on the ground to stand, a stick snapped behind her, and the sharp point of a blade pricked the back of her neck. Black terror froze her for a moment.

"I was just telling my man here that I would dearly love a wench's soft body under mine."

Disgust roiled through Eve as she held her hands up in the air. She'd try reasoning with them, and if that didn't work, she'd need just the right time to reach for and obtain her dagger strapped to her side. "I'm no wench, sir," she said. "I'm the, um—" Her mind flailed for a moment, knowing she could not say she was the lost heiress of Linlithian Castle. "I'm the cousin of Lord Decres of Linlithian Castle. Do you know him?" Her heart pounded so hard it hurt her chest.

Hands grasped her, suddenly jerked her to her feet, and twisted her around harshly. Two men stood before her, their faces greatly obscured by the darkness, but she knew when one of them smiled as his teeth flashed in the blackness. "I know Lord Decres, certainly."

"Oh thank God!" she cried out, practically slumping with relief. "Can you take me to him? I, well, my party was overcome, and I need aid." She bit her lip, praying these men were not trained in detecting changes in tone as Grant was.

She felt the man's fingers come to her waist before she'd realized he'd moved. He jerked her violently to him as his comrade laughed. New fear blossomed and stole her breath as his blade came to the side of her neck. "She wants us to take her to her cousin," the man said to the other.

"Yes, my lord," said one man, shorter and smaller than the broad-shouldered man.

"We shall," the taller man said to Eve, squeezing her waist painfully, "after we have a bit of fun with you."

His words curled around her heart like icy talons. "Sir, I am a lady and a Decres." She prayed her voice didn't sound as fearful as she felt.

"And I'm Guy de Beauchamp," he said with distinct mockery. The blade at the side of her neck pressed deeper into her skin, piercing it. She gasped as he chuckled and slid his hand from her waist, up between her breasts, to clutch her neck. He leaned in to her, the evidence of his desire pressing into her belly. Nausea roiled her stomach, even as his lips came close to her ear, making her skin crawl. "Do you know who I am?" he said, his voice calm and cool.

"Yes," she bit out, her fear giving way to rage. "You're Guy de Beauchamp, as you just told me, but what that is supposed to mean to me, I neither know nor care!"

The hand around her neck pressed into her windpipe, and she automatically brought her hands up to his as fear-spiked rage had her raking at him to release her. She struggled for air as he *tsked* in her ear. "My lady," he said, the words heavy with sarcasm. "Take a care with your tongue or I'll be forced to cut it out."

His hold on her lessened, and she gulped in greedy, desperate breaths. "The king surely will not like you abusing a lady!" she gasped.

His hand left her neck and slid around her back to crush her to him. She shuddered at his touch, so different from Grant's. "The king gives me full impunity to do as I wish. He needs my coin and would not dare deny me," he said, his hot breath hitting her face. She tried to strain away, but he gripped her like a vise. "If I want to ravage and pillage my way across Scotland and England, and my men do, as well, the king will allow it, as long as I continue to provide warriors and coin to aid him in crushing the Scots."

De Beauchamp's words landed like a blow to her heart. King Edward, if this was true, was no king she could ever pledge loyalty to. Was Grant's king such a man as King Edward? She thought not, considering how honorable not only Grant but all of his men and Ross had treated her.

Her mind raced with how to save herself, and the only way she could see was deception. She said a silent, fervent prayer that she sounded believable. "I see. Please forgive me, Lord de Beauchamp. If our good King Edward grants you this right, then I'm happy to oblige."

"Spoken like a true cousin of the cunning, conniving Lord Decres," de Beauchamp said. His seeming familiarity with her uncle and his character parted her lips in worry, yet she shoved the concern to the back of her mind to address later when her innocence was not in peril. "George, my man, take your leave. I don't need an audience to bed the wench. Go tend the horses," de Beauchamp ordered, his hand coming to her breast and clutching it.

A scream sprang forth from her mind and filled her with a desperate need, but she swallowed it as George said, "Yes, my lord," and turned to do as he was bid.

De Beauchamp released her and pointed his sword at her. "Take off your clothing."

Never had she been so glad for an order in her life. "As you command, my lord," she said, pleased her tone was steady and normal. She had the unexpected thought that Grant would be impressed. She judged the distance between her and de Beauchamp, and concluded he was close enough for her to plunge her dagger into his black heart. Smiling, she bent down and grabbed at the skirt of the gown Sister Mary Margaret had saved of hers, the one she'd put on to have better access to her dagger. Her hands shook, so she took several slow, deep breaths, as she pulled up her skirts bit by bit. When her fingers touched the leather of the dagger sheath, she allowed her skirts to drape over her hand.

"Will you undress for me, as well?" she asked, trying to sound inviting.

De Beauchamp grinned. "I do so love an eager wench." He tossed his sword negligently to the ground by his feet.

And that's when she attacked.

Chapter Twelve

A violent scream rent through the cacophony already in Grant's head. He pulled up on the reins of his horse, stilling the beast immediately so he could pause and discern what direction the scream had come from and if it had been Eve's.

Another bellow—this one unmistakably Eve—came from ahead of them, beyond the crest of the hill. Fear sprang within him and rushed through his veins, gushing in his ears and drowning out all sounds but those of his breathing. He knew he was barking orders to Ross and Kade, but he did not know what he said. It didn't matter. He was acting on instinct now, as he had been trained to do, and all his instincts were directed at saving Eve and killing whoever or whatever was hurting her.

He sent his horse into a full gallop, disregarding any danger to himself, yet staying astute enough to duck any low-hanging branches. The steep path up the hill wound narrowly around a ledge, and his horse neighed, as if balking at the dangerous climb. Grant urged the beast on, and the horse complied, though his hooves slid on the rocks several times.

As his destrier pounded up the trail, thunder boomed above him, and when he crested the hill, lightning cracked the sky and illuminated the scene before him. Someone held

Eve in the air, and she flailed her arms and kicked wildly at a second man who stood in front of her.

Shock yielded quickly to scalding fury. He tugged his horse to a shuddering halt, ripped his sword from its sheath, and jumped down, not even waiting until he could land with sure feet. And it cost him. His knee touched down for a moment, and in that instant, the second man ripped the front of Eve's gown. She howled her rage, Grant feeling it in every inch of his body.

He roared his own fury, and the man who'd ripped Eve's gown looked at him, just as Grant closed the distance separating them. He did not hesitate, striking the man holding his wife first. He sent his sword through the man's back, yanked it out, and kicked him sideways to get him and Eve out of the way of the other man, who was swinging his own sword up into an arc for a blow.

Grant met the man's sword above his head with his own. Steel crashed against steel, sending vibrations down his arm, but his fury burned and only retribution would put out the fire. He shoved the man's sword down, stabbed him in the gut, and jerked his weapon out, only to plunge it forward again into the stranger's chest to deliver the killing blow. Even before the man had fully fallen, Eve lunged at her attacker, screaming and wielding a dagger. As the man fell to the ground with a thud, Grant caught Eve around her waist, but she twisted, like a trapped animal desperate to escape. Between her screams and her cries, he could not understand what she was saying at first, but as he hugged her flailing body to his, he thought he made out the words *kill him*.

"Eve." He pressed his lips to her ear, as Kade and Ross came racing toward them, swords draw. "They're dead."

"I know!" she said between sobs. "I wanted to kill him! I

tried to do so. I tried. I tried." Her words gave way to her crying.

"We'll give ye a moment," Ross said, to which Grant nodded.

As the two men walked away, Grant pulled Eve back from the dead men so that she'd not have to look at them. Once they were a fair distance away, he turned his still-mumbling wife to him. "Eve, did they hurt ye?"

She shook her head, and he released a breath he'd not realized he'd been holding, but then she nodded. He froze. God's teeth, what had they done to her? "Did they—" He swallowed, trying to form the words. "Did they take yer innocence?"

She stiffened in his arms. "Why do you care? Because you want to be certain that you are the one to take it? So our marriage is true?"

"God, nay, Eve." He cupped her face in his hands. "I swear to ye it's nae that. Ye are my wife truly in my heart now, though I ken ye dunnae wish it. When I said my vows to ye, it sealed me to ye for life. I'm supposed to protect ye, and I failed."

"I'm supposed to be able to protect myself," she sniffed, and to his surprise, she pressed her forehead against his chest. Her body trembled, and a physical ache to wipe away her hurt sprang up in his gut. He brought one hand to her back and the other to her freesia-scented hair, and as she cried quietly, he gently rubbed her back while running his hand through her soft hair.

"I stabbed him," she said. "I stabbed him just as I'd been taught, but he deflected my blow well enough that it did not kill him. I cannot defend myself as I thought." Another sob escaped her.

"Shh." He gently brought both hands back to her face.

His fingers rested against her silken skin, moist with her tears. "Ye *did* defend yerself," he said, realizing instantly that he could have used this moment to get her to relinquish the notion of defending herself. If he agreed with her that she could never protect herself against her enemies, then she'd not try. But that, he thought with shock, would not make her safer but put her in more danger. He saw clearly now what his guilt over his mother's death had clouded. Her knowing how to wield a weapon had not killed her. Foolish choices had. Eve was his to protect, and he would, but her knowing how to protect herself was also a good thing.

He let out a ragged breath, feeling as if he was releasing a torment he had long harbored within him. "I imagine if ye'd nae stabbed the man, he would have defiled ye before I found ye. I will work with ye and teach ye how to be the best fighter ye can be, but I will have yer vow that ye'll nae go looking for trouble."

Eve's eyes went wide. "But you said you did not want me to wield a weapon."

"Aye," he acknowledged. "And I still dunnae, but if ye need to, if danger comes to ye, I'd have ye ken the verra best way to defend yerself." There was a great pressure in his chest and a need to say more, to try to put him and Eve on a good path. He'd meant what he'd said, that they were bound now for life. "Eve, I ken ye were fleeing to yer uncle to try to dissolve our marriage. I'll nae stop ye if it's what ye really wish."

"You'll let me go?" she asked, and he thought he heard dismay in her voice—or he hoped he did.

He kissed her forehead, the bridge of her nose, and then lightly brushed his lips to hers. "Nay, lass. Nae without a fight."

"Because of Linlithian," she grumbled.

"If ye'd asked me that yesterday, I'd have said aye," he admitted, guilt hitting him in the gut. She stiffened, and he prayed the proper words to show her what he was feeling would come to him quickly. She was rapidly coming to mean something to him, and he didn't know how to tell her. So he did the only thing he could think to do. He captured her soft lips with his and tried to make her understand his burning desire, growing need, and burgeoning wish to discover what they could be together.

His kiss lit a fire in her veins as it had done before, but it also filled her chest with warmth. His words about working with her, his acknowledgment that he'd been a fool, rang in her mind for a moment, but then all thoughts fled as his featherlight kiss coaxed her to let him in. She did, and their tongues twined slowly, exploring each other and learning each other. She quivered at the sweet tenderness and dreamy intimacy of his kiss. As her own desire for him grew, she pressed her hand to his chest, and his heart thundered against her palm. She groaned at the realization of just how much she excited him. And when she groaned, he growled, and his kiss became a forceful domination of her mouth that left her weak-kneed and clinging to him.

When he pulled back from her, regret painted his face. He slid his strong hands to the back of her neck, as if they belonged there, as if there was nothing so right as him touching her. And it did feel right.

"We need to see to the dead men," he said.

Her brow furrowed. "Do you mean bury them?"

"Aye. They dunnae deserve it, but if others come looking for them, it's best the bodies are nae found. They dunnae need a reason to chase us."

She glanced toward the bodies silhouetted in the moonlight. An odd numbness descended upon her. "The man who wished to ravage me," she said, swallowing, "he was a lord. He said King Edward gave him impunity to do as he wished." She huddled close to Grant, needing to feel his strength for a moment. Without words, he cradled her in his arms, and his uneven breathing whispered across her cheek as he waited silently and patiently for her to speak. Unexpected hope sparked inside her. The encounter with de Beauchamp had not only left her with questions regarding her uncle but it had changed what she thought she wanted in regard to Grant.

"The man, de Beauchamp—"

"De Beauchamp!" Grant cut in, clearly shocked. "I did nae recognize him in the darkness!"

She looked up at Grant's face, his strong profile making her itch to trace a finger over his jawline. "Did you know him?"

"I met him in London, the day my brother was killed. De Beauchamp is one of the king's favorites," Grant said with such clear disgust that Eve felt it, too.

She shook her head. "If that man is a favorite of King Edward, then the King of England is no king I can support."

"What are ye saying?" Grant asked, and though she could not see his gaze clearly, she could feel his eyes upon her, searching.

She gripped his arms, the hard muscle under her fingertips flexing. Her heart began to pound as she thought about what she was about to not only accept but support with her words. "I wish to learn more about your king and the fight for the throne between him and King Edward. Will you tell me?"

"Aye, lass," he said, brushing a kiss to the top of her head. It was an innocent gesture, but also intimate, and her heart squeezed at the tenderness he was unknowingly showing her. He'd been taught not to show his emotions, and she knew he'd tried to abide by his father's wishes after his mother's death, but part of him was a deeply caring man, and that gave her more hope than anything.

When he started to pull away from her, she grabbed his arm. "De Beauchamp said that the king needed his coin and would not dare deny him. He said if he wanted to ravage and pillage his way across Scotland and England, and let his men do so, as well, the king would allow it as long as de Beauchamp continued to provide warriors and coin to aid King Edward in crushing the Scots. Is that true, Grant?"

"It is, my lady," came Ross's voice from behind Grant. She peered around Grant to find Ross and Kade standing there. She had not even heard them come up, but Grant did not look at all surprised that they were there. She'd have to ask him later if he had a special trick for hearing people who were trying to sneak up on him.

Grant moved to her side and took her hand in his, squeezing it. "We'll let Eve decide for herself what she thinks about King Edward," Grant said. "After we bury the bodies, we'll tell ye what we ken of yer king."

"Not my king!" she said reflexively, distraught by the image of women being ravaged by English knights.

"I do believe my wife may be a Scot at heart," Grant said proudly.

My wife. Eve rolled the words around in her mind, allowing them to sink in. That truth did not bother her nearly as much now as it had that morning.

Eve yawned and leaned her head against Grant's shoulder when he patted it. Just as she got comfortable, he slid his arm around her waist and brought her into his side. The man was a veritable source of heat all by himself. She marveled at that fact for a moment before scooting closer to him. Though Ross had lit a fire for them to cook the rabbit Kade had killed, it was not a big fire, and the temperature outside had dropped considerably. Still, with the logs crackling pleasantly and her belly full from the rabbit, Eve could almost have imagined them sitting and exchanging lovely stories—except the tales Ross and Kade had told so far had not been pleasant.

They'd been recounting horrific acts done by King Edward. She now knew the fight for the Scottish throne had begun with the death of the Scottish king Alexander III, though no one had realized it at the time. It made Eve's heart squeeze to think of the king dying because he was so impatient to get to his new bride. His eagerness drove him to ride out at night in great fog, despite his men warning him not to, and he apparently rode his horse off a cliff. She thought then of his young, innocent granddaughter, Margaret, who was his only surviving descendant.

She inherited the throne at the tender age of three, and because she was so young, a body of men known as the Guardians of Scotland had been appointed to rule Scotland until Margaret reached twelve summers, and then she would rule with their guidance. But she, too, died on the way to meet her affianced, who it seemed had been King Edward's young son. Eve sniffed thinking upon someone so young having a marriage contract made for them to a stranger. She knew it happened all the time, but she disliked it, nevertheless.

It seemed it was the young girl's death that was the final

catalyst for the war they were now in. Many men, Scottish and English, vied and argued that they had the best claim to the Scottish throne, and ironically, King Edward had been called upon by the Guardians to decide which contender had the best claim and should rule Scotland.

Eve sat upright, and Grant released her. "What did you say the process was called when Edward decided who would rule your country?"

"The Great Cause," Ross replied. "In the end, the two men with the strongest claim were John Balliol, who the Comyns supported, and Bruce's grandfather, who is now dead. I believe ye ken the rest of the history."

"Well, I've recently heard that your king killed a Comyn, and that the MacDougalls support the Comyns, which is why they are your enemies."

"That's stating it simply, lass," Grant stepped in, threading his fingers through hers. She liked the way her hand felt in his larger, protective one. She looked over at him, and he was staring ahead into the fire. He'd not told her any tales of King Edward yet, and she suspected he had remained quiet so she would not think he was trying to convince her one way or another.

"Tell me what you know of King Edward," she said.

He focused on her, a grim look upon his face. "He long ago chose Balliol over Bruce because he recognized instinctively that Balliol was a weak man, a man he could bend to his will, and Bruce was nae."

"Do you think it was King Edward's intention all along to eventually take the Scottish throne?" she asked.

Grant let out a long, slow breath before he answered her. "I think when King Alexander died, King Edward recognized the opportunity and began to plot. Do ye ken what the English call yer king?"

"He is not my king," she repeated and squeezed Grant's hand. "Of this, I am now certain."

He nodded and squeezed her hand back. "They call him the Hammer of the Scots. They call him this," Grant said, "because he did not simply turn a blind eye to the atrocities his men have committed, King Edward ordered most of them."

She felt her mouth slip open. "Why would he order the rape, pillaging, and murder of the very people he wants to rule?"

"Because he is nae a benevolent ruler. He is a tyrant. He wishes to control a land and a people that dunnae belong to him. He dunnae care about the Scottish people. He wants more land and more vassals so he can put more coin in his coffers. Every promise he has made he has broken." He stopped and shook his head before continuing. "When this all started, he vowed to give back to Balliol and Bruce, the two main contenders in the end, control of their kingdoms and castles within two months. When the time came to do so, he demanded they pledge loyalty to him or he would destroy their homes. He has burned entire villages when they attempted to defy him. He's ordered his soldiers to cut down women and children. *Women and children!*" Grant repeated, his voice so full of agony that tears sprang to her eyes.

Tension crackled around the fire, which she felt with every beat of her heart. "He swept into our land—*ours!*" Grant pounded his fist against his chest. "We did nae seek this fight, Eve, but we will nae back down from it. We kinnae. If we do, he will bend us until he breaks us. He will work us tirelessly and tax us endlessly, even more than he's already done, so that he can fight his wars to control even more lands with our coin and our men. He dunnae care about Scotland. He covets power. He has stripped our country of its treasure and has tried to destroy every last thing that symbolizes Scottish pride.

"He took our king's crown and his throne. He took our crown jewels. But he kinnae take our will to fight him; he kinnae take our loyalty. It must be given, and it will nae ever be given to him!"

Kade and Ross both offered hearty and loud agreement, and Eve found she wished to shout an agreement of her own, but she did not think Ross and Kade, and perhaps even Grant, would believe her. Instead, she leaned closer to Grant and said, "I wish to go to my uncle tomorrow and tell him that I am good and truly wed to a Scot." Her belly tightened with her words, and her breath caught in her throat in anticipation of what Grant might say.

He inhaled sharply, and then his warm breath fanned her face as he let it out. His hand came to her chin as his lips came to her ear. "Are ye telling me that—"

"Yes," she whispered. Grant did not love her, nor she him, but there was hope between them and so much possibility. In the short time she had known him, he'd shown her his honor, his strength, and his hidden tender side. And the world had shown her the peril she was in. She'd been taken hostage and then nearly ravaged. She could very well never make it to her uncle, never have the chance to choose her own husband. She'd thought herself safe since she knew how to wield weapons, but she'd been wrong. She was not safe. But she'd be a lot more protected as Grant's wife than she would otherwise.

"I will make our marriage true this night," she said low so only he could hear, "but first I will have your vow to help me find my sister and to allow me to not simply *win* the favor of the men of Linlithian but to help you *lead* them."

His answer was to take her hand and tug her to a standing position. "Eve is tired," he announced.

Her cheeks burned suddenly, as she was certain Ross and Kade must suspect something. But the men simply nodded, for which gratefulness filled her.

Grant led her away from the fire and down a short path through the woods to a shelter he'd set up earlier after he, Kade, and Ross had buried the men. The shelter, made of Kade's and Ross's plaids stretched on thick sticks, was a good distance from the fire, but near a stream, and set back in a little circle of trees. He pulled one side of the plaid up and waved her inside. The space was small, but it was big enough for the two of them to lie down. She shivered suddenly with both anticipation and fear of the unknown.

When he entered the shelter, he swallowed up all the room with his massive height and build, and when he dropped the flap of the tent, nearly all the light from the moon was extinguished. Her vulnerability pricked her awareness, but she inhaled a breath to calm her nerves. With him, she would be safe. As if he sensed her burgeoning trepidation, he drew closer, a swish in the darkness. His heat invaded her space before his warm fingers touched her hands and then slid up her arms like a whisper to cup her face.

"Ye are certain ye want this? Want me?" he asked.

If there had been any lingering doubt, the fact that he'd asked her the question, even as need threaded his tone, wiped away any doubt that might have remained.

"Yes," she whispered.

He released his hold on her, which surprised her, and then a rustling sound filled the small space. "What are you doing?" she asked.

"Settling my plaid on the ground for ye. 'Tis bad

enough that there is nae a bed for this night. I'll nae have ye stuck rolling in the dirt."

She grinned at him, though she knew he could not see her face. "You're very thoughtful."

"I'm nae!" he protested, as if she'd said something horrid about his person.

She swallowed her laughter. Grant's natural tendency was to be thoughtful, but he'd clearly been raised to bury the gentler side of himself, to rarely even acknowledge its existence. She did not fault his father for bringing Grant up that way, for the man likely had been trying to raise strong sons to lead his clan. Yet, she felt the thoughtful side of Grant would help him be a better leader. She'd have to think on ways to prove this to him.

"Well, I do appreciate not having to lie in the dirt," she finally said.

When he stood, he was so near her that his bare chest touched her breasts, and all at once, her heartbeat exploded. His hands came to her back and ran the length of it ever so gently, and then again, lingering on the curve of her waist before his fingers trailed lower to her hips, then upward once more, gently skimming her taut breasts and coming to her collarbone.

"What are you doing?" she asked, her voice no more than a husky whisper of need.

"I'm memorizing ye, *mo bhean mhaiseach*."

"What does *mo bhean mhaiseach* mean?" she asked, wincing at her slaughtered pronunciation.

"It means," he said, roving his hands from her collarbone to her heavy breasts, "'my beautiful wife.'" His fingers brushed her nipples, which became instantly hard, and then he brushed them again, circling them, and ripping a moan from her lips.

"Do ye like that?" he asked, his voice a seductive demand.

She had no notion whether he was asking if she liked him calling her his beautiful wife or if she liked what he was doing to her, so she said, "Yes," as he slid his fingers under the neckline of her gown and tugged it and her léine down to expose one of her breasts, which was instantly covered with gooseflesh from the cool night air. But within a breath, he leaned down and took her other breast in his hand to tease her nipple while the bared one was claimed by his hot, seeking mouth.

She jerked in shock, then arched toward him with the exquisite pleasure of it and the desperate need to ensure he did not stop. She could hear herself practically mewling like a kitten, but she didn't care. She brought her hands to his shoulders, wanting to push his head nearer but embarrassed to show such boldness, such wantonness. Yet, when he began to pull her nipple harder into his mouth, whatever shyness she possessed disappeared. She curved her hands over the corded muscles of his shoulders, ran them up the back of his neck, and twined them into his thick hair, only to push his head closer to her.

He growled at the gesture, but she knew it was an appreciative growl as he pressed his body firmly to hers, the proof of his own desire hard like steel against her belly. Her heart jolted and her pulse pounded as he released her bud just enough that he could tease her with his tongue. He circled her straining bud until she screamed with pure pleasure, and when she opened her mouth to do so again, his lips covered hers in a frantic, demanding, and possessive kiss.

His hands worked quickly to relieve her of her gown, and she surprised herself when she began to tug his braies down. His hips were narrow, his thighs strong, and when her fingers brushed his staff, he jerked and she stilled immediately. She had no notion how they would fit together. Trepidation pricked her haze of desire, but when his hand covered hers and he molded her fingers around his hot manhood, curiosity overcame her fear. She slid her hand up his staff, pleased when he moaned and thrust against her.

"That feels good?" she asked.

"Aye. Too good. I want ye too much for ye to do that again, or ye'll be in danger of me falling on ye like a rutting beast."

She giggled at that, closing her fingers around his hard maleness. "And what makes you think I mind a rutting beast?" she teased.

"Ah, lass," he said, capturing her mouth for a lusty kiss before breaking the contact. "For yer first time, ye need to be prepared so it will nae cause ye too much pain."

"Too much pain?" she squeaked, the fear trying to return.

"Aye." He wrapped one hand around the back of her neck as the other hand traced light swirls over her belly, making her quiver. She was suddenly incredibly aware that she stood naked as the day she was born in front of a man. Her cheeks burned with embarrassment, but she refused to back away from what she'd started now.

"There is a little seal inside ye," he said, roving his hand lower until his fingers came shockingly to rest between her legs. She caught her breath and tried to push his hand away, but his fingers outmaneuvered her and, to her even greater shock, slid through the hair there to part her.

"What are you doing?" she gasped as his fingers touched upon a spot that almost brought her to her knees. It throbbed to life, sucking all the air out of her lungs and all the thoughts out of her head. As he moved his fingers in tiny circles over the spot, her body felt as if it was a knot slowly being wound tighter and tighter. She tingled all over, and her blood rushed through her veins, causing a humming in her ears.

Her senses crackled like lightning, and when his fingers moved faster and exerted more pressure, the strength to hold herself up left her. But Grant was there. His hand slid to her back and held her as his other hand tortured her sweetly until she cried out as a downpour of fiery sensations exploded in her. Wave after wave of ecstasy throbbed through her, and she slumped into him, her cheek coming to the corded muscles of his chest. His heart thundered against her skin.

"Now," he said in a silken tone that held the promise of a thousand wicked sins to come, "ye are ready for us to join." Before she could reply, he swooped a hand under her legs, lifted her, and brought her gently to his plaid.

He moved between her thighs and hovered above her. "Eve," he said, his voice holding an odd tension, "I vow to ye, I will always protect ye. My home is yer home. My family is yer family. And to answer yer earlier question, Linlithian is nae the only reason I would nae give ye up without a fight."

Her heart fluttered wildly at his words. She opened her arms to him, beckoning him, welcoming him. "Come to me. Make me yours."

He delved his hands under her bottom and lifted her. "It will only hurt for a minute," he said, and then he slid slowly into her, filling her and stretching her and then piercing her core. She bit down upon a scream. Yet as fast as the tide of fear rose, it fell as her body seemed to expand to fit his. It helped immensely that Grant held himself perfectly still.

"Are ye all right?" he asked, his voice as taut as a bow.

Was she? She looked up at her husband, seeing only a vague outline of his warrior's body. "I think so," she said, wiggling just a little to test it.

He groaned at her movements, and she smiled. Already the pain was subsiding and desire was returning. "You can move if you wish," she offered.

"I dunnae think I've ever wished for anything more, lass," he said. With exquisite care that she could feel by the rigid muscle of his thighs, she skidded her hand up his taut abdomen and equally stiff arms. In that moment she understood the amount of self-control it was taking for him to hold still within her. Tenderness for him gripped her, and as he began to move his hips, she met his movements step by step. Together, they found a rhythm and then not much later, perfect harmony. Her body melted against his as a new tide rose to take her. She gasped in sweet agony as Grant cried out his own release, and together they reached a place she'd never imagined.

When it was over, he collapsed beside her, then pulled her to his sweat-slicked body and slid his arm under her head. She turned into him, laying a hand on his chest and her cheek on his shoulder. Heavy breathing filled the silence, but soon it gave way to long, slow breaths that filled her with drowsiness and made it impossible to keep her eyes open.

Eve had no notion how long she'd been asleep when she woke, but she had a desperate need to relieve the wine she'd drunk. It was still very dark in the tent so she didn't think she'd been asleep for too horribly long. Her arm was thrown over Grant's body, and she could feel the deep rise and fall of her husband's chest as he slept. She grinned into the darkness at how soundly Grant was sleeping. Kade and Ross had said that Grant slept very little and very lightly, but he was good and asleep now.

Thanks to her, she thought with a little giggle. She slapped a hand over her mouth and froze, sure he'd awaken, but he did not stir. Grant Fraser slept the sleep of the dead because she'd worn him out. She had to swallow more laughter, and then gingerly, she lifted her arm from his body and peeled herself away from the luxurious heat he provided. She dressed quickly in only her léine since she did not intend to venture where Kade or Ross might see her, if they were even awake, and she tiptoed past Grant.

As she exited the shelter, she was glad for the brightness of the moon. She glanced up, recalling a memory of talking to the moon with her sister. "Mary," Eve whispered, "I'm going to find you. Please, please be alive." Eve closed her eyes and wished with all her heart, and then she opened them and looked around the lush alcove of the forest where Grant had made their shelter. Just beyond the trees, the water of the stream she'd glimpsed earlier glimmered in the moonlight. It was not so far that she needed to go back for her slippers and risk waking Grant. Eagerness to wash had her hurrying her steps, despite the soreness she felt from the joining.

The soft wet grass tickled her feet as she walked, and the chill breeze cooled her skin. The stream was a bit farther than she'd first judged, but it was not so far that she was concerned. She knelt at the stream and pulled up her léine to wash herself. When she was done, she cupped some water in her hands, closed her eyes, and splashed it on her face. Behind her, a hand brushing her back made her jerk, but then she smiled. "I tried not to wake you," she said.

But instead of Grant responding, a hand clamped over her mouth, sending a jolt of terror straight to her heart.

"Hello, Niece," came a deep, distinctly English voice in her ear.

Niece?

She stilled, realizing that it had to be her uncle Frederick. And then another realization hit. If he was here, now, lurking about, coming at her from behind, then he was not good as she'd always hoped. And he was likely the reason her family had been destroyed. Panic welled within her, and she brought her hands up to claw at his face, but he caught her wrists with his free hand and pulled her arms down against her stomach.

"Lord?" a man whispered from the darkness. "What are your orders?"

"Kill them," her uncle said in the coldest voice she'd ever heard. "And then return back to the castle."

Rage mingled with complete panic drove her to action. She bit down as hard as she could on her uncle's hand, and he released her with a curse. She opened her mouth to scream, but then a fist hit her square in the face, and all she heard were the echoes of her own scream in her head as the world around her went completely black.

Chapter Thirteen

The corpses of the men Grant killed littered the ground. Kade and Ross, who were bloodied from their own battles, faced him. Early-morning sunlight shone down on him, making him squint and causing Kade to raise a hand to shield his eyes. Ross did not blink, nor did he attempt to shield his eyes. He stared unblinking at Grant. "Maybe Eve went willingly with her uncle."

"Nay," Grant responded, his body tensing.

"These are Decres's knights, Grant!"

Grant glanced at the armor of the dead man nearest to him. It had a falcon and a sword emblazoned on it. "She betrayed ye."

"She did nae betray me," he said, working his jaw back and forth to loosen it.

"She did nae scream to alert us," Ross pointed out.

Ross's damn persistence that Eve had betrayed them irritated the devil out of him. "There are a hundred reasons Eve may nae have screamed," Grant said, "and ye ken it as well as I do. Someone could have covered her mouth. Or hit her upon the head to put her to sleep."

"Or killed her," Kade offered.

Grant felt as if someone had just stabbed him in the chest. Was Eve *dead*? No. Why would they kill her and not leave her body? Unless…

A notion came into his head that made him want to bellow with rage. He shoved past both Ross and Kade and headed toward the stream. It was deep in places, and he'd not thought to look for a body.

Her body.

Why in God's name had he not looked yet?

He strode into the water, ignoring the calls from Ross and Kade. He waded toward the deeper section of the stream, though it was not so deep that he could not touch bottom. He scanned the area for a floating body, for Eve's body. Bile rose in his mouth as he skimmed the water again and again, seeing her image in his head just as he'd last seen her in reality—a peaceful look upon her face, eyes closed, and red hair fanned out around her like a fiery halo.

"Eve!" he roared, his voice echoing back to him into the dark chambers of his heart and the long, deep tunnels of his mind. "Eve!" But there was no response. She was not there. And if she was not there, where was she?

"Grant!" Ross said as he grabbed Grant by the arm and tugged at him. Grant hadn't even noticed the man had entered the stream. "What the devil are ye doing?"

"Looking for my wife," Grant said, shoving Ross away. His chest squeezed into a fist, and breath was hard to come by. "She's *not* dead." He said it more to assure himself than anything. "Her uncle must have her. He'd nae kill her. He'll want her alive to use her."

"Grant," Ross said, "Ye must consider what I said. What if she betrayed ye? What if she left willingly?"

He shook his head. "She'd nae."

Ross put a hand on his shoulder. "How do ye ken? Ye have nae kenned her long."

Grant turned to fully face his friend, prepared to argue, but a niggle of doubt stopped him for a moment as he considered what Ross was saying. "It dunnae matter. She's my wife. We made our marriage true last night, and even if we had nae, I would go after her to ensure she was nae harmed."

Ross sighed. "There's that troublesome honor again."

"'Tis nae just honor that drives me to my wife," Grant said, unable to say more because he could not properly communicate his feelings. All he knew for certain was that she was in his blood now, and he would ride straight into danger, straight toward death, to save her. "If luck is with us, we will reach them before they arrive at Linlithian." Once her uncle had her within those walls, rescuing her would take an army and an all-out attack, and Grant feared what might happen to her in the meantime. Her uncle may not risk killing her, but he could hurt her in ways Grant did not wish to imagine.

Once they waded out of the water, they started toward Kade, who stood with the horses beside what was left of the shelter Grant had made for himself and Eve. As they neared Kade, Grant frowned. "What are ye holding?"

"Yer wife's gown and slippers." Kade met Grant's gaze. "I dunnae think she left ye willingly. I dunnae ken many women who would depart in nothing more than their léines."

"Give them to me," Grant ordered, clutching the items that Ross handed him. He brought the gown to his nose, not caring that Ross and Kade were watching him, and inhaled Eve's scent. He would get her back. He had to. And not just because she was his responsibility as Ross had suggested. Eve had opened a door within him that he'd intended to keep shut, and now that it was open, there wasn't a hope to close it. He wasn't even sure he would want to if he could.

Eve returned to consciousness with a start and a gasp. She scrambled off the bed she was in and ran to the door. She tried to open it, but it was locked. She beat on it, but no one answered. Shaken and confused, she moved back to the bed and sat, pulling her knees up to her chest and becoming aware of her half-dressed state. She shivered from the cold room...or was it from anger or fear?

She shoved at the fear within her. She could not allow it; yet the emotion did not care for her denial. It clawed at her insides, scratching and ripping the armor of bravery and hope she wanted to cloak herself in. Why was she so terrified? She'd faced many horrible things already in her life and lived through them. Yet, the black fright threatening to consume her felt greater than anything she could recall.

Realization came to her like a mountain of snow crashing upon her. Her uncle's words roared to life once more, nearly bursting her eardrums with their intensity: *Kill them.* Her head rang with the noise of the words. *Kill them,* it came again. She pressed her hands to her ears and screamed until her throat burned with her effort, as if someone had lit a torch in her throat. Her screams turned to racking sobs that she could not quell. She sat huddled on the bed, chin pressed to her knees, and she cried as she had not cried since losing her mother, father, and sister. But now, now she had lost her family for good. Her uncle was evil. The last of her blood relations had been lost to her if Mary was gone, and if she could never find her. And what of Grant? He would have been her new start, her new family, and she had not understood how bad she wanted it, needed it, until this moment.

Grant. Grant. Grant. His image came to her, and she

cried so hard that she could not catch her breath. Sadness pressed on every part of her, until she felt she would simply die from the weight of it. She rolled onto her back, squeezed her eyes shut, and cried until her nose was stuffy, her head aching, and her vision blurry. When there was simply nothing left to shed and the cover beneath her head was soaked with tears, she stopped and lay there silently, recalling the night before and all the hope she'd found so unexpectedly.

It was that memory of that hope that got her to push herself to sitting and open her eyes. She could not simply crumble, even if Grant was dead, the mere thought of which left her gasping again for breath. She would not be a pawn in whatever plot her uncle had planned. Determination brought her to her feet, and she looked around the room, stilling when she realized she had been put in her old bedchamber.

She gasped with relief as she raced to the large wardrobe that concealed a door that led to her sister's room—or once had led there. Eve tried to push it as she cast worried glances over her shoulder. When it became apparent that merely pushing it would not budge the wardrobe, she leaned her back against it, braced her feet against the floor, and shoved with all her might, grunting with the effort. The wardrobe creaked but did not move. Girding herself with resolve, she braced again and shoved, and this time, the wardrobe moved the slightest bit. But just as hope flooded her, the door to her bedchamber rattled.

Eve launched herself at her bed, pulling the coverlet over her bare legs just as the door opened and a guard appeared on the threshold with Clara by his side. Her friend had dark bruises under her eyes and a cut lip that made Eve cry out. The two women practically collided, hugging.

"Make her presentable quickly," the guard said in a curt tone. "My lord wishes to get the wedding over with immediately." And then he slammed the bedchamber door, and the distinct clink of it being locked filled the room.

God above! If her uncle intended to wed her, he was either certain Grant was dead or he simply did not know she was already wed to Grant. Eve looked at Clara's pale, worried face. "Clara," she said in a whisper, taking her hands, "I'm sorry I did not listen."

Clara bit her lip and nodded. "Eve." The woman's voice broke on a sob, which was astonishing. In all the years Eve had known Clara, never had she seen the woman cry. Clara had been like iron—unbreakable. "You know how I do so love to be right," she said, her eyes filling with more tears, "but in this instance, I would give my life to have been wrong about your uncle and spare you the pain."

"Shush," Eve said in a low voice so the guard on the other side of the door wouldn't hear. She gave Clara an apologetic look. "I'm so very sorry that I did not believe you."

Clara squeezed Eve's hands. "It's worse than I feared, though…"

Eve gave a brittle laugh. "What can be worse than my uncle betraying my father? Worse than him having my parents killed, all so he could wed me to a man he could control and thus, control the castle." Clara opened her mouth as if to speak, but Eve had so many thoughts tumbling in her head and a desperate need to sort them out. "Do you know to whom Uncle Frederick intends to wed me? I cannot imagine who it could be. Who is so loyal to my uncle that he wouldn't simply take control of the castle for himself, and—" The utterly distraught look on Clara's face caused Eve to pause. "Clara, what are you not telling me?"

"I'd have already told you, child, if you would but take a breath and allow me to speak."

"Speak, speak," Eve encouraged.

"Eve…" A visible shudder ran through Clara, and Eve found that she, too, was trembling in fearful anticipation. "Your uncle intends to wed you himself. It's what he has always intended."

A wave of nausea roiled in Eve's stomach. "But—" she sucked in a sharp breath, the sickening feeling increasing until she was certain she'd be ill "—that cannot be."

"It is," Clara said, unbending. "I heard it with my own ears."

"No." Flashes of memories of Eve sitting on her uncle's lap and listening to his stories filled her mind, and bile stung her throat. "You must have heard wrong," she whispered furiously.

"Eve," Clara said in the stern tone she'd used often when Eve was younger, "I did not hear wrong. Your uncle told his man when I was in the room. They thought me still unconscious from the beating they gave me. He intends to wed you. He intended to do so years ago."

"But I am his niece," Eve said, horrified. "I was a ch-ch-child," she sputtered.

"He's a disgusting pig," Clara said, never having been one to mince words. She set her hands on Eve's shoulders and looked her in the eye. "He believed we both drowned and were swept away when they could not find our bodies, so he contented himself with ruling the castle at the king's whim. But it seems King Edward is getting harder and harder to please, and your uncle very much wants to legally be entitled to the castle. That way, the nobles will side with him if the king tries to take it from him."

"But if he thought us dead—"

"He has a spy in the MacDougall keep. It seems the MacDougalls are the clan that aided your uncle in his plot to attack Linlithian. He did not have troops of his own, so he promised them coin to aid him. There's much more to tell you, but—"

"We must escape," Eve finished. She wanted to tell Clara about Grant and how she was now wed—or she had been, at least. A knot of torment lodged in her throat at not knowing whether Grant lived or not, and if she stayed here and told her uncle she was wed, he might kill her. She'd rather not take that chance.

She glanced to the wardrobe. No one had ever known about the secret passage except for Eve, her sister, and her parents. Her father had ordered them never to tell another soul. He'd said betrayal could come from the person one least suspected. God above, but he'd been right, as had Clara. Eve's anger at Clara had long since faded. Standing here with her battered lady's maid now, who had given up years of her life to stay with Eve in hiding and who was now risking her life for her—again—Eve was grateful, not angry. She must tell Clara just how grateful she was, but she would have to do so later. Right now, the most important thing was escaping. She motioned to the wardrobe, then waved Clara to follow her. Clara's brow furrowed, but she followed Eve to the wardrobe.

"There is a hidden tunnel that leads to the stables," Eve whispered. Clara's eyes widened. "If we can gain the stables, perhaps we can escape."

"What is this 'perhaps' nonsense?" Clara said, winking at Eve. "We will escape!"

"We must move the wardrobe." Eve set her back against it as she'd done earlier and braced her feet. Clara got into position beside her, and together, they shoved on the wardrobe, which moved with such a loud creak that they both froze, only daring to glance at the door.

"What are you two doing in there?" came the guard's harsh voice, followed by the sound of keys rattling. Eve looked to the wardrobe. It had been moved just enough for someone to slip into the passage. They'd never make it out now that the guard was coming in. If he didn't catch them in the passage, which he likely could, he'd be close on their heels and alert the other guards the minute they all came out at the other side.

"Go!" Eve hissed at Clara and pushed her friend toward the passageway.

"No," Clara whispered back. "Not without you!"

"We'll never both make it, but you can if I lie sufficiently. If we both stay, there will be no hope, and while Uncle Frederick will not kill me yet, but you—"

The door started to creak and Eve shoved Clara into the passage, but Clara grabbed Eve's hand. "Who can I even go to for help?"

"Make your way to the Fraser hold, Dithorn, and demand to speak to the laird. I—" Eve gulped, realizing she did not know who would be laird if Grant had been killed. "Ask to speak to Esme Fraser. Tell her that I need help. Tell her, please." Would Esme gather men for her? Would they even listen to Esme? Eve had no notion, but she had to try.

"But your uncle," Clara wailed low. "What if he forces you to wed him before I return?"

Eve refused to believe Grant was dead until she had proof, and if he was alive, then she could not truly be wed to another. "Then I will wed him," she rushed out. She did not have time to explain because the door creaked again. "Go!" she commanded and rushed to the door just as it was opening. Before the guard could step into her bedchamber, Eve shoved her way out and slammed the door behind them. Her heart was pounding as she looked at the guard. "I'm ready to be wed. My silly old lady's maid is lightheaded, and I've ordered her to lie down so she doesn't ruin the wedding by doing something annoying, like fainting. I know my uncle would hate that."

The guard—thanks be to God—did not look all that astute. He frowned at Eve, and then nodded. "Your uncle does not like to be kept waiting."

"As well he should not," she said, very careful to keep her tone normal. "As lord of this castle, he is an important man. Come," she said, turning away from the bedchamber door. "Take me to him." She held her breath, hoping the guard would comply.

He nodded and led her toward the stairs and then down the narrow, circular passage. She had not walked that particular passage since moments before she'd seen her father murdered years ago. Hopelessness tightened her throat, constricting her breath. The stairs wound round and round, past small windows that allowed rays of light to shine into the dark stairwell, and memories flashed in her mind: Her and her sister running with ribbons over their heads. Her mother singing as she walked hand in hand with Eve down the stairs. Her father carrying her up the stairs when she'd hurt her knee.

Her uncle had taken everything from her. She would get vengeance. Somehow, some way, she would get back what was hers. Grant would not like her plotting revenge and risking herself, she thought with a small smile. She prayed she got the chance to see him once again, even if but to argue that she should be able to be a part of bringing her uncle low.

As the guard led her to the great hall, Eve's mind raced to uncover what she could do to avoid being wed shortly. She could think of nothing, and that knotted her belly with fear, which twisted and knifed through her when the great hall door was opened, revealing her uncle standing there beside a priest, the rest of the room empty. Her uncle looked much the same, except instead of his previously all brown hair it was peppered with white. He was as tall as she'd remembered and thin with a hawklike nose and beady eyes. The priest leaned close to him and whispered something. Eve did not recognize the man, though, and she frowned, wondering what had happened to Father Michael. Had he died? He'd been the priest of Linlithian Castle for as long as Eve could remember. He had christened Eve and her sister, and Father Michael had always listened to Eve when she had a problem. He had been so very kind and good. Everyone had loved him.

Eve sucked in a sharp breath as an idea of how to possibly delay—or gain help doing so—came to her.

"Ah, Eve!" her uncle boomed and spread his arms wide, as if she should simply walk into his treacherous embrace. She shuddered inwardly, but what her uncle expected was exactly what she had to do. "Eve, come." He motioned to her. "Don't be vexed with me for the way we were first reunited, my dear. Everything I did was done to keep you safe."

"Of course, Uncle Frederick," she replied, shocked at how calm she managed to sound.

She said a quick prayer that her uncle caught a pox that took his lying tongue, and she forced her feet to move. She walked toward him and the priest as if she were walking through thick mud. Her legs did not want to cooperate with her. Each step made the nausea increase so that by the time she reached her uncle, her stomach roiled like violent waves in the sea and perspiration dampened her brow.

Please, God, do not let him notice.

Brown, watchful eyes locked on her. "You've changed much, Eve. You're a beautiful woman now."

She wished she were a woman with a dagger, she thought with burning anger. She'd plunge it straight into his black heart. She forced a smile. "You are too kind."

"Clara told me how you two managed to escape those wretched Scots. 'Tis a pity your sister did not. I've searched high and low for her, Eve, and I could not find her."

Lies. Her uncle spewed lies like the sky released rain—freely.

Her uncle frowned. "Where is Clara?"

Her uncle did not have a single care for Clara, of that Eve had no doubt. He simply wanted her in the room so he could use her to threaten Eve if she did not do as he demanded.

Eve motioned nonchalantly toward the great hall door. "She was feeling faint, so I ordered her to lie down in my bedchamber."

"I see." His eyes narrowed for a moment, as if he was contemplating having the guard fetch her.

"She told me I am to wed today," Eve announced, hoping to distract him. "Who will be my husband?"

Her uncle exchanged a look with the priest, who gave an almost imperceptible nod. It was a good thing she had not hoped to find an ally in this priest. She would have been sorely disappointed. He obviously did whatever her uncle bade him without question. "Eve, the king wishes us to wed," her uncle lied again. Eve allowed a bit of her horror to show. After all, her uncle would not expect her to hear this news and not be surprised. "He wants Linlithian to stay in our family, and our wedding is the only way to ensure this and keep your father's men appeased."

It was interesting to her that her uncle had said *your father's men*. As if he had never gained the knights' true loyalty. "Do my father's men hold his memory dear?" Eve asked, searching her uncle's expression for a sign of the truth. Annoyance flickered across his face, and she knew then that they did. That gave her great hope, for it meant they did not find her uncle a good ruler in some way.

"Yes." He offered a tight smile, which did nothing to mask his anger. "They searched for you and your sister for years," he added, annoyance lacing his tone.

Her and her sister! Hope flared in her. Mary surly had to be alive.

"They will be pleased to serve you, and of course, you will be pleased to serve me, yes?"

She wanted to ask about Mary, but even if her uncle knew something, which she did not think he did, she felt certain he'd never tell her. "I will serve you always as you deserve, Uncle," she said, thinking upon serving him with a dagger to his gut. She forced herself to muster another smile for him. "But before we wed, I would like to speak to Father Michael and confess my sins. Where is he?"

Please, please, God, let Father Michael be alive.

A fierce frown came to her uncle's face. "I don't think—"

"A minute if you will, Lord Decres," the chubby priest interrupted, then smiled placatingly at Eve. "I'm Father George."

Eve curtsied as was expected, though the man did not deserve such reverence.

Uncle Frederick looked as if he would deny the priest's request for a moment's time, but he finally nodded, and he and Father George moved a few steps away. Eve stared at

the priest's mouth as he spoke, trying to read his lips.
Let her. What harm. Goodwill breeds cooperation.

Uncle Frederick flashed a forced smile toward her. "I'll send for him. He's even slower than he used to be, and he now resides in a cottage beyond the woods of my land."

"You mean *my land*," she said, unable to stop herself.

Her uncle flushed red, and his lip curled back. "What is yours will become *mine* when we are wed. I will be your lord."

"Of course." She forced the words out through clenched teeth and prayed she did not sound or look as angry as she felt.

Her uncle motioned for the guard. "Go now, Tormod, and fetch Father Michael."

"Let me, Lord Decres," Father George said. "It may take a word from another priest to remind Father Michael of his duty to come and listen to Lady Decres's confession and properly absolve her."

What utter lies! Eve fumed where she stood. There was no doubt in her mind that the corrupt priest before her wished to go to Father Michael to threaten him not to aid Eve.

Uncle Frederick nodded and motioned between Eve and the guard. "Return her to her chambers," he said. She bit her lip on a burst of hope. Once she was in her bedchamber again, she could escape as Clara hopefully had. The guard started to turn her but paused as her uncle said, "On second thought, put her in my chambers, which are soon to be *ours*, and send my chambermaid to her. There's a tub in my chambers, and clearly, you have need of one, as the washing Clara gave you did nothing to cleanse you. I'd have you bathed and presentable before our wedding."

Her head pounded with rage, but she nodded. She could not afford to argue and risk her uncle sending someone to fetch Clara and use her to get Eve to do his bidding.

Chapter Fourteen

It was nearing nightfall when they finally reached the Valley of Blood and Linlithian Castle came into view. And by the time they made their way into the woods that surrounded the outer perimeter of the castle, darkness had descended in the sky—and in Grant's heart and mind. All he'd been able to think about since discovering Eve was taken was that he had failed to protect her. That thought was immediately followed by myriad torturous scenes that all featured Eve. There was Eve being ravaged or Eve being killed. Or Eve being ravaged and then killed. Every scene played out with Eve being viciously hurt until Grant groaned at the images racing relentlessly through his mind.

"I ken ye dunnae like what I'm saying," Ross snapped, "but it must be said."

Grant halted his horse and turned toward Ross. "I did nae even hear what ye said."

Ross and Kade pulled their horses to a stop beside Grant's. "We are riding to our likely deaths," Ross said. "I ken ye wish to rescue Eve, but we need a plan. We kinnae just ride up to the gate and demand to be let in."

Grant tugged a hand through his hair in frustration. He knew his friend was right.

He stared at the castle in the distance. Tall ramparts surrounded every side, each manned by at least one guard.

He could not approach from left or right, because tall hills were on either side of the land. If he approached from the front or back, they'd see him coming the moment he exited the woods, and the only way they'd not shoot was if they believed him to be an ally or one of their own returning from a journey. Grant had nothing to make them seem like an ally or a Decres. He dismounted, as did the others, while he considered what to do.

"Our best hope," he said, the words sticking upon his tongue, "is to wait and ambush a Decres knight or someone visiting the castle. We could cloak ourselves in their clothing, if there was more than one of them." The moment he spoke the idea he knew it would not do.

"That's an excellent plan," Kade said.

Grant shook his head. "Nay, it's a terrible plan. How long might it take for someone to pass by? It could be today, tomorrow, or a sennight or longer before someone ventures through the valley toward the castle." He jerked a frustrated hand through his hair. "I kinnae wait that long."

"Nay," Ross agreed, something in his voice telling Grant that Ross had been waiting for him to come to this revelation. "I think we must create a distraction, so ye can slip into the castle."

"What sort of distraction?" came a woman's voice from his right. She popped up out of the bushes, her silver hair seeming to glisten in the moonlight.

Grant, Kade, and Ross all drew their swords. "Who are ye?" Grant demanded.

The tiny woman crossed her arms over her chest, and Grant could just see her arch her brows. "I'm a friend to Eve Decres," the woman said, her voice cautious. "Who are you?"

"I'm Grant Fraser, laird to the Fraser Clan and Eve's

husband," Grant replied, the words making his chest squeeze. He was amazed at how protective he was of her.

"Husband?" she repeated, shock and disbelief clear in her voice and on her face. "Eve cannot be wed to you."

"Whyever nae? Because I'm a Scot?"

"No, because she said she would wed her uncle!"

"I told ye that ye could nae trust her," Ross barked.

Before Grant could snap at Ross to be quiet, the woman turned toward Ross. "How dare you," she bellowed, much in the same fashion that Eve had. Suddenly, Grant understood how Eve had learned the art of being heard. This woman was Clara! And for such a small woman, she was incredibly loud. "Take that back." She shoved her finger into Ross's chest.

A mutinous look came over his face, but Grant shook his head at his friend. They did not have time for such arguments. Grant cleared his throat and faced the woman. "Ye must be Clara."

Her jaw dropped slightly. "Y-yes. How did you—"

"I told ye," Grant cut in, forcing a smile to his face, "Eve is my wife. We went to the convent to rescue ye, but ye weren't there." Then awareness that Clara had escaped but Eve had not slammed into him. "Where is Eve?"

Clara's moonlit eyes welled with tears.

"Ye best start from the beginning," Grant said gently. "But I beg of ye, make it quick."

The woman nodded. "Eve's uncle was the one who betrayed her family," she said in a rush. "He promised coin to the MacDougalls if they would kill his brother and wife, and take Eve and her sister. He even led them into the castle himself! When the plan was completed, the MacDougalls were to be given Mary, as well as the coin, for their efforts, and Eve was to be 'rescued' by her uncle." Clara snorted.

"In truth, Frederick only wanted the Decres warriors to think he'd rescued Eve from savage Scots so they would not protest overly much when he wed her under the guise of keeping her safe."

She looked from Grant's face to his hands as they instinctively curled into fists. Anger and repulsion pulsed within him. "Continue," he urged. "Please."

She nodded. "Eve was propelled over the cliff by the horse we rode when we were trying to escape, and I jumped in after her. When they could not find our bodies, they assumed us dead. But, of course, we were not."

"And ye took Eve to the convent for safety," Grant said.

Clara nodded. "I was suspicious that her uncle had been behind the attack, and I knew Eve would never be safe until she reached eighteen summers. Her father was wise and persuaded Edward to let Eve wed a man of her own choosing at that time, and then that man would one day inherit Linlithian. It helped Eve's father's argument greatly that the queen was a romantic and by the king's side the day Eve's father made the request for Eve to choose her husband—a good, honorable husband," she said, eyeing him.

"I am honorable," Grant replied, eyeing the woman back.

"Are you?" Clara asked, tilting her head. "How, then, did Eve come to be wed to you? If she even is!" Her voice rose, her own protectiveness over Eve flaring in the dark night.

"Eve is my wife," he said, struggling to maintain his patience. He could literally feel time slipping away, yet he could not make decisions about how to proceed without knowing as much as he could about the enemies he would face. "She is my wife in every sense of the word."

He'd meant to ease the woman's mind, to help her understand that he would die to protect Eve, but when Clara's lips slipped open and she gasped, he knew his words had not been clear enough.

"You ravaged her?" Clara hissed.

He took a deep breath. "Madame, I assure ye, I did nae." Despite the cool night air, irritation heated him.

"You must have," she accused. "Eve would never have wed you, let alone joined with you and sealed her fate."

"Well, she did," Kade snapped. "And ye kinnae speak to my laird that way. Lady Eve wed him quick as a fox when she kenned he'd nae aid her in rescuing ye if she did nae."

Grant groaned.

"You are a barbarian!" Clara screamed, and though he hated to do it, he grabbed the woman and clamped his hand over her mouth, lest she bring Decres and his men straight to them.

Guilt over what he'd forced Eve to do niggled at him. He'd not felt any misgivings over the acts required of him since the day his mother had died, but since meeting Eve, doubt seemed to be his constant companion, and he did not care for it at all. Doubt was weakness, and he could not be weak and protect everyone who needed him.

"I'm a Scot, and we do what we must," he told her. "And much of what we must do has been forced upon us by *yer* king. Now, if ye continue to argue with me, Eve may well be ravaged this night, but it will nae be by me. If I remove my hand, ye must be quiet, do ye ken me?"

Clara nodded, and Grant immediately released his hold on her. "Where was Eve when ye last saw her?" he asked.

"In her bedchamber," Clara replied. Her tone had gone from outraged to worried. "We were going to escape through a secret tunnel, but then the guard heard us and she said I must go, that we would never both make it out on time."

"Where does the tunnel lead?" If she'd used it to get out of the castle, it stood to reason that they could use it to get into it.

"To the stables," Clara said. "From there, you have to cross the outer courtyard to exit the keep. I stayed to the shadows, and I crawled from the keep to the woods. 'Tis the only way, as the area is open and the guards could more easily see you if you stood. I believe you could get to the stables, but there are guards everywhere. They'd kill you on sight. It would be folly for you to attempt it." Her voice broke, and he knew she was trying not to cry.

"As I said," Ross spoke, "we must create a distraction."

"How?" Clara demanded. "Whoever does it would be sacrificing their lives, most likely."

Grant's gaze locked with Ross's, his mind turning over what he'd learned. Eve may have agreed to wed her uncle, but she knew well that her marriage to him was true now. She could not wed one man when wed to another. "She must have planned to wed Decres only if she had to. A marriage made true cannot be dissolved."

"She was ready to sacrifice herself for me." Clara began to sob. "So…so I c-could escape. I will be the one to create the distraction, as it should be."

Pride in Eve and anger at Decres nearly choked Grant. He was glad Eve was brave, but he'd told her not to court trouble, and she'd gone and done exactly that. "Nae," Grant said. "It will be me. Eve is my wife."

Clara's mouth slipped open, but after a moment she said, "You would give your life for Eve?"

"Aye," he assured the woman.

Clara nodded. "Eve has chosen wisely, then," she said.

"If Frederick believes he is wed to Eve, he will join with her. He may…" Clara swallowed loudly. "He may already have done so." Tears leaked down the woman's cheeks. "He would do that in his bedchamber."

The thought of another man touching Eve, of taking her against her will, made Grant shake all over and his blood rush through his veins. "I'll rush the castle on my horse," he bit out. "And when I do, ye must slip in, Ross. Kade, ye take Clara and make yer way to Dithorn."

"I'll not leave Eve," the woman protested.

Grant's patience snapped. He had not time to spare. "Kade—"

"Aye, laird. Ye need nae say more," Kade replied and scooped Clara off her feet and muffled her wails. "I'll see ye at Dithorn." He turned to march toward his horse.

"Ye ken I will do what ye ask, Grant," Ross said beside him, "but this is folly. Ye'll be killed this night. Perhaps if we wait, someone will venture by that we can ambush, or we can leave to get aid and return for Eve."

Ross spoke wisely. Grant knew it, and yet… "I kinnae wait," he said. "And I kinnae simply ride away and leave her."

"This foolhardiness is why I'll nae ever wed," Ross replied with a sigh. "Ye are heading toward death, but I will do all I can to ensure yer wife and I dunnae join ye there."

"Thank ye, Ross," Grant said, turned, and started shoving through the bushes in the direction of the castle. "God, be on our side," he said, and started to glance toward the sky, but a torch lit the darkness to illuminate a priest riding away from the castle and toward them on a horse. Grant stopped in his tracks and set a hand on Ross's shoulder. "That is the quickest God has ever answered me," he said with a grin.

The knock at her uncle's bedchamber door came much later than Eve had expected. She'd thought the priest would have rushed to return to the castle, but she'd been in the bedchamber quite a long time. She rose on trembling legs, the folds of the ornate gown her uncle had insisted she wear billowing to the ground to swish at her feet. Bile rose in her throat as the door opened, and then her eyes widened in shock at the sight of the two priests standing there. Their robes were drawn over their heads and low on their faces. Eve opened her mouth to demand to know who they were, but before she could get the question out, she noticed the man assigned to guard her lay crumpled on the ground behind the priests.

"What in God's name—"

"I hear ye love the state of marriage so much that ye intend to take a second husband," one of the men said, shoving his hood back to reveal his face.

"Grant!" she cried out, shock and relief rendering her immobile for one moment, before joy sent her flying into the protective embrace of his arms. "Did you encounter Father George? Are these his and Father Michael's robes? However did you—"

A savage kiss stopped her question for a brief moment. Then he broke the contact and motioned her to step out of the way.

"Aye, and aye. But 'tis a tale for when we escape this castle," he said as he bent and grabbed the unconscious guard by the arms. Grant looked up at Ross, who had been disguised as the second priest. "Are ye just going to stand there, or are ye going to aid me?"

Ross glowered at Grant. "I was waiting for ye to snap

another order, as ye've been doing since this ill-advised foray into the castle," he growled, even as he grasped the guard's legs. He and Grant carried the guard past Eve and into the bedchamber. They deposited him onto the floor with a *thud*.

Grant stood, swept his gaze around the bedchamber, and then looked at Eve and frowned. "What are ye wearing?"

Eve gave a nervous laugh. "The wedding finery my uncle demanded."

A tender look came over his face. "I'm sorry to have been right about him, Wife."

Her throat suddenly tightened with the need to slump into Grant's arms and cry. She felt she'd suffered another great loss today. She had loved her uncle and trusted him, and he'd proven treacherous. Grant took her hand and squeezed it, seeming to understand what she was feeling without saying it. Gratefulness filled her.

"We have to flee," he said. "Luck was on our side on the way in, but it will nae be long now before the guards we knocked unconscious are discovered. Thèn—"

Horns began to ring all at once. A chill swept Eve's body, and she moved closer to Grant. "That horn signals an intruder in the castle."

"What's the best route of escape?" Grant asked.

Eve hesitated for a brief moment, thinking back to her life here, which seemed so very long ago. The only way out was through the keep and down the valley; they'd never make it. Her uncle's men would overcome them. Unless...

"We'll go straight out the front entrance in plain sight, but you will need to knock out two more guards."

Grant smiled, as did Ross. "I like how quick ye think, Wife. It so happens we left two guards down the passage.

We'll return in a moment."

She nodded, moving toward the unconscious guard. "I'll take his clothes," she said, motioning to the man on the floor.

"I'll agree to that this time, but ye should ken, I dunnae share what is mine," he said with the hint of teasing, "and ye are mine."

She knew he was making light, likely so she would not be as scared. She winked at him. "'Tis good to hear, Husband, for I don't share what is mine, either, and *you* are mine."

By the time Eve had gotten the guard's clothing off and had disrobed herself, Grant and Ross returned with two more uniforms. Embarrassment heated her cheeks when Ross's eyes widened upon her as she stood dressed in only her léine. Grant elbowed his friend, even though Ross immediately averted his eyes.

"Wipe that picture of Eve from yer mind," Grant ordered as he began to strip off his plaid and braies to don the clothes he held in his hands.

"I assure ye, it's already gone," Ross said, moving to the window behind them and facing it as he dressed, as well.

Eve and Grant locked eyes as they hurriedly dressed, and for the brief moment her husband's chest was bare, all she could think upon was how he'd felt under her touch. Her neck and chest heated with the thoughts of her husband, and he gave her a knowing look, as if he too was recalling their night together. Suddenly, he pulled her to him and pressed his lips to her ear.

"Stay behind me," he said, putting his helmet on and then brushing his thumb over her lips before picking up his sword, which had been hidden under the priest's frock, and sheathing it.

She frowned and snatched up one of the guard's daggers that Grant had not yet picked up from where he'd placed the weapons on the ground. "I'll stay beside you, or I may even lead," she said, determined to take her bravery back. She shoved past Grant, but he grabbed her hand.

"Eve—"

"Nae a one of us will be alive to stay anywhere if we dunnae flee now," Ross growled, donning his helmet.

As if he'd called the hounds of Hell down upon them, the door burst open, and a guard, brandishing a sword, barreled into the room.

※

Even as Grant drew his sword to save Eve, she lunged at the guard and plunged her dagger into his gut. The guard's eyes grew wide, and wider still, as Grant finished him with a clean blow to the chest. Before the man fully fell to the floor, sword clattering, Grant grabbed his wife, tugged her around the falling warrior, grasped the helmet she had yet to put on, and shoved it onto her head.

"Ye need a lesson in obedience," he growled, seeing his mother's face and then an image of Eve dead.

"Well, you will have to save it for later," she said as a dozen guards appeared at the top of the stairs.

"Do you have Lady Decres?" the guard at the front of the line demanded.

"No," Eve spoke before Grant could. She'd pitched her voice low, but was it enough to fool the guards?

"Search the courtyard, then," the guard said. "We'll continue to search the castle. Whoever's in here has surely come for her."

Eve nodded, and the guards turned and ran down the

passage. The moment they were out of sight, Grant, Eve, and Ross made for the stairs. Grant had to pull Eve back to get ahead of her and position her between himself and Ross. When they reached the main floor, the door to the castle had opened wide, and knights flooded the courtyard and the valley beyond as far as Grant could see.

"If anyone stops us let me speak," Eve whispered. "They will know you two are Scots the minute you open your mouths."

Grant nodded, knowing she was likely correct. His English accent was passable, but Eve could pitch her voice better than he could mimic the English brogue. Sweat dampened his back and brow as they walked into the courtyard and began to wind through the men going in various directions. The noise all around him did not compare to the rushing in his ears. Never had he been afraid in battle. He'd always been able to detach himself, to think only of the moment, but with Eve beside him, all he could think was that a single blow could kill her. Worry gnawed at him, and he did not care for it at all. The urge to take her hand or put his arm around her was near overwhelming, but that would draw attention to them. Knights were deployed in various directions, and Grant committed their paths to memory for when he returned to take the castle for his wife. And this time, it would be as much for her as for Scotland.

They made their way through the courtyard without incident. When they reached the gates manned by four guards, one of the guards raised his hand for them to stop. "Lord Decres said no one leaves the castle grounds without seeing him first."

Grant curled his hand around the hilt of his sword, prepared to kill if necessary. "He just ordered us to search the woods," Eve said, doing a surprisingly good impression of a man's voice. "You can stop us, but I'd not if I were you. Lord Decres is in a foul mood since Eve went missing."

"Go, then," the guard said, waving at the one manning the gates. Grant hesitated, not wanting him and Ross to move through the gate without Eve, but he forced himself to move when the guard barked, "I said you can go! Do your legs no longer work?"

He came through the gate, as did Ross. When Eve passed the guard manning the gate, however, the man said, "Halt!"

Grant's heart exploded as he turned to see Eve stop and the guard rush toward her. The man raised his sword to the sliver of exposed skin at Eve's neck. "You called Lady Decres by her given name."

"Yes," Eve responded, and Grant winced. He could hear the change in her tone, but could the guard here it?

"Last night Lord Decres ordered us all to never become familiar with Lady Decres," the man said. "We were to keep our distance, and always remember that she has lived a long time in Scotland. She is not to be trusted. Yet, *you* called her Eve…"

Perspiration rolled down Grant's back, and he took a step toward Eve, judging the distance between them. There would be no way to reach her in time if the guard made a move. Yet, he could not stop himself. He took a step toward them, and the guard's gaze flicked to Grant before returning to Eve. "What do you say for yourself?"

"It was—" Her voice had pitched yet higher, and this time it sounded distinctly like a woman's.

Grant and the guard lunged for Eve simultaneously. Another guard came at Grant from the right, and Grant sliced the man across the stomach. Behind him, swords clanked once, twice, and then Ross cried out, "Die, English swine!" A body thudded to the ground. "Good riddance."

Grant strode toward Eve who was swinging her dagger at the guard, whose back was now to Grant. He drew his sword back when he was within striking distance, and as he did, the man lunged forward again. As Grant sliced his opponent's back, the man yelped and staggered forward, tripping and coming to his knees. Relief poured over Grant. Eve had not been hurt.

"Go!" he roared at her as he swung his sword in a death blow to the kneeled guard's stomach while Eve ran past the two of them. The knight's eyes went wide as he dropped his sword and fell face-first to land at Grant's feet.

Relief gripped Grant once more, but then Ross bellowed from behind him, "Eve, nay!"

Grant turned, seeing only a blur of Eve launching herself in front of him. She grunted and fell into him, crumpling into his arms. He gripped her to him, and shock froze him for a breath. Then rage unlike anything he'd ever known flooded his veins, surging from his heart to his limbs. He looked up and saw a horseman riding toward them, bow drawn, and behind the man, in the distance, Decres's men rode hard toward them while Ross, to Grant's shock, fled past him.

Grant jerked his gaze away from Ross and back to Eve. Her eyes were closed, and she was limp in his arms. When he moved his hand to her back, he felt an arrow protruding from her body. Fear ripped through him, shredding him.

"Unhand my niece!" Decres roared as he approached. The horrified look that swept his face when he looked at Eve told Grant that Decres hadn't realized he'd missed his target and shot Eve instead. Grant kneeled, laid Eve down, and came up with his sword in his hand.

"My men will reach us before you can strike me and get away," Decres shouted.

"Ye have nae ever seen how fast I can kill a man," Grant snarled, shifting his sword from his right to his left hand while drawing his dagger with his right. He jerked it up, and threw it straight at Decres's black heart. It stuck true, and the man was falling forward to his death as Grant was bending to reach for Eve. When he came up, Ross galloped toward him, leading Grant's horse.

"Ye did nae think I'd left ye, did ye?" Ross asked.

Grant snapped his jaw closed as he laid Eve across the destrier and mounted behind her. "Thank ye," he breathed to his friend as they turned the horses and rode toward freedom.

Chapter Fifteen

"Will she die?" Grant asked, hovering behind Esme, who was the healer of the clan and was bent over Eve, tending to her puncture wound. Esme had sent everyone else, including a loudly protesting Clara and a grumbling Thomas and Allisdair from the room. His sister worked best alone, but she had not even attempted to make him leave. A good thing, too, as he would not have parted from Eve no matter if the king himself ordered it. He looked down at Eve, and his gut twisted. A sheen of perspiration covered her brow, and she was white as the thick fog that covered the rolling hills in the morning. She could not die. He could not fail to have protected yet another person he cared for.

Cared for. The term was not enough to describe the depth of emotion that Eve evoked. She stirred a storm inside him that threatened to destroy him if he lost her. He could not explore the myriad soft emotions trying to break through the barrier he was desperate to hold in place. He could not face the tenderness, the longing, the lo—He blocked the thought before it could fully form. His pulse pounded, as did his temples. Hollowness filled him. "Will she die?" he asked again, his voice a whisper.

"I kinnae say, Brother. She's caught in the throes of a fever. How long did ye say she's been like this?"

Had he said? Tiredness made his thoughts feel like sludge. They had journeyed from Linlithian to Dithorn in a day when it normally took two. He'd never ridden so hard or so fast, and he'd fled for his life many a time. They'd lost the Decres knights who had been pursuing them soon after reaching the woods. Eve's men, for they were Eve's men by rights, were not well trained in tracking men. He'd rectify that once he took the castle back in Eve's name.

"Grant?" Esme asked, her fingertips brushing his shoulder. "Go take a respite. Ye kinnae aid Eve at the moment, and ye are barely standing on yer own two feet."

"She's been like this since midafternoon yesterday," he said, only just remembering he had not answered his sister's question.

Esme nodded. "If fever is going to set in, 'tis about the time it takes to do so."

Eve moaned just then and thrashed her arms. He bent down beside her and set his hand to her forehead. "Shh, Eve," he whispered, his chest squeezing. "I'm here." Immediately, she stilled, and he relaxed.

"Ye care for her," Esme said, the awe in her voice apparent. He nodded, too damned tired to deny it to his sister, even though it was private. He'd not even explored it, the deep endless cavern of it, himself. A powerful ache took hold of his chest and squeezed until he took a shuddering breath.

"Don't leave me," Eve cried out, thrashing her arms once more. "Don't leave me, don't leave me."

Grant gripped her wrists in a gentle hold and placed her arms by her sides as he whispered to her. "I'll nae ever leave ye, ye wee stubborn lass. Dunnae ye leave me." Eve sighed and stilled once more, but he frowned at the searing heat from her body. He glanced at his sister. "Is there nae anything we can do to ease her discomfort?"

"Sometimes cool baths help," Esme said. "I can—"

"Nay, I wish to do it," he said. "Tell me what to do."

"Simply dip a rag in cool water and run it over her skin." Esme walked to the washbasin and brought it to him. Grant pulled the bedcoverings down past Eve's long, slender legs. She was wearing only a thin léine, and the outline of her lush breasts and curve of her hips through the linen made him want to run his hands over her body and worship her. Protect her. "Eve," he whispered close to her ear, "I vow I'll nae ever let harm come to ye again," he said as he lifted the léine to drag the cool rag over her taut belly.

"Such a promise is impossible to keep, Grant," Esme said, "and she would nae like to be treated as if helpless."

"Nae helpless," he corrected. "Protected. I promised her that I'd teach her to defend herself, and she vowed to me that she'd nae go courting trouble, a vow she broke immediately."

Esme scowled at him. "Only a man would see a woman saving his life as the woman courting trouble. Did ye want her to stand there and watch as the arrow her uncle shot at ye struck true?"

"Aye," he said, his temper flaring. "That's exactly what I wanted, since it meant her risking her life otherwise. 'Tis my duty to protect her, and 'tis her duty to stay alive!" he thundered, an image of his mother coming unbidden to his mind. He turned away from Esme's probing stare and dipped the rag in the cool water once more, then trailed it up each of Eve's arms before laying it on her forehead.

Esme kneeled beside him. He could feel her looking at him, but he kept his stare on Eve. For one, he wanted to see any change in his wife that might occur. But also, Esme had the uncanny ability to read people's inner thoughts sometimes, and he'd rather keep his plaguing guilt over his mother's death to himself.

"If that is the only duty ye allow her, Grant, she will grow to hate ye. The two of ye will nae ever have a marriage of love."

Love? The word struck a chord deep in him. It echoed in his ears and reverberated in his mind. He could not love her. He could not allow it. Clenching his teeth, he fought against the rise of emotions in him once more. Devil take it. He wasn't sure he wanted any part of such a thing. Just caring for Eve had made him crazed. What would love do? He'd loved his mother, and losing her had sent him reeling for months and had changed him forever. Loving Eve would be even worse. He knew it to the depths of his soul.

"I dunnae need love," he choked out, the feeling that he could not breathe gripping him once more. "We have desire, and I like her, certainly—"

Esme snorted at that. "Ye fool yerself."

Possibly. Hell, quite probably. But all his warrior instincts told him to fight the tide of his feelings for Eve, a tide that was threatening to sweep him away. "Then let me," he finally ground out when Esme poked him.

"Grant Fraser," Esme growled, "just why do ye think Mother went to our enemy clan to aid them?"

"Foolishness," he snapped as he ran the cool, wet rag over Eve's legs now. She kicked out then; she would have kicked him in the face if he hadn't caught her ankle gently and lowered her leg to the bed.

"That's yer wife stating her opinion," Esme said, matter-of-fact.

"She can have all the opinions she wants, but I'm her husband and her laird, and she will obey my orders."

"Mother liked to feel needed, and Da made her feel

useless," Esme went on, ignoring him. "He allowed her nothing but trivial duties, and her mind and spirit were too great for that." His sister met his eyes. "Eve is like Mother."

He looked away and studied Eve, half-amazed at how simply looking at her made his chest ache and half-concerned that she had such an effect on him. Eve was very similar to his mother in many ways. "I'll make her feel important," he vowed aloud. She did not need to be a warrior to feel important. Running the castle was a great duty, and his wife would be the one to oversee it all.

Esme yawned. "Are ye certain ye dunnae want to lie down?"

He nodded, brushing a loose tendril of hair from Eve's damp forehead. "I want to be here if she needs me."

"Because ye care for her much more than ye are admitting to me or yourself," Esme said to his annoyance. He waved a hand at her, and she chuckled. "I'll return in the morning, but if ye need me or if her fever increases"—her voice dropped low with concern—"come rouse me immediately. There's a root called bane weed that I can give her if truly needed. It has been known to aid fever, but it also carries a great risk of making a woman unable to bear children. I myself have had to give it to two women, and neither of them have conceived a child since taking it."

He nodded, praying to God he did not have to make that choice for Eve, for he knew how he'd choose.

After Esme left his bedchamber, he dipped the cloth in the water and gently drew down Eve's léine to sponge her chest, neck, and face. Unexpected desire stirred deep within him, but he pushed it away. It would be a long while before he allowed himself to touch his wife. He would ensure all of her strength had returned first, so she did not overtax herself and have a setback as Loranna, Simon's late wife, had. She had been injured, and seemed to be recovering, so she took up her duties at the castle once more, and her fever had returned and became so severe that she died.

Grant dropped the rag into the water basin, leaned back in the chair, and closed his eyes, recalling the past. Grant had thought Simon indifferent to Loranna's death, as his brother had left while she had been sick, and Loranna and Simon had been estranged. But he'd discovered later that Simon had not actually known how much danger Loranna had been in from the fever. Grant turned his right arm over to look at the inside of his wrist where the brand he'd given himself was. He traced his finger over the mark.

God, how he'd wanted to be in his brother's circle of renegades, but Simon had kept him out to protect him, almost to the detriment of their relationship. He'd thought Simon a traitor because Simon had kept what he was doing a secret for so long. Thank God they had reconciled before he'd died. Still, Grant balled his hands into fists. They'd lost much time as true brothers due to the rift, and for that, Grant was to blame. But he would avenge his brother. He had not forgotten the MacDougalls or what they had done. He would not let Simon down again. He would get vengeance, but it would be carefully achieved so as not to put any of his men in unnecessary danger. And his first order of business would be to go to Linlithian and establish himself as the new lord. It should be a simple matter of returning there with Eve by his side, but he was not such a fool as to go without a contingent of men to hold order against any of Decres's knights who may not wish Grant as their new lord.

Nor was he so naive as to simply believe it would be that easy when the matter relied on King Edward keeping his word to acknowledge Eve as the rightful heir. He'd seen the English king break his vows to men too many times, to take back land he had given or castles that had long belonged to families, merely because it pleased him to do so. No, Grant needed to be prepared for the worst possible scenario: that he would have to battle the Decres knights, King Edward, and quite possibly the MacDougalls, for control of Linlithian.

The images he'd noted while at Linlithian rolled through his mind now. He sat with his eyes closed, the need for sleep tugging at him, but he battled it by recalling all the details that would be useful in seizing the castle. Now that Frederick Decres was dead, the king would make a move. Grant had hoped to take Linlithian before the king had even been aware of what he was doing and establish Eve there to hopefully gain the trust and favor of the men who once served her father, but that opportunity was likely now gone.

He knew King Edward was not far from Linlithian, and the Decres knights would surely send a messenger to him before Grant could return with Eve, or even Clara in Eve's place if she was too weak to travel.

With nothing but time, he lay there carefully considering how to take Linlithian by force and how to win over the Decres warriors—or banish them from the castle, if necessary. And then he turned his mind to Eve's sister, Mary. He wanted to reunite Eve with her, if possible, and in order to do that, he needed to know all the details of the night that Eve had last seen her. He would ask Eve, of course, but she was young and had likely forgotten much. But Clara might remember something useful. Next time he spoke with her, he'd question her about it.

Eve stirred suddenly and then moaned, but it was different from before. Grant's eyes flew open, and he sat upright, reaching for her hand. She whimpered in her sleep when he touched it, and then she snatched her hand back, curled into a ball, and began to shriek.

"Eve!" He shoved out of his chair and thought to take her in his arms, but she cried out even louder when he touched her again. Stark fear battered him as he looked between Eve and the door. He had to get Esme, but he didn't want to leave Eve alone.

The door crashed open with a bang, and Thomas ran in. "What is it? What's wrong with Eve?"

"Fetch Esme!" Grant barked, not even questioning what Thomas had been doing lurking at the door.

His younger brother nodded and hurried out of the room. Grant turned his attention back to Eve, reaching for her again but stopping short of touching her. He didn't want to cause her any more pain. She writhed and moaned on the bed, now clutching her skull.

"My head!" she bellowed. "You are splitting my head in two!"

"Eve, hold on," Grant urged, feeling as if worry was shredding him.

"Stand back," Esme demanded as she pushed past him with Clara at her side. She set a hand to Eve's forehead and hissed. "The fever is much, much worse, Brother. I fear…I fear it will kill her." She turned to Grant with tear-filled eyes. "I brought the root. What do ye want me to do?"

Grant returned his gaze to Eve, skimming over Thomas, who was standing there gaping, and Clara, whose face was drained of all color. "Give it to her," he choked out, a numbness descending upon him.

"Ye recall what I said—"

He waved Esme to silence. "Aye. Eve's life means more to me than an heir she might give me."

Grant did not miss the relief that passed over his sister's

face or Clara's rush of breath that she pushed from her lungs. Had the women doubted that he would choose Eve over an heir?

"Hold her by the shoulders," Esme ordered.

Grant did as she said, and Esme pried Eve's jaw open, dropped the tiny bits of root into her mouth, then held a wine goblet to her lips and tilted a bit of liquid in. She shut Eve's mouth and held it closed as Eve fought her. Clara moved to Eve's other side and whispered reassuring things to her. When Eve finally settled, Esme released her and then indicated for Grant to do so, as well, but as he did, tears began to leak from Eve's eyes.

Guilt stabbed at him. Would she be angry when she learned the truth or would she understand that it had been the only way?

"She will understand eventually," Clara said, as if she'd read his mind. "After the pain of discovering she will likely not have a child passes, she will understand."

He nodded, appreciating Clara's kind words, but all he wanted now was to be with Eve. "Leave us, please," he commanded Esme, Thomas, and Clara, glad that they immediately obeyed. Grant sat staring at Eve, who panted with pain. A physical need to touch her burned inside him like a fire raging out of control, but he held himself still until the panting ceased, and she lay there, still as the dead.

His heart nearly stopped at the thought. He carefully put his finger under her nose, and her warm breath wafted over his skin. Abruptly, she turned on her side at the edge of the bed, and he gently lay down beside her, tentatively touching first her back and then her shoulder, arm, and hip. When she sighed and scooted back toward him, he trembled with relief. He moved closer to her, and gently encircled her in his protective embrace.

"Ye are a fighter, Wife," he whispered into her hair. "Now if only I can make ye a listener, I think we will be verra happy."

He lay there, listening to her deep, steady inhales and exhales, and gratefulness that Eve had lived made his throat tighten and his eyes water. God's teeth, the woman made him soft as dough. He'd have to work on that. But sleep, which he'd not had in what seemed like forever, beckoned to him now with his wife nestled in his arms, resting peacefully. So finally, he allowed himself to give in to the desperate need, breathing her freesia scent as he drifted toward oblivion.

"Grant?" Bryden's voice came from the door as he knocked.

Grant carefully rose from the bed and made his way to the door, opening it and stepping into the passageway.

"How is Eve?" Bryden asked.

"Better," Grant replied, a rush of relief tingling through him.

"I've news ye are nae going to like."

"Get on with it," Grant said, impatient to return to Eve. She was his main concern at the moment. Though, God's truth, as laird, the clan should always come first; he could not make it so in his mind.

"MacDougall warriors were spotted near the borders of our land," Bryden said.

Grant's hands fisted at his side as rage beat like a drum within him. They were circling like vultures for Eve. Word of her uncle's death must have reached them. "Double the warriors on guard."

Bryden nodded. "What of Lady Eve? When she is well

enough and ventures out should I assign a man to guard her?"

"I want ye to guard her personally, but stay back so that she dunnae ken it. My wife is verra independent, and I'd rather she nae feel like a prisoner."

"Of course," Bryden agreed. He gave Grant a concerned look. "When was the last time ye ate?"

"I dunnae recall," Grant said as his stomach growled. With Eve so sick, he'd had no appetite or desire for food. He was her husband. It was his job to ensure she lived, and he would do everything in his power to make certain that he did not fail, including going without food and sleep when she needed him. And Eve had most definitely needed him. She needed him still.

"Come and sup," Bryden said.

Grant shook his head, seeing Clara come to the top of the stairs at the end of the passage.

"Cousin, ye need to eat. I'll sit with Eve if—"

"Nay," Grant snapped. He knew Bryden was trying to help, but he'd not leave Eve.

Clara strolled toward them and paused by Bryden. "Why don't you have one of the serving wenches bring a platter of food for Grant?"

A momentary look of annoyance skittered across Bryden's face, but he nodded. Grant assumed his cousin did not like an English woman making a suggestion, even if it was a good one. He'd have to speak to Bryden later when there was time.

"Eve is resting peacefully," he offered Clara as Bryden strode toward the stairs.

"I'm glad. I came to check on her and see if I could offer aid. I confess I'm no healer like your sister, and I've been so worried. I spoke with Esme, and she says the bane weed will most likely make Eve nauseated."

He jerked a hand through his hair. "What have I done?"

Clara patted his arm. "The only thing you could—just as I did the night I took her to hiding so long ago."

Clara mentioning the night Eve's parents had been killed and her sister Mary had disappeared reminded Grant he wished to speak with her about it.

"I wish to talk to ye about the night Eve's parents were killed and her sister went missing. I wish to talk to ye about yer escape."

"What do you want to know?" Clara asked.

He liked that the woman did not mince words. "Tell me what ye can recall of Mary. Did she ride alone? Was she on foot? Was someone looking out for her as ye were for Eve?"

"Mary was riding with John, the stablemaster. She was but a wee lass of five summers. He was seeing to her safety, even as I was seeing to Eve's. But they fell and were trampled. Why?"

There was no way to soften the shock of what he was going to tell her, so he simply spit it out. "There is a verra good chance that Mary and John are alive."

"What?" Clara's face went pale. "But…but—"

"I ken yer shock, but the song the bards always sing about the missing heiress of Linlithian includes a part about her missing sister, and that would be Mary."

Clara nibbled on her lip as she nodded slowly. "Yes, it would." She suddenly gripped Grant by the forearm. "The plan that John and I came up with to get the girls to safety was to ride out to the Calder clan."

"They're an enemy clan of ours," Grant said, thinking immediately of Millicent. His former leman had been a Calder before wedding one of Grant's guards, who was now deceased. "I ken someone who might be able to aid me in getting safely into the Calder holding and having an audience with the laird to see if John and Mary ever made it there."

The plan was sound, but it would be best not to tell Clara of his former relationship with Millicent. He'd broken it off when she'd proven to be a spiteful woman and only allowed her to stay at Dithorn because he'd promised his guard on his deathbed that he would always give Millicent shelter as long as she wished it. He suspected, though, that neither Clara nor Eve would approve of him traveling to the Calder holding with a woman with whom he'd previously joined. Yet, that was exactly what he'd have to do to gain entry without the threat of being killed. Since Millicent had been born a Calder, she could go back to her clan freely to see whatever family was still there, and as the man accompanying her, he would be guaranteed safety while they were there.

"I sent messengers on several occasions to the Calder laird," Clara said. "At first, I received no response when I inquired about John Talbot and Mary, and last time, about a year ago, I received a message that said there was no one there by those names and there never had been. I fear speaking to the Calder laird will bring no answers," Clara said, her voice unhappy.

"It may nae," Grant agreed, "but if there is any possibility that doing so will lead me to reuniting Eve with her sister, maybe—"

Understanding lit Clara's eyes. "You fear she will blame you for the bane weed," Clara said on a low voice.

He clenched his jaw but nodded. "Aye. I would give her a reason nae to hate me."

Clara smiled gently and squeezed his arm. "I do believe you've already given her many reasons, but if you could find her sister, it would mean the world to her. She's had to bear a lot of sadness, and I think part of why she was able to remain so strong was the hope that she would return to Linlithian one day and recapture the happiness she'd known as a child, which had included her uncle as part of her family."

"She will have a chance to be happy there," he said, willing it to be so. "We will live here, of course, but while I'm establishing control of the castle, we will stay there, and once it's established and I have my man in place to oversee it, we will visit often not simply because I need to but because I ken she will want to. She is my family, and I want her to be happy."

"Yes, of course," Clara said slowly, "but Eve wants to feel the love she once felt." She eyed him expectantly.

"Ye're here," he said, purposely avoiding her probing stare.

"For now," Clara replied. "But once I know Eve is settled and happy, I'll go."

"Where? Ye're more than welcome to stay on as part of the clan."

"I thank you," she said, "but I have duties I swore to uphold long ago, and Eve is but one of those duties."

"Do ye care to tell me more?"

Clara smiled secretly. "I cannot, but I'll tell you this: men are not the only ones who can be warriors. We women are mighty, and our weapons are not always swords. Words often cut as sharp as a blade."

"God's teeth, woman," he said on a chuckle, "dunnae tell Eve that. She wishes to wield swords, and if she wields words, too, I'll be outmatched."

She surprised him by winking. "What makes you think you are not already?"

He opened his mouth to answer when Eve suddenly cried out. Fear sent him bolting through the door with Clara on his heels. Eve was standing by the bed, doubled over, retching violently, but before he could reach her, she collapsed.

Murmured voices invaded Eve's dreams. She tried to open her eyes to see who was there, but it felt as if someone had nailed her eyelids shut. They would not budge.

"Let me watch her, Grant," came a voice she recognized as Clara's. Happiness warmed Eve's heart knowing that Clara was safe and there with her. She tried to smile, but her cheeks and her lips would not cooperate, and when she attempted to speak to Clara, what came out of her sounded more like a cat's pitiful cry than words.

"Nay," Grant finally answered. "Ye see, she cried out in her sleep when she thought I might leave her."

"Bah!" was Clara's response, making Eve want to laugh. "She was probably crying out for some peace and quiet. You've sat by her bed for three straight days telling her horrific battle tales—"

"She likes them," Grant protested. "She becomes verra still and quiet when I tell her of all the battles I've fought."

"And you sing her all those awful Scottish ballads," Clara muttered.

He'd sung to her? And sat by her bed? And told her stories?

Eve strained to make her lips form the smile that wanted to burst forth.

"Both God and Eve like my singing," Grant said in an overly confident tone. "There!" Suddenly, she felt strong hands under her shoulders. "She's smiling." And then she was pressed against a rock... Or was that her husband's chest?

Eve tried harder and harder to pry open her eyes. When they finally did, blinding light made her gasp. "Dear God, 'tis bright in here!"

"Eve!" Grant said on what sounded like a happy sigh. He kissed the top of her head, and his arms tightened around her ever so slightly. Then he pulled back, and she stared in shock at her husband's haggard face. He had many days' worth of beard growth, which would have been rather becoming if not for the dark circles under his eyes. She frowned as she studied him further. His normally blue eyes were so bloodshot she could hardly see the blue.

"You look like death knocked at your door," Eve blurted.

"He has nae slept," Esme said from behind Grant.

Eve blinked her eyes, which were now watering from the light, and then attempted to focus on Clara and Esme, who'd both moved to her bedside.

"We tried to get him to sleep," Esme clucked.

"This man you married is sinfully stubborn, Eve," Clara said, giving Grant an approving look that made Eve want to laugh. Her husband had obviously won Clara's approval. Eve frowned, trying to recall why she was in bed and unaware of how Grant had won over Clara.

"What's the matter, *mo bhean mhaiseach?*" he asked.

His beautiful wife. She rather liked that endearment.

"Is yer back paining ye? Yer stomach?" he asked, an odd, tight look coming over his face as he laid his large palm over her stomach in an almost protective manner.

She considered his questions for a moment, concentrated on how she felt, and then gasped. "I was shot!" Grant,

Esme, and Clara nodded. "By Uncle Frederick," Eve added, her voice catching. All three of them nodded again. She had so many questions. She started to sit up, but a wave of nausea overcame her, and she slapped a hand over her mouth, fearing she'd be sick.

"I'll get the sickness pitcher!" Esme cried out and scurried away only to come right back with a large pitcher that she shoved at Grant, who held it up to Eve.

"Retch in here, Eve," he ordered as Clara came to her other side with a wet cloth, which she laid atop Eve's head.

Eve swallowed several times, and the nausea passed. "It's better now," she said, moving to sit up again, but this time much more slowly. She glanced around at the concerned faces and offered a weak smile. "I take it I've been sick a few times?" Given how they'd been prepared for it, her assumption seemed sound. The uneasy look they all exchanged baffled her, though. "Don't look so concerned," she assured them. "Your healer gave me something for pain, yes?"

Esme nodded. "I'm the healer. And aye, I gave ye something for the pain the arrow caused ye, but 'tis bane weed that makes ye nauseated."

"Bane weed?" Eve's brow furrowed.

"I'll be the one to tell her," Grant interrupted, misery lacing his tone.

His tone and the worry in his eyes caused gooseflesh to sweep across her arms. "What is it?" she asked, fear blossoming in her.

Grant looked to Esme and Clara. "Leave us," he ordered.

"Clara is not of your clan, and you cannot go about commanding her, Grant," Eve chided, as she fully expected her stubborn friend to ignore his demand, and she did not want him angry at Clara.

To her utter shock, Clara said, "'Tis fine, Eve. I'll be just outside the door if you need me."

Well, of course, she needed Clara! They had much to discuss, and she really did want to apologize again for how horrid she'd been when they had parted at the convent, especially given how Clara had been correct about her uncle.

Oh!

"My uncle… What happened? How did we get away? We have to return," she rushed out, her words coming as fast as her thoughts did. "Linlithian is mine." She looked to Grant. "Ours. 'Tis ours. We must—"

Grant pressed a finger gently to her lips as he sat on the edge of the bed facing her. Then rested his hands on her hips. Deep in her belly, her core tightened with awareness of her husband and the desire he made her feel. "Dunnae fash yerself, Eve. I will take Linlithian for ye."

No, *they* would do it together. It was her right!

She opened her mouth to argue, then promptly closed it. It was wise to know when to pick one's battles, and now was not the best time. She felt weak, and she needed strength to persuade her husband to take her with him. Instead, she forced herself to nod. "What happened to my uncle?"

Grant took her hands in his, worry dancing in the depths of his blue eyes. "I killed him Eve. I'm sorry."

The news made her want to weep, which angered her. Her uncle had killed her father and mother and had caused her to lose many precious years with her sister, or possibly even forever. Maybe her parents had not died by his own hands, but by his order. And he'd tried to kill Grant! She knew she should not feel sad to hear of his death, yet she did. "I don't know why I'm sad," she muttered, even as hot tears began to fill her eyes and roll down her cheeks to drip off her face.

Grant brushed his fingers over both her cheeks and then gently leaned forward and kissed her. "Ye're sad, *mo bhean mhaiseach,* because despite what he did he was your family, ye loved him."

She sniffled and nodded. Trying to ignore the sadness, she said, "I doubt I look very beautiful at this moment." Her eyes already felt puffy, and if she'd been lying in bed retching, she must look a fright.

"To me," he said, sliding his strong fingers into her hair to cradle her head, "ye look beautiful."

"You have terrible eyesight, then, Husband," she grumbled.

"Nay, lass. I see ye, and ye are beautiful. Ye will make—" He stopped himself mid-sentence, his brows dipping together as he frowned. He inhaled a long, slow breath. "Ye do make me verra proud. Ye are so braw."

She had the strangest feeling that whatever he'd been about to say was not that. "Something odd is occurring here," she grumbled. "I do not care for secrets, even ones meant to protect me. So simply spit out your thoughts."

"Ye caught a terrible fever because of the arrow," he said softly.

"And?" she prodded. She could tell he was hedging, which was not in character at all given how blunt he'd been since they'd first met.

"I feared ye would die, as did Esme. She told me she could give ye something called bane weed, which would save ye from death by fever, and I had her do so." He paused, as if in thought. "As Esme told ye, that's what made ye sick to yer stomach. Ye retched for an entire day and night."

"Well, goodness," Eve said, squeezing his hand. "Were you worried I'd be vexed about that? You two saved my life. I—"

"Eve." The pain she heard in his voice made her catch her breath.

"Yes?" she whispered.

"The bane weed Esme gave ye," he started, then audibly swallowed. "It's kenned to make women nae able to have bairns."

She heard his words, but she was not comprehending what he'd said. "What do you mean it's known to do that? I can still have children, yes?" Her heart began to thunder as he simply stared at her, his lips parted, a pained expression on his face.

"Likely nae." His answer sounded as if he'd choked it out. She rather felt like someone was choking *her*. Breathing had become difficult, and she tried to suck in a deep breath, but it was more like a short gasp. Her hand fluttered to her neck, and when she laid her fingertips against her skin, the wild flutter of her heartbeat thumped against the pads of her fingers.

Likely not. His words echoed loudly in her ears. Likely she would never hold a baby of her own in her arms. Likely she would never rock a child to sleep, feed them, bathe them, watch them grow. Likely she would not be able to give Grant an heir, which he would want as laird of his clan. Yes, he had a brother, but men wanted sons.

She bit her lip as the thoughts came as fast as the tears. Would he take a mistress to bear him a child, then? Could she deny him such a thing? Would he even take her feelings into account? She had to know.

"But...you need an heir," she said, unable to outright

ask such a horrid question. Her breath caught with both hope and fear.

"Aye," he agreed.

It felt as if he'd reached into her chest and ripped out her heart. In that moment, sound rushed at her from all around—her thundering heart, his breathing, children laughing from the keep below—and she realized, with horror, that her husband had stolen her heart like a thief. How could that be? A hundred slivers of things he'd shown came to her at once. Honor. Loyalty. Bravery. Tenderness. How could it not have happened, was the better question…

Her throat tightened. He had her heart and her castle, what did she have of his? She certainly could not have his love if he was going to join with another woman. She did not care that it was the need for an heir that propelled the decision. Her father never would have done such a thing to her mother. Because her father had *loved* her mother.

Grant started to reach for her, and she pushed his hand away and turned her face from his. "I'd like to be alone," she said.

"Eve…"

Her name was a plea upon his lips, but the pain in her heart turned to anger. Anger she could stand; the pain, the loss of the chance to be a mother, was too great to bear. She had no true family, and a child would have been that for her. And her sister, if Eve could ever find Mary, but in this moment, it seemed utterly hopeless.

"Go away," she said stonily, pain trying to force itself through her anger. If she could just hold on to her anger, maybe she would not feel the pain. She did not want to feel it. She'd vowed in her darkest hour of wretchedness after her parents' deaths that she would not allow pain to consume her, but she felt consumed in pain now. It burned her from the inside out. How much loss was one person supposed to bear?

"Eve," he said, his tone uneasy in a way she'd never heard before, "we must talk about Linlithian."

The pain broke through her circle of rage, and she felt as if it would cleave her in two. *Childless. Parentless.* The words pounded in her head. She grasped frantically at the anger, yanking it up to use it as a sword. "Linlithian!" She curled her hands into fists, facing him once more. "Of course you wish to talk of Linlithian! Do not fear, Laird Fraser!" Wariness swept his face, and he removed his hands from her thigh. She fought the urge to touch him. She would not beg for him or his love—ever. "I will help you gain Linlithian even if it kills me to do so. It is all that matters now!"

To *him*, that was…

As the tears coursed down her cheeks, she realized that if someone told her Linlithian had burned to the ground, she might well cheer. "Leave me be now," she finished in a near-broken whisper. "Leave me be."

He rose without a word, without attempting to persuade her to let him stay. Her heart twisted, but she bit her lip until a metallic taste touched her tongue. She shoved the need for him as deep as she could and turned away. The moment the door closed, she buried her face in the covers and wept.

Chapter Sixteen

"How is she?" Clara and Esme asked the moment Grant had shut the bedchamber door.

"Nae good," he replied, a strangling pain in his chest making him rub it. "She's upset."

"As expected," Clara said. "Any woman would be upset to discover she likely could not have children."

Millicent appeared around the corner holding wash. "What's this?" she asked. "Yer new wife kinnae have bairns?" Her brown eyes warmed with mischief.

Grant narrowed his eyes at the woman. "Ye misheard," he said. "Now move along and finish yer chores. When ye are done, come see me in my study."

Millicent flashed a seductive smile that made his neck heat with embarrassment. He'd have to make her understand right away that nothing would be occurring between them.

"Of course, my laird," she replied before taking her leave down the passageway.

Grant waited until she was completely out of sight and then turned to his sister and Clara once more. Both women were staring at him, arms crossed over their chests.

Before he could say anything, Esme snapped, "If ye are thinking of taking up with that woman again—"

"Esme," he began, frustrated, but she ignored him.

"—I'll brain ye!" She held up her fist threateningly. "I ken ye think ye need an heir—"

"Esme," he said in warning now, his own temper flaring.

She scowled but kept going. "That woman is poison. She must be magical in the bed for ye to—"

"Cease talking *now*, Esme," Grant cut in, "or ye'll find yerself wed tomorrow."

That finally, mercifully, got his sister to quiet, but the damage was done. Clara was glaring at him.

"The lass *was* my leman once, but I have need of her for what we discussed the other night outside of my bedchamber," he explained to Clara, not wishing to expand in front of Esme. He loved his sister, but she was impetuous at best and she made dangerous decisions at worst. If she was irritated enough with him, she might just tell Eve.

Clara's eyes widened, and she nodded. Esme looked as if she wished to ask, but he leveled her with a dark look. She pressed her lips together with a snort and muttered, "Men and their secrets."

Grant took a long breath, seeking patience. "I've ordered Bryden to guard Eve."

Esme plunked her hands on her hips. "And just where are ye off to, Brother?" she snapped. Grant was pleased his sister wanted to protect Eve, so he bit down on his reprimand. "Yer wife has been ill! Dunnae ye think ye should stay by her side?"

He was the last person Eve wanted by her side right now, but he hoped that if and when he returned with her sister, it would lessen her anger at him and help assuage her grief. "I've a matter to see to now, so—"

"Is Millicent the *matter*?" his sister demanded.

He slid his teeth back and forth as his eye began to

twitch. "Esme, what I do as *yer laird* is my business, but 'tis nae as ye think."

"Ye men," she growled. "Ye think we women are but chattel!"

He put up a silencing hand. He knew his sister well. Once she had worked herself into a knot, it would take her time to undo herself, and he was hoping to depart before nightfall. "Now, keep yer opinions to yerself, especially around Eve, or I vow my threat to marry ye off will nae be a threat any longer."

Eve awoke to an empty bed for the third day in a row, and pain lanced her heart once more. Devil take Grant for making her fall in love with him. She tried to call up the anger she'd felt toward him for giving her the bane weed, but that particular anger had dissipated and understanding had taken its place. If Grant had been dying and there had been something that could save him but leave him unable to give her children, she would have given it to him, too.

Sighing, Eve carefully scooted from the bed. She was pleasantly surprised to find she felt very strong today, unlike the past three. Clara had given her soup for all three meals yesterday and had insisted it was needed for her to heal, so Eve had to finish it all. It seemed Clara had been right again…

Eve made her way to the wardrobe and took out one of the gowns Esme had lent her until new ones could be made. As Eve slipped it on, her thoughts turned to Grant once more, questions and fears battering her. The question still remained whether he had judged her life as more important than her ability to give him an heir because of her own worth or because he needed her to gain the allegiance of her father's men. As much as it may hurt, she had to know the truth. It would guide her in her own actions. It would help her determine whether to open her heart to him even more or to build a wall and protect it from him as much as she possibly could.

She also needed to speak with him about Mary. It may be hopeless to try to find her sister, but she must try, and she needed Grant's aid. Eve bit her lip, recalling how young her sister had been on that fateful night. Eve's own memories of the night were dulled. Would Mary, having been only five summers, even remember Eve?

With a sigh, she put on her slippers, stood, and ran a brush through her hair, which Esme, who had been unusually quiet the last few days, had washed for Eve. She hoped she looked presentable. She certainly did not want to look horrid when she saw Grant. The thought of him lying with another woman, even just to attain an heir, knotted her stomach and made her mouth go dry. She knew, without a doubt, that she could not tolerate such a thing. Where would it leave them if that was what he intended? The question twisted Eve's insides even more, but she shoved it away for now. It would not do to fret over that which she did not yet even know.

She departed their chamber and made her way through the castle looking for Grant. She checked the great hall, and found it empty except for a serving wench. The woman was picking trenchers up off the table, so Eve strolled up to her and cleared her throat to get her attention. The young woman turned to her, and her brown eyes went wide. "My lady," she said, dropping into a curtsy. "I'm pleased to see ye up and about. Can I get ye something to eat?"

Eve shook her head. "No, thank you. Have you seen my

husband?"

"Oh, the laird is gone. I could nae say where, though, or for how long, but I would imagine Ross or Kade would ken."

"Thank you," Eve murmured, wondering irritably where Grant had gone. She headed to the courtyard and found Ross and Kade leading a training session. Thomas stood nearby, watching.

"Eve!" the lad cried out and rushed over to her. He gave her a quick hug. "Are ye better?"

"I'm much improved," she said with a smile. "Can you tell me where Grant has gone?"

Thomas shrugged. "I dunnae. He did nae say to me, mayhap Ross or Kade ken."

"So I've been told already," she muttered, finding it odd that Grant simply left her and was apparently quiet about where he was going. She looked toward Ross and Kade, who were sparring some distance away. "Where is Grant?" she asked, raising her voice.

Both men ceased their fight. Kade opened his mouth as if to answer, but Ross gave a quick shake of his head. Eve had the sinking feeling she was not supposed to see it. "Where has he gone?" she demanded now.

"He had business with another clan," Ross answered. "Hopefully he will return tonight."

Her heart clenched. He had not even told her he was leaving. But then, she *had* been angry at him when they last had seen each other.

"Ye should nae be out of bed," Ross added. "Grant would nae like it."

She frowned at him. "Well, since Grant is not here, I suppose it does not matter what he'd like," she snapped. Without another word, she turned on her heel and marched off to the kitchens to find Clara, who had mentioned teaching the lasses in the kitchen how to cook better.

When she entered the kitchens and found Clara instructing the soup girls, Eve couldn't help but laugh. Clara was as bossy in the kitchens as she was in everyday life, but Eve loved her for it.

Clara turned directly toward her. "You should not be out of bed!"

Eve was beginning to feel as if there was a conspiracy to keep her in her bedchamber. She pulled Clara to the side, away from prying ears. "Do you know where Grant went?"

"To the Calder clan's holding," Clara immediately replied. "I believe he had business there." Her gaze shifted away from Eve.

Suspicion furrowed her brow. "That is exactly what Ross said. What sort of business?"

Clara slowly brought her gaze back to Eve's. She nibbled on her lip for a moment and then said, "I believe he needed to speak with the Calder laird on a matter of importance."

When Eve opened her mouth to ask exactly what, Clara exclaimed, "Oh dear me! The soup is boiling over! Take yourself back to the bedchamber, Eve. I'll be there shortly to bring you some." And then she turned her back on Eve before Eve could say more.

She couldn't put her finger on exactly what was going on, but something was afoot. She made her way out of the kitchen and, instead of going to her bedchamber, decided to look for Esme. But no one seemed to know where she was, either.

After a frustrating morning, Eve took the path down to beach and found Esme at the edge of the water practicing with her sword. Eve cleared her throat as she approached

Grant's sister.

Esme startled anyway. "Ye should nae be—"

"No!" Eve snapped. "I should not be abed. Why is everyone trying to force me to stay there? And why did your brother go to the Calder holding?"

"The Calder holding!" Esme gasped, lowering her sword point to the ground. "I kenned it! I did nae want to ken it, but I did."

"You knew what?" Eve asked, alarm bells ringing in her head.

"I—" An anguished look swept across Esme's face. "I really should nae say, but ye have a right to ken it. But first, Eve, I vow he cares for ye. 'Tis nae all his fault. Father raised my brothers to put duty before all else, before their hearts especially, and when Grant *did* put his wishes before his duty, trouble resulted—first for Grant and then our mother. So ye see—"

"Esme," Eve said sharply, sensing by the woman's increasing tone that she was just getting started, "I love your brother," she blurted. Esme's mouth formed an O, and Eve nodded at her obvious shock. "I was surprised to realize it, as well. So, you see, I must speak with him. I must learn if he saved me out of love, or for how I can aid him with the Decres warriors."

"Oh, Eve," Esme said, and Eve's heart sank to her slippers. Esme rushed to her, clasped her arms, then hugged her. "I believe he loves ye and dunnae even ken it."

Eve's eyes widened, a bit of her fear subsiding until Esme shook her head.

"I dunnae believe for a breath that he saved ye because of Linlithian." Esme paused then, nibbling on her lip. "He threatened me—aye, he did—but I dunnae care, I'll run away if he tries to force me to wed." She gave Eve an apologetic look, and on a large gulp of breath, she said, "Clan Calder is his former leman Millicent's clan."

Eve flinched as if Esme had hit her.

"I am scairt he's putting duty before his heart," Esme continued, every word like a fresh lashing. "I am scairt he went to speak with the Calder laird, as would be custom if he intended to put a bairn in Millicent's belly."

Eve pressed a hand to her mouth, feeling violently ill. She could not stay here. She did not know where she would go, but she could not stay here.

Esme sucked in her lower lip, then popped it out. "Eve, I am sorry. I should nae have told ye."

Eve could not show Esme the depth of her despair. And Clara… Eve was positive that Clara knew what Grant was about and kept the secret from her. Eve fought back the tears that wanted to fall. She could forgive Clara for the secret she'd harbored about her uncle, but not for this. She had to flee. She didn't care that she had nowhere to go; she simply wanted to get away. She forced a calm that she did not feel. Esme may well try to stop her if she knew Eve was going to leave. "I think I'll take a walk to think upon all of this."

"Let me accompany ye," Esme said.

"No," Eve replied. "I need to be alone."

Esme shoved her sword at Eve. "Take Fate. 'Tis nae ever good to walk unarmed, and I have my daggers with me. I can wield daggers much better than the sword."

Eve grasped it at the hilt, but Esme did not release it at first. "Eve, I've been thinking upon the bane weed, and I asked our previous healer if she had ever given it to a woman who had later had children. Though no one *she* gave it to ever conceived, she thought she remembered hearing of a woman who had at some point. I ken it's nae much hope, but…"

Eve reached out and squeezed Esme's hand. "Thank you," she said, meaning it. But Esme's words did not offer her hope. Any hope for Eve and Grant had been completely destroyed the moment Esme had told her of Millicent.

Eve took her leave and made her way up the steep, rocky mountain to the bridge where she had first met Grant. Then she crossed the bridge toward the thick woods that led to the edge of the Fraser property. She could just walk away, but she had nowhere to go. Even if she somehow made it to Linlithian, Grant was legally the rightful laird now, as long as King Edward cooperated. All she was, was his barren wife.

Overheated and plagued by a pounding head, Eve sat on a stump, willing herself not to cry. What did she have left? Before she could form an answer, something rustled behind her, and when she whirled around, Bryden was there.

"God's teeth," she said, looking up at the man. "You scared me."

Bryden raised his hand, shielding his eyes from the sun. In the other hand, he held his sword.

"Are you expecting trouble?" Eve asked.

"I'm always prepared when close to the border between our land and the MacDougalls'," he replied. "What are ye doing so far out here?"

Something in his manner was odd to her. He was shifting a great deal, and he kept glancing around, as if he was expecting someone else. Eve curled her fingers tightly around the handle of Esme's sword, her heart racing. Slowly, she rose from the stump to her feet. He had not answered her question, but she did not truly care. "Were you following me?" she asked, her heart now thudding in her ears.

Bryden flashed an odd grin. "Aye. Grant himself commanded it, which was perfect."

"What?" she asked, searching anxiously for the meaning behind his words.

"What he means," came a voice from behind her, "is that the Frasers will nae ever question, will nae ever even consider, that he might have been the one to hand ye over to us, Eve."

She swung toward the voice, and her heart stuttered at the sight of Aros MacDougall. She clenched her teeth. "There is no point in taking me, Aros. I'm wed to Grant."

"There's every point," he replied. "Yer husband is riding into a trap at this verra moment, and soon, ye'll nae be wed anymore." She choked back a cry. "Soon, he'll be on the road to return to Dithorn and his guard will lower, and my father and men will be waiting there in the woods." Her stomach turned as she began to tremble. "They will cut him down, then take his head and put it on a spike."

The absolute lack of emotion in his voice chilled her. Behind her, she could feel Bryden move closer, and she tensed, wondering if she could possibly kill them both. She had to keep their attention. "Do you truly hate him that much, or is it that you want Linlithian that bad?"

There was a long, brittle silence. "It's more complicated than that, Eve," Aros said.

She swung toward Bryden, who was directly behind her. She'd have to take a step back to even strike at him. "And you! Grant is your laird! Your cousin!"

"*I* should be laird," Bryden snarled. Eve took a step back and hoped it appeared as if it was out of fright. "My father was the eldest son, but Grant's father stole the lairdship when my father died, and it went to Simon and then Grant.

It's mine. I'm a better ruler!"

Eve took another step away, putting enough distance between herself and Bryden to injure him. She could cut him down at the legs, she was certain of it, and Aros would not harm her too badly if she could not disarm him. He needed her.

"Enough talk," Aros said, slashing a hand in the air.

"Give me the sword, Eve," Bryden demanded.

"You want the sword?" As he nodded, she whipped it hip height while drawing it toward him and sliced it straight across his legs. With a scream, he fell at her feet, reaching toward his bleeding shins. "There you go," she snapped and turned to fight Aros.

As Grant rode home toward Dithorn, accompanied only by Millicent, he thought on Eve's sister, Mary, whom he'd found. She was a timid creature, very unlike his wife. He could understand it somewhat. She'd not had the benefit of being with Clara, someone who loved her, as Eve had, and she had been even younger than Eve when separated from her family, whom she did not even remember now. Grant sighed at that, and sifted through the rest of what he'd discovered.

John had brought her to the Calder clan as planned, but he'd died shortly after from the wounds he'd sustained fighting the MacDougalls. Mary had been taken in by a family, but they had been less than kind. Now she was wed to a man she clearly cared for, and she had no wish to recall a past that was painful. He'd tried to persuade her to at least see Eve, but he was not certain it had done any good. He'd seen the fear in her eyes. She was hiding from memories she did not currently have. Maybe seeing Eve would bring them to the surface, and she feared that, yet Grant could not help but think recalling her past might help her finally overcome it and the fear it brought her. Yet, if she was going to come to that understanding, it would likely have to be on her own accord.

He swiped a hand over his face. Mary had said she would think upon seeing Eve again, but it would be on her terms if she ever did so. He prayed she did. He had to tell Eve that Mary was alive, and it twisted his gut to think how it was going to hurt Eve that Mary did not want to see her.

"I need to relieve myself," Millicent said, interrupting his thoughts.

Grant eyed her warily from his horse. Since leaving Dithorn a sennight ago, Millicent had slipped into his bed no less than twice, and once she'd slid her gown down to show her bare breasts before he'd realized what was occurring. He'd spoken to her sternly and then threatened to leave her at the Caldor keep. She'd behaved since then, but he'd not take chances. "Need I remind ye—"

"Ye need nae," she said, pursing her lips. "Ye are loyal to yer barren wife." Millicent smirked as she looked at him. "We shall see how long that loyalty lasts when ye dunnae have an heir." She pulled up on her reins and dismounted, forcing him to do the same. They were close to Fraser land but not quite there yet, and he was keenly aware that MacDougalls could be lurking about.

"Go there, behind those bushes." He waved to the thick shrubs. That way, she'd be out of his sight but not so far away that he would not hear her scream for help.

"We could both go," she said in a suggestive voice.

"Millicent," he said, his tone a warning.

"Fine." She shrugged. "I dunnae ken why ye dunnae

take my offer. Ye may love yer new English bride, but ye still need an heir." She marched away, grumbling loudly.

He opened his mouth to deny what Millicent had said and then snapped it shut, stunned by the certainty that Eve had ensnared him body and soul. He could no longer ignore or deny it. Every second away from her had been torture. At night, he'd spent countless hours thinking of her lush body, her eyes flashing in defiance, her chin jutting out when she wished to show a brave face, the subtle pitch of her voice when she attempted—and failed—to lie well. She had defied him, charmed him, scared him witless, astounded him, enraged him, and bewitched him.

The guilt over his mother's death was still there, but in this moment, as he was going back to his wife with nothing to offer her but himself, he knew that he would give her all of him. All he wanted to do now was return home and tell Eve how he felt, in the hope it would be enough.

"Grant!" Millicent screamed, yanking him from his reverie.

He instinctively raised his sword, and MacDougall and two other men raced from the woods where Millicent had been, brandishing their swords.

MacDougall stopped and motioned to his men. "Kill him!"

The first warrior charged him, and Grant cut him down easily with a swipe across his neck. Then the other two attacked simultaneously. They came toward him from the left and the right, and MacDougall shouted, "I'll make certain Lady Eve sees yer head on a spike before I have Aros wed and bed her."

Rage pumped out of his heart, rushing through his veins to propel him into action. He swung out to his left and plunged his sword into the MacDougall warrior there, while releasing his dagger to the right, which landed in the forehead of the third MacDougall warrior. They fell to the ground one after the other, and then he turned to meet Laird MacDougall himself, who was coming at him. Grant had no fear as he raised his sword to meet MacDougall's. He could not lose; Eve needed him.

Their swords clanked, and the vibrations of metal upon metal sank into his bones. MacDougall might be older than Grant was, but the man was powerful and a well-seasoned warrior. He cut Grant across his forearm. Grant, in turn, made contact, slicing open his enemy's chest, making the man drop his sword with a gasp. Fury burned Grant's throat as an image of Simon filled his mind, and he brought his sword up to end MacDougall's life exactly as the man had ended Simon's. When the body followed the head to the ground, Grant started to slump with relief, but another scream, this one distinctly Eve's, filled the silence.

He started to turn toward Eve and then recalled Millicent. Cursing, he ran to where she'd gone to relieve herself and found her hovering, crying. "Get to the castle," he ordered harshly, "and tell the watchmen to sound the war bell." With that, he raced toward Eve's voice.

Eve glanced down at the rocks and the swirling sea behind her and then back at Aros. He motioned to her with his free hand. "Come to me, Eve. Ye dunnae wish to jump."

No, she certainly did not. It would be the death of her! But now that she'd been disarmed, she needed to think of something. She backed up again, the ground beneath her heel disappearing, and she screamed.

Aros lunged toward her, and in that instant, she tried to

jump to the side, but the ground they both stood upon suddenly gave way. Another scream ripped from her throat as she grabbed a root sticking up from the ground and her body slammed into rock, then dangled there. She glanced over her shoulder, then squeezed her eyes shut on the horrid picture of Aros hitting the rocks below. Her hand began to burn and slip, and she screamed again. "Help! Help!"

Please, God. Help has to be coming...

The root loosened a bit, causing her to release a bloodcurdling bellow, and she squeezed her eyes shut, sure she was about to die. Her thoughts went instantly to Grant.

"Eve!"

Afraid she had conjured his voice out of desperation, she slowly opened her eyes. But there he was, on his belly and leaning over the edge, fear and determination in his blue eyes and a half smile on his lips.

"Grant," she breathed.

His right hand grasped her wrist, and with a grunt, he pulled her up the side of the cliff, and when her head reached the ledge, he slid his left hand to her waist and hauled her all the way over with a grunt. She landed on him, and he immediately cupped her face. "Eve." Raw emotions filled his voice. "God, Eve." He kissed her hard on the mouth once, twice, then pulled away. "I beg of ye," he croaked, a half smile on his lips, "quit courting trouble."

Before she could respond, his men began to race toward them. At the front of the pack were Ross and Kade, and they had Bryden hanging between them by either arm. When he saw her, his eyes widened. As Grant pulled her to her feet, Bryden shouted, "Eve tried to kill me so she could flee with Aros!"

Eve gasped and turned to Grant. The look of rage that

came to his face made her try to tug her hand free of his hold, but he gripped her tighter and brought her with him as he strode toward Bryden. He stopped when they were face-to-face. "Eve would nae ever betray me, Cousin," Grant said in a chilling tone. "Tell me yer true sins now, or I'll leave ye in the thief's hole until ye're nae but dust."

Bryden began to blubber, admitting his plot to take the lairdship from Grant. Eve stood there, marveling at her husband's icy control and how he'd shown so much faith in her. She decided then and there that she had failed this man, who had shown her nothing but honor and loyalty since the day they'd met. She had believed the worst when she should have first sought to hear it from him.

As he started to call orders to his men, telling them to mount their horses and sweep the castle, he released her. "Eve, go to the keep with Kade. I need to see to Bryden."

His wary look told her he expected her to argue, so she took great pleasure in smiling and saying, "As you wish, Husband."

Chapter Seventeen

*E*ve awoke to a brush of lips upon hers. When she opened her eyes, Grant hovered over her, moonlight streaming in from the window and across his face and bare chest. Desire sprang up in her belly and lower in her core, but she pressed a halting hand to his shoulder, even as she felt the evidence of his desire for her. They must talk, sort through things, and if she allowed him to kiss her again, she feared desire would sweep her away.

"How did the scouting go?" she asked.

"We found no more MacDougalls on our land."

The impatience in his voice and the way he moved his hips against her made her smile, and coiled her insides tight. "And Bryden?" she asked breathlessly as Grant pressed his hips more solidly against her.

"In the thief's hole. Tomorrow he will be taken across the sea and left at Dragoon."

"What is Dragoon?"

Grant leaned forward and kissed her neck, making her shiver. "Dragoon is where traitors are taken. 'Tis deep in the heart of the Dark Woods. If he makes it out alive, he may live free, but he will nae ever be a Fraser again."

She frowned, not sure she wanted him to make it out alive but not wanting to wish death upon anyone else, either. "How many have made it out alive?"

Grant kissed her forehead, her eyes, and her nose before answering. "None that I ken."

When he went to kiss her mouth again, she turned her head. "Tell me of Millicent," she said.

He released a long, weary breath and rolled off her to lie beside her. She turned to look at him, studying his profile, which revealed nothing but the fact that her husband's face was very strong and very handsome. "Who told ye of Millicent?" he finally asked.

Her heart squeezed at his words, which seemed to indicate the worst. "Your sister. I forced it out of her," she added in an effort to protect Esme.

She thought he'd be mad, but he surprised her by laughing. "It pleases me how ye and Esme try to protect each other. I want to protect ye, as well."

"I know," she said. "And *that* pleases me, but not if it means I am living a lie."

His hand found hers, and he twined their fingers together. She took comfort knowing he wanted to touch her as she wanted to touch him. "I took Millicent to the Calder holding to ensure they gave me admittance since we are nae allies. Millicent was a Calder before she was a Fraser."

"And she was once your leman." Eve did not bother to mince words.

A derisive sound came deep from her husband's throat. "My sister should nae have told ye that. I can only imagine the worry it has caused ye."

"I doubt you can," she replied, attempting to make light of it.

He moved atop of her, his powerful leg pushing between her thighs and his arms caging her in. Tension radiated from him. "Ye have my heart, Eve," he whispered, shocking her. "And because ye have that, ye'll be the only woman to ever have my body, even if that means I dunnae have an heir."

She did not even realize she had started crying until his fingers were upon her face, gently brushing away her tears. "Ye nae being able to give me a bairn dunnae make me love ye less, but more."

"You love me?" she whispered, her heart feeling as if it would burst.

"Aye, lass. Completely. Gloriously. Hopelessly. Forever and always from this breath until my last."

"I love you too with all my heart," she said.

"I dunnae ken why God has blessed me so, but I'll nae question it," he replied and brushed his lips across hers ever so lightly, and when he pulled back, he said, "I ken the strength ye must draw on to endure the sorrow of nae being able to have bairns, and it makes me love ye even more." More warm tears leaked out of her eyes and down her cheeks. "Since I'm the reason ye kinnae have a bairn," he said, his voice hitching with obvious agony, "I'd hoped to find yer sister and reunite ye with her so that maybe ye would hate me less."

His admission stole her ability to speak for a moment, and then she rose to kiss him. "I could never hate you. I could definitely be vexed with you." They both laughed at that. "But I love you so very much."

He nuzzled his face in her neck and then pressed his mouth to her ear. "Eve, I will try my best to show my love always, but this is new for me, and if I stumble—"

"I'll help you up," she promised, pressing her lips to his neck.

His lips were on her again, but this time the kiss was one of two people truly finding each other underneath the armor they had worn for the world.

When they broke the kiss, Grant said, "I found yer sister." Shock slammed into her while he continued. "I dunnae ken if she'll see ye. She was taken in by a cold family, but she's wed now to a man she seems to love. She's timid, though, and fearful, and she does not truly recall ye and is fearful to try to do so, but she said she will think upon seeing ye."

Eve nodded, her throat too tight with emotion to speak. Finally, she swallowed. "She is the last of my old family. I want her in my life. But if she does not wish it—"

"Ye have a new family to love ye," Grant finished. "Let me love ye now, Wife."

Her answer was to kiss his chest, trailing up to his neck and his lips. Then he took control. His lips captured hers, persuading her to open her mouth for him, and when she did, the pleasure she took from the way he swirled his tongue with hers surely had to be sinful, but not nearly as sinful as the way she cried out when he took her nipple with tantalizing possessiveness. His tongue caressed the sensitive bud while his hands slid down her belly, tracing a sensuous path to ecstasy.

His fingers expertly found the spot hidden behind her curls, the one that made her moan and arch her back toward him, pressing her hips up to get more of his touch. His fingers branded her at her core, and she throbbed with need. Passion pounded the blood through her heart, chest, and head, and as her pulse exploded, so did his touch, becoming frenzied, circling and massaging without giving quarter, until her entire body tightened. When she thought she could not take another moment, she screamed out for him, needing to feel him inside her. He took her then with a savage intensity, driving into her and claiming her as his.

Together, they found a tempo that bound them, and as

they moved, she caressed the broad plane of his back, his strong shoulders, and then down to his buttocks, feeling the muscles flex with each delicious slide into her. Heat rippled from him to her, and she could sense his need building to match hers. She moaned with pleasure when he touched somewhere deep inside her, and then her world seemed to explode as her body did the same. Her last coherent memory was his cry of release and the warmth of Grant flooding into her.

The length of Eve was pressed heavily against Grant, warm, soft, and womanly. She was the most perfect creature he'd ever known, even while snoring—and aye, but she could snore. A deep feeling of peace overcame him as he ran his fingers lightly over his wife's back. She sighed happily in her sleep. The turbulence of the passion they had shared amazed him, and he closed his eyes in desperate need of sleep. But just as he did, it seemed only a moment later that a knock came at their door.

"Grant!" Ross called.

He scooted out from under Eve, donned his plaid, opened the door, slipped out, and said, "This better be of utmost importance."

Ross nodded. "Eve's sister has come to see her, and she's brought nearly four hundred Calder warriors to aid us in taking Linlithian."

"Well, even though it's the middle of the night, I'll wake my wife for that," he said with a smile.

"'Tis morning, Grant."

Grant frowned and glanced toward the window. He stared in shock; Ross had spoken the truth. Chuckling,

Grant slapped his friend on the back. "Ye must find a wife, Ross. They are verra good for one's sleep. We'll be down directly."

Ross nodded, and Grant made his way back to Eve and gently shook her awake. She grumbled a bit but finally opened one eye. "I had the most amazing dream," she said with a yawn.

"What did ye dream of?" he asked, unable to resist tucking her hair behind her ear.

She pressed his hand to her face and smiled up at him. "I dreamed that my sister came to see me, and—"

"Eve, she's downstairs," he said, shock rippling through him. Eve's eyes widened, then tears filled them. "What's this?" he asked, kneeling in front of her. "Why are ye sad?"

"No," she said excitedly, sitting up. "I'm not sad. I'm happy. Do you know what else I just dreamed?"

"Nay, and I dunnae care at this moment," he teased, cupping her enticing breasts.

She grabbed his hand and moved it to her belly, her lavender gaze locking with his. "I dreamed we had a son with gray eyes."

Grant curled his fingers softly, protectively over his wife's stomach. "Well, ye dreamed of wedding for love, and ye did." He winked at her. "And ye dreamed yer sister was here, and she is. So I'd say we've a verra good chance of having a gray-eyed son from a lavender-eyed beauty. Ye ken what that means, though?"

"I must not court trouble?" she asked with a laugh.

"Exactly, Wife, exactly."

Epilogue

"Eve, I distinctly recall that your husband's last words to you before he left to attend King Robert, were that you 'should not court trouble,'" Mary chided.

"Teaching the art of swordsmanship as Grant has taught it to me is not courting trouble," Eve replied with a grin before ducking Esme's oncoming swing with Fate.

Eve straightened with a grunt and then a gasp when her unborn baby kicked, making his presence known. She patted her stomach and cooed to her son, even as she whipped up her sword to meet another of Esme's attempts to best her and knocked Fate out of her hands. Esme frowned as the Decres warriors who were gathered in the courtyard of Linlithian cheered.

Eve took a bow, nearly pitching forward because of her rather large stomach, but Esme and Mary were there on either side of her, as they had been for her entire pregnancy. Clara clucked her tongue, shook her head, and strolled toward Eve. "I agree with Mary," Clara said. "Grant would most definitely consider this courting trouble. 'Tis too much exertion for the state you are in."

"I much preferred it when you were always on my side," Eve said, arching her eyebrows. She did not bother to ask where Clara had been. She knew she would not get an answer, but she also knew that whatever Clara was doing had something to do with a promise she had made long ago, one that had her aiding the Scottish cause.

Clara chuckled. "I'm certain you did. You *did* promise him you'd not have the baby before he returned." Eve smiled at her old friend, glad that Clara had arrived at Linlithian yesterday after such a long absence.

"And I'll not," she replied, feeling Grant's sudden presence as she always did the moment he was near. She swept her gaze around and found him—tall, strong, and confident—striding toward her looking battle-worn but happy. As he drew closer, the air changed, her heartbeat quickened, and her body tingled. They'd both had high walls around them before they'd met, and she supposed when they'd torn them down, a hard fall had been inevitable. They'd shattered, she had realized one night, into a million pieces, and the two of them had become one.

The Decres warriors and the Fraser warriors parted to let him through, and he stopped in front of her, smiling down at her before brushing his lips to her and placing his large hand protectively over her belly. "How is my son?"

"Almost ready to appear I think," she told him as the child kicked once more.

He nodded, as if he'd known, and she knew part of him had. His connection to her was just as strong as hers to him. He scooped his arms under her legs and lifted her off her feet. Cheers erupted around them as he turned to carry her to their bedchamber.

"Did Bruce get to safety?" she asked, placing her hand on his chest.

"I hope so," Grant replied.

She frowned. "You hope so?"

"I saw him across the water safely, but then I felt yer need for me here." Grant touched her hand to his heart. "So

I left Ross to finish seeing to the king's escape."

"You left Ross to finish the duty?" she repeated, astonished.

"Aye, Eve. Ye are my first duty always. And the most pleasant, I might add." With that, his lips parted hers in a soul-reaching kiss that whispered a pledge of love, family, and faith in all the tomorrows to come.

If you love Scottish romance, I think you might like my HIGHLANDER VOWS: ENTANGLED HEARTS series. Book 1 in the series is WHEN A LAIRD LOVES A LADY, and you can purchase it, and start reading it with chapter one below.

Chapter One

England, 1357

Faking her death would be simple. It was escaping her home that would be difficult. Marion de Lacy stared hard into the slowly darkening sky, thinking about the plan she intended to put into action tomorrow—if all went well—but growing uneasiness tightened her belly. From where she stood in the bailey, she counted the guards up in the tower. It was not her imagination: Father had tripled the knights keeping guard at all times, as if he was expecting trouble.

Taking a deep breath of the damp air, she pulled her mother's cloak tighter around her to ward off the twilight chill. A lump lodged in her throat as the wool scratched her neck. In the many years since her mother had been gone, Marion had both hated and loved this cloak for the death and life it represented. Her mother's freesia scent had long since faded from the garment, yet simply calling up a memory of her mother wearing it gave Marion comfort.

She rubbed her fingers against the rough material. When she fled, she couldn't chance taking anything with her but the clothes on her body and this cloak. Her death had to appear accidental, and the cloak that everyone knew she prized would ensure her freedom. Finding it tangled in the branches at the edge of the sea cliff ought to be just the thing to convince her father and William Froste that she'd drowned. After all, neither man thought she could swim. They didn't truly care about her anyway. Her marriage to the blackhearted knight was only about what her hand could give the two men. Her father, Baron de Lacy, wanted more power, and Froste wanted her family's prized land. A match made in Heaven, if only the match didn't involve her...but it did.

Father would set the hounds of Hell themselves to track her down if he had the slightest suspicion that she was still alive. She was an inestimable possession to be given to secure Froste's unwavering allegiance and, therefore, that of the renowned ferocious knights who served him. Whatever small sliver of hope she had that her father would grant her mercy and not marry her to Froste had been destroyed by the lashing she'd received when she'd pleaded for him to do so.

The moon crested above the watchtower, reminding her why she was out here so close to mealtime: to meet Angus. The Scotsman may have been her father's stable master, but he was *her* ally, and when he'd proposed she flee England for Scotland, she'd readily consented.

Marion looked to the west, the direction from which Angus would return from Newcastle. He should be back any minute now from meeting his cousin and clansman Neil, who was to escort her to Scotland. She prayed all was set and that Angus's kin was ready to depart. With her wedding to Froste to take place in six days, she wanted to be far away before there was even the slightest chance he'd be making his way here. And since he was set to arrive the night before the wedding, leaving tomorrow promised she'd not encounter him.

A sense of urgency enveloped her, and Marion forced herself to stroll across the bailey toward the gatehouse that led to the tunnel preceding the drawbridge. She couldn't risk raising suspicion from the tower guards. At the gatehouse, she nodded to Albert, one of the knights who operated the drawbridge mechanism. He was young and rarely questioned her excursions to pick flowers or find herbs.

"Off to get some medicine?" he inquired.

"Yes," she lied with a smile and a little pang of guilt. But this was survival, she reminded herself as she entered the tunnel. When she exited the heavy wooden door that led to freedom, she wasn't surprised to find Peter and Andrew not yet up in the twin towers that flanked the entrance to the drawbridge. It was, after all, time for the changing of the guard.

They smiled at her as they put on their helmets and demi-gauntlets. They were an imposing presence to any who crossed the drawbridge and dared to approach the castle gate. Both men were tall and looked particularly daunting in their full armor, which Father insisted upon at all times. The men were certainly a fortress in their own right.

She nodded to them. "I'll not be long. I want to gather some more flowers for the supper table." Her voice didn't even wobble with the lie.

Peter grinned at her, his kind brown eyes crinkling at

the edges. "Will you pick me one of those pale winter flowers for my wife again, Marion?"

She returned his smile. "It took away her anger as I said it would, didn't it?"

"It did," he replied. "You always know just how to help with her."

"I'll get a pink one if I can find it. The colors are becoming scarcer as the weather cools."

Andrew, the younger of the two knights, smiled, displaying a set of straight teeth. He held up his covered arm. "My cut is almost healed."

Marion nodded. "I told you! Now maybe you'll listen to me sooner next time you're wounded in training."

He gave a soft laugh. "I will. Should I put more of your paste on tonight?"

"Yes, keep using it. I'll have to gather some more yarrow, if I can find any, and mix up another batch of the medicine for you." And she'd have to do it before she escaped. "I better get going if I'm going to find those things." She knew she should not have agreed to search for the flowers and offered to find the yarrow when she still had to speak to Angus and return to the castle in time for supper, but both men had been kind to her when many had not. It was her way of thanking them.

After Peter lowered the bridge and opened the door, she departed the castle grounds, considering her plan once more. Had she forgotten anything? She didn't think so. She was simply going to walk straight out of her father's castle and never come back. Tomorrow, she'd announce she was going out to collect more winter blooms, and then, instead, she would go down to the edge of the cliff overlooking the sea. She would slip off her cloak and leave it for a search party to find. Her breath caught deep in her chest at the simple yet dangerous plot. The last detail to see to was Angus.

She stared down the long dirt path that led to the sea and stilled, listening for hoofbeats. A slight vibration of the ground tingled her feet, and her heart sped in hopeful anticipation that it was Angus coming down the dirt road on his horse. When the crafty stable master appeared with a grin spread across his face, the worry that was squeezing her heart loosened. For the first time since he had ridden out that morning, she took a proper breath. He stopped his stallion alongside her and dismounted.

She tilted her head back to look up at him as he towered over her. An errant thought struck. "Angus, are all Scots as tall as you?"

"Nay, but ye ken Scots are bigger than all the wee Englishmen." Suppressed laughter filled his deep voice. "So even the ones nae as tall as me are giants compared te the scrawny men here."

"You're teasing me," she replied, even as she arched her eyebrows in uncertainty.

"A wee bit," he agreed and tousled her hair. The laughter vanished from his eyes as he rubbed a hand over his square jaw and then stared down his bumpy nose at her, fixing what he called his "lecturing look" on her. "We've nae much time. Neil is in Newcastle just as he's supposed te be, but there's been a slight change."

She frowned. "For the last month, every time I wanted to simply make haste and flee, you refused my suggestion, and now you say there's a slight change?"

His ruddy complexion darkened. She'd pricked that MacLeod temper her mother had always said Angus's clan was known for throughout the Isle of Skye, where they lived in the farthest reaches of Scotland. Marion could remember her mother chuckling and teasing Angus about how no one knew the MacLeod temperament better than their neighboring clan, the MacDonalds of Sleat, to which her mother had been born. The two clans had a history of feuding.

Angus cleared his throat and recaptured Marion's attention. Without warning, his hand closed over her shoulder, and he squeezed gently. "I'm sorry te say it so plain, but ye must die at once."

Her eyes widened as dread settled in the pit of her stomach. "What? Why?" The sudden fear she felt was unreasonable. She knew he didn't mean she was really going to die, but her palms were sweating and her lungs had tightened all the same. She sucked in air and wiped her damp hands down the length of her linen skirts. Suddenly, the idea of going to a foreign land and living with her mother's clan, people she'd never met, made her apprehensive.

She didn't even know if the MacDonalds—her uncle, in particular, who was now the laird—would accept her or not. She was half-English, after all, and Angus had told her that when a Scot considered her English bloodline and the fact that she'd been raised there, they would most likely brand her fully English, which was not a good thing in a Scottish mind. And if her uncle was anything like her grandfather had been, the man was not going to be very reasonable. But she didn't have any other family to turn to who would dare defy her father, and Angus hadn't offered for her to go to his clan, so she'd not asked. He likely didn't want to bring trouble to his clan's doorstep, and she didn't blame him.

Panic bubbled inside her. She needed more time, even if it was only the day she'd thought she had, to gather her courage.

"Why must I flee tonight? I was to teach Eustice how to dress a wound. She might serve as a maid, but then she will be able to help the knights when I'm gone. And her little brother, Bernard, needs a few more lessons before he's mastered writing his name and reading. And Eustice's youngest sister has begged me to speak to Father about allowing her to visit her mother next week."

"Ye kinnae watch out for everyone here anymore, Marion."

She placed her hand over his on her shoulder. "Neither can you."

Their gazes locked in understanding and disagreement.

He slipped his hand from her shoulder, and then crossed his arms over his chest in a gesture that screamed stubborn, unyielding protector. "If I leave at the same time ye feign yer death," he said, changing the subject, "it could stir yer father's suspicion and make him ask questions when none need te be asked. I'll be going home te Scotland soon after ye." Angus reached into a satchel attached to his horse and pulled out a dagger, which he slipped to her. "I had this made for ye."

Marion took the weapon and turned it over, her heart pounding. "It's beautiful." She held it by its black handle while withdrawing it from the sheath and examining it. "It's much sharper than the one I have."

"Aye," he said grimly. "It is. Dunnae forget that just because I taught ye te wield a dagger does nae mean ye can defend yerself from *all* harm. Listen te my cousin and do as he says. Follow his lead."

She gave a tight nod. "I will. But why must I leave now and not tomorrow?"

Concern filled Angus's eyes. "Because I ran into Froste's

brother in town and he told me that Froste sent word that he would be arriving in two days."

Marion gasped. "That's earlier than expected."

"Aye," Angus said and took her arm with gentle authority. "So ye must go now. I'd rather be trying te trick only yer father than yer father, Froste, and his savage knights. I want ye long gone and yer death accepted when Froste arrives."

She shivered as her mind began to race with all that could go wrong.

"I see the worry darkening yer green eyes," Angus said, interrupting her thoughts. He whipped off his hat and his hair, still shockingly red in spite of his years, fell down around his shoulders. He only ever wore it that way when he was riding. He said the wind in his hair reminded him of riding his own horse when he was in Scotland. "I was going to talk to ye tonight, but now that I kinnae…" He shifted from foot to foot, as if uncomfortable. "I want te offer ye something. I'd have proposed it sooner, but I did nae want ye te feel ye had te take my offer so as nae te hurt me, but I kinnae hold my tongue, even so."

She furrowed her brow. "What is it?"

"I'd be proud if ye wanted te stay with the MacLeod clan instead of going te the MacDonalds. Then ye'd nae have te leave everyone ye ken behind. Ye'd have me."

A surge of relief filled her. She threw her arms around Angus, and he returned her hug quick and hard before setting her away. Her eyes misted at once. "I had hoped you would ask me," she admitted.

For a moment, he looked astonished, but then he spoke. "Yer mother risked her life te come into MacLeod territory at a time when we were fighting terrible with the MacDonalds, as ye well ken."

Marion nodded. She knew the story of how Angus had ended up here. He'd told her many times. Her mother had been somewhat of a renowned healer from a young age, and when Angus's wife had a hard birthing, her mother had gone to help. The knowledge that his wife and child had died anyway still made Marion want to cry.

"I pledged my life te keep yer mother safe for the kindness she'd done me, which brought me here, but, lass, long ago ye became like a daughter te me, and I pledge the rest of my miserable life te defending ye."

She gripped Angus's hand. "I wish you were my father."

He gave her a proud yet smug look, one she was used to seeing. She chortled to herself. The man did have a terrible streak of pride. She'd have to give Father John another coin for penance for Angus, since the Scot refused to take up the custom himself.

Angus hooked his thumb in his gray tunic. "Ye'll make a fine MacLeod because ye already ken we're the best clan in Scotland."

Mentally, she added another coin to her dues. "Do you think they'll let me become a MacLeod, though, since my mother was the daughter of the previous MacDonald laird and I've an English father?"

"They will," he answered without hesitation, but she heard the slight catch in his voice.

"Angus." She narrowed her eyes. "You said you would never lie to me."

His brows dipped together, and he gave her a long, disgruntled look. "They may be a bit wary," he finally admitted. "But I'll nae let them turn ye away. Dunnae worry," he finished, his Scottish brogue becoming thick with emotion.

She bit her lip. "Yes, but you won't be with me when I

first get there. What should I do to make certain that they will let me stay?"

He quirked his mouth as he considered her question. "Ye must first get the laird te like ye. Tell Neil te take ye directly te the MacLeod te get his consent for ye te live there. I kinnae vouch for the man myself as I've never met him, but Neil says he's verra honorable, fierce in battle, patient, and reasonable." Angus cocked his head as if in thought. "Now that I think about it, I'm sure the MacLeod can get ye a husband, and then the clan will more readily accept ye. Aye." He nodded. "Get in the laird's good graces as soon as ye meet him and ask him te find ye a husband." A scowl twisted his lips. "Preferably one who will accept yer acting like a man sometimes."

She frowned at him. "*You* are the one who taught me how to ride bareback, wield a dagger, and shoot an arrow true."

"Aye." He nodded. "I did. But when I started teaching ye, I thought yer mama would be around te add her woman's touch. I did nae ken at the time that she'd pass when ye'd only seen eight summers in yer life."

"You're lying again," Marion said. "You continued those lessons long after Mama's death. You weren't a bit worried how I'd turn out."

"I sure was!" he objected, even as a guilty look crossed his face. "But what could I do? Ye insisted on hunting for the widows so they'd have food in the winter, and ye insisted on going out in the dark te help injured knights when I could nae go with ye. I had te teach ye te hunt and defend yerself. Plus, you were a sad, lonely thing, and I could nae verra well overlook ye when ye came te the stables and asked me te teach ye things."

"Oh, you could have," she replied. "Father overlooked

me all the time, but your heart is too big to treat someone like that." She patted him on the chest. "I think you taught me the best things in the world, and it seems to me any man would want his woman to be able to defend herself."

"Shows how much ye ken about men," Angus muttered with a shake of his head. "Men like te think a woman needs *them*."

"I dunnae need a man," she said in her best Scottish accent.

He threw up his hands. "Ye do. Ye're just afeared."

The fear was true enough. Part of her longed for love, to feel as if she belonged to a family. For so long she'd wanted those things from her father, but she had never gotten them, no matter what she did. It was difficult to believe it would be any different in the future. She'd rather not be disappointed.

Angus tilted his head, looking at her uncertainly. "Ye want a wee bairn some day, dunnae ye?"

"Well, yes," she admitted and peered down at the ground, feeling foolish.

"Then ye need a man," he crowed.

She drew her gaze up to his. "Not just any man. I want a man who will truly love me."

He waved a hand dismissively. Marriages of convenience were a part of life, she knew, but she would not marry unless she was in love and her potential husband loved her in return. She would support herself if she needed to.

"The other big problem with a husband for ye," he continued, purposely avoiding, she suspected, her mention of the word *love*, "as I see it, is yer tender heart."

"What's wrong with a tender heart?" She raised her brow in question.

"'Tis more likely te get broken, aye?" His response was

matter-of-fact.

"Nay. 'Tis more likely to have compassion," she replied with a grin.

"We're both right," he announced. "Yer mama had a tender heart like ye. 'Tis why yer father's black heart hurt her so. I dunnae care te watch the light dim in ye as it did yer mother."

"I don't wish for that fate, either," she replied, trying hard not to think about how sad and distant her mother had often seemed. "Which is why I will only marry for love. And why I need to get out of England."

"I ken that, lass, truly I do, but ye kinnae go through life alone."

"I don't wish to," she defended. "But if I have to, I have you, so I'll not be alone." With a shudder, her heart denied the possibility that she may never find love, but she squared her shoulders.

"'Tis nae the same as a husband," he said. "I'm old. Ye need a younger man who has the power te defend ye. And if Sir Frosty Pants ever comes after ye, you're going te need a strong man te go against him."

Marion snorted to cover the worry that was creeping in.

Angus moved his mouth to speak, but his reply was drowned by the sound of the supper horn blowing. "God's bones!" Angus muttered when the sound died. "I've flapped my jaw too long. Ye must go now. I'll head te the stables and start the fire as we intended. It'll draw Andrew and Peter away if they are watching ye too closely."

Marion looked over her shoulder at the knights, her stomach turning. She had known the plan since the day they had formed it, but now the reality of it scared her into a cold sweat. She turned back to Angus and gripped her dagger hard. "I'm afraid."

Determination filled his expression, as if his will for her to stay out of harm would make it so. "Ye will stay safe," he commanded. "Make yer way through the path in the woods that I showed ye, straight te Newcastle. I left ye a bag of coins under the first tree ye come te, the one with the rope tied te it. Neil will be waiting for ye by Pilgrim Gate on Pilgrim Street. The two of ye will depart from there."

She worried her lip but nodded all the same.

"Neil has become friends with a friar who can get the two of ye out," Angus went on. "Dunnae talk te anyone, especially any men. Ye should go unnoticed, as ye've never been there and won't likely see anyone ye've ever come in contact with here."

Fear tightened her lungs, but she swallowed. "I didn't even bid anyone farewell." Not that she really could have, nor did she think anyone would miss her other than Angus, and she would be seeing him again. Peter and Andrew *had* been kind to her, but they were her father's men, and she knew it well. She had been taken to the dungeon by the knights several times for punishment for transgressions that ranged from her tone not pleasing her father to his thinking she gave him a disrespectful look. Other times, they'd carried out the duty of tying her to the post for a thrashing when she'd angered her father. They had begged her forgiveness profusely but done their duties all the same. They would likely be somewhat glad they did not have to contend with such things anymore.

Eustice was both kind *and* thankful for Marion teaching her brother how to read, but Eustice lost all color any time someone mentioned the maid going with Marion to Froste's home after Marion was married. She suspected the woman was afraid to go to the home of the infamous "Merciless Knight." Eustice would likely be relieved when

Marion disappeared. Not that Marion blamed her.

A small lump lodged in her throat. Would her father even mourn her loss? It wasn't likely, and her stomach knotted at the thought.

"You'll come as soon as you can?" she asked Angus.

"Aye. Dunnae fash yerself."

She forced a smile. "You are already sounding like you're back in Scotland. Don't forget to curb that when speaking with Father."

"I'll remember. Now, make haste te the cliff te leave yer cloak, then head straight for Newcastle."

"I don't want to leave you," she said, ashamed at the sudden rise of cowardliness in her chest and at the way her eyes stung with unshed tears.

"Gather yer courage, lass. I'll be seeing ye soon, and Neil will keep ye safe."

She sniffed. "I'll do the same for Neil."

"I've nay doubt ye'll try," Angus said, sounding proud and wary at the same time.

"I'm not afraid for myself," she told him in a shaky voice. "You're taking a great risk for me. How will I ever make it up to you?"

"Ye already have," Angus said hastily, glancing around and directing a worried look toward the drawbridge. "Ye want te live with my clan, which means I can go te my dying day treating ye as my daughter. Now, dunnae cry when I walk away. I ken how sorely ye'll miss me," he boasted with a wink. "I'll miss ye just as much."

With that, he swung up onto his mount. He had just given the signal for his beast to go when Marion realized she didn't know what Neil looked like.

"Angus!"

He pulled back on the reins and turned toward her.

"Aye?"

"I need Neil's description."

Angus's eyes widened. "I'm getting old," he grumbled. "I dunnae believe I forgot such a detail. He's got hair redder than mine, and wears it tied back always. Oh, and he's missing his right ear, thanks te Froste. Took it when Neil came through these parts te see me last year."

"What?" She gaped at him. "You never told me that!"

"I did nae because I knew ye would try te go after Neil and patch him up, and that surely would have cost ye another beating if ye were caught." His gaze bore into her. "Ye're verra courageous. I reckon I had a hand in that 'cause I knew ye needed te be strong te withstand yer father. But dunnae be mindless. Courageous men and women who are mindless get killed. Ye ken?"

She nodded.

"Tread carefully," he warned.

"You too." She said the words to his back, for he was already turned and headed toward the drawbridge.

She made her way slowly to the edge of the steep embankment as tears filled her eyes. She wasn't upset because she was leaving her father—she'd certainly need to say a prayer of forgiveness for that sin tonight—but she couldn't shake the feeling that she'd never see Angus again. It was silly; everything would go as they had planned. Before she could fret further, the blast of the fire horn jerked her into motion. There was no time for any thoughts but those of escape.

Series by Julie Johnstone

Scottish Medieval Romance Books:

Highlander Vows: Entangled Hearts Series
When a Laird Loves a Lady, Book 1
Wicked Highland Wishes, Book 2
Christmas in the Scot's Arms, Book 3
When a Highlander Loses His Heart, Book 4
How a Scot Surrenders to a Lady, Book 5
When a Warrior Woos a Lass, Book 6
When a Scot Gives His Heart, Book 7
When a Highlander Weds a Hellion, Book 8
Highlander Vows: Entangled Hearts Boxset, Books 1-4

Renegade Scots Series
Outlaw King, Book 1
Highland Defender, Book 2
Highland Avenger, Book 3

Regency Romance Books:

A Whisper of Scandal Series
Bargaining with a Rake, Book 1
Conspiring with a Rogue, Book 2
Dancing with a Devil, Book 3
After Forever, Book 4
The Dangerous Duke of Dinnisfree, Book 5

A Once Upon A Rogue Series
My Fair Duchess, Book 1
My Seductive Innocent, Book 2
My Enchanting Hoyden, Book 3
My Daring Duchess, Book 4

Lords of Deception Series
What a Rogue Wants, Book 1

Danby Regency Christmas Novellas
The Redemption of a Dissolute Earl, Book 1
Season For Surrender, Book 2
It's in the Duke's Kiss, Book 3

Regency Anthologies
A Summons from the Duke of Danby (Regency Christmas Summons, Book 2)
Thwarting the Duke (When the Duke Comes to Town, Book 2)

Regency Romance Box Sets
A Whisper of Scandal Trilogy (Books 1-3)
Dukes, Duchesses & Dashing Noblemen (A Once Upon a Rogue Regency Novels, Books 1-3)

Paranormal Books:

The Siren Saga
Echoes in the Silence, Book 1

About the Author

As a little girl I loved to create fantasy worlds and then give all my friends roles to play. Of course, I was always the heroine! Books have always been an escape for me and brought me so much pleasure, but it didn't occur to me that I could possibly be a writer for a living until I was in a career that was not my passion. One day, I decided I wanted to craft stories like the ones I loved, and with a great leap of faith I quit my day job and decided to try to make my dream come true. I discovered my passion, and I have never looked back. I feel incredibly blessed and fortunate that I have been able to make a career out of sharing the stories that are in my head! I write Scottish Medieval Romance, Regency Romance, and I have even written a Paranormal Romance book. And because I have the best readers in the world, I have hit the USA Today bestseller list several times.

If you love me, I hope you do, you can follow me on Bookbub, and they will send you notices whenever I have a sale or a new release. You can follow me here:
bookbub.com/authors/julie-johnstone

You can also join my newsletter to get great prizes and inside scoops!
Join here: https://goo.gl/qnkXFF

I really want to hear from you! It makes my day!
Email me here:
juliejohnstoneauthor@gmail.com

I'm on Facebook a great deal chatting about books and life. If you want to follow me, you can do so here:
facebook.com/authorjuliejohnstone

Can't get enough of me? Well, good! Come see me here:
Twitter:
@juliejohnstone
Goodreads:
https://goo.gl/T57MTA

Made in the USA
Columbia, SC
05 August 2019